# Summer at Squee

## ANDREA WANG

ISBN: 978-0-593-11131-4

Trim: 5½ x 8¼

On Sale: March 5, 2024

Ages 8–12 | Grades 3–7

320 pages

$18.99 USA | $24.99 CAN

Kokila

D1431555

# Summer at Squee

## ANDREA WANG

ISBN: 978-0-593-11131-4
Price: $16 x x x
On Sale March 8, 2024
Ages 8-12 / Grades 3-7
320 pages
$16.99 USA / $22.99 CAN

# SUMMER AT SQUEE

## ANDREA WANG

Kokila

KOKILA
An imprint of Penguin Random House LLC, New York

First published in the United States of America by Kokila,
an imprint of Penguin Random House LLC, 2024

Visit us online at PenguinRandomHouse.com.

Library of Congress Cataloging-in-Publication Data is available.

ISBN 9780593111314

1 3 5 7 9 10 8 6 4 2
[Vendor Code]

This book was edited by Joanna Cárdenas, copyedited by Jacqueline Hornberger, proofread by [TK],
and designed by Asiya Ahmed. The production was supervised by Tabitha Dulla, Nicole Kiser,
Ariela Rudy Zaltzman, and Caitlin Taylor. | Text set in Amasis MT Pro

*For Anita, Ezra, and Feo, with love and gratitude for the memories of summers past, present, and future.*

# CHAPTER ONE

The banner ripples across the front of St. Agnes Hall. WELCOME TO SCCWEE—SUMMERTIME CHINESE CULTURE, WELLNESS, AND ENRICHMENT EXPERIENCE! My chest twinges, which makes sense now that I know the heart is made up of muscle fibers. For an entire year, I've longed for camp with every single one of those cells. It's like my heart is physically tied to this place and every day apart stretches those fibers more and more, until I feel like I'm going to snap.

Dad pulls into a parking space in front of St. Agnes Hall. The moment the car comes to a complete stop, I spring out and wrap my arms around Lyrica, who is waiting on the curb.

The tension I've been feeling for months unravels in an instant. "I'm here! Let the Squee times begin!" The camp's name is so long, we all just call it "Squee."

"Phee!" my best friend squeals, hugging me back. "You're finally here. I can't wait to set up our room!"

"Let's go, then!" I spin around only to lock eyes with Dad. He's standing next to the open trunk, his eyebrows raised. "Oh, right. I need my stuff first."

My younger brother, Matthew, climbs out of the car and bumps fists with Lyr.

"Hey, Matty," she says, using the nickname I gave him when he was born and that has stuck ever since. "First time at overnight camp. You must be super excited!"

He grins mischievously. "I can't wait to break into the snack closet. Emerson said he'd show me how."

Lyr leans closer to Matty. "Can you get me some White Rabbit candy?" she murmurs conspiratorially.

"Swedish Fish for me, please. And tell Emerson it's not fair that he's only showing *you* how to get into the snack closet. He's my big brother, too."

Matty laughs. "I promise to tell you the secret so you can steal your own candy next time."

"Phoenny!" Dad calls from the back of the car. He wrestles my giant suitcase out of the trunk, and it lands on its side with a loud thunk. "What is in this thing? Did you pack my old law books for some summer reading?"

I rush over, and Lyr helps me lift it onto its wheels. "How did you guess?" Dad's fondest dream is for all three of his kids to follow in his footsteps, become lawyers, and join his law firm. I don't want to burst his bubble, but I'd rather eat his huge legal dictionary than read it. Better yet, I'd tear out all the pages and make one of those paper dresses I've seen on social media. "Actually, it's just full of clothes and props for camp activities," I tell him.

It's not exactly a lie. Other kids bring Rubik's Cubes to show off their skills at the Variety Show. Lyr brings her digital piano, which must be at least four feet long. Me? I don't go anywhere without my sewing machine if I can help it. I also packed a bunch of different fabrics, spools of thread, and all the tools I thought I might need. I'd love to make something for each of my friends if I have time. Without them, I might not have gotten through seventh grade. Even if I don't have a bestie at school anymore, I still have my camp besties—the Squad.

Dad heaves my second suitcase out of the trunk and shakes his head in disbelief. "Well, I can't imagine you forgot anything," he says, "but if you did, give me a call." He hands Matty his duffel bag and shuts the trunk. "Have a great two weeks. I'll see you at the Showcase. In the meantime, do me a favor and look after your mom and brothers, okay?"

I roll my eyes at Dad. "Emerson is sixteen and a counselor-in-training. CITs are supposed to look after *us*." Nevertheless, I hook my pinkie around his to promise, hug him goodbye, and pull my suitcases into the building.

A boy runs into the lobby and skids to a stop. "Matty! Look!" He raises a hoverboard above his head like a trophy. "Come try it out!"

"Cool!" Matty says. He kicks his duffel under the desk and the two take off without a backward glance.

Beside me, Lyr laughs. "Good luck keeping an eye on that one. Come on, let's go get our room keys."

I glance around the lobby. Our moms are nowhere to be seen, but their voices carry through a set of double doors to our left. Mom is the director of Squee, and Lyr's mom, whom I call Chǔ Auntie, is the assistant director. Every year, they ask us to come early so we can help with last-minute errands. Once camp starts, they're usually so busy we see them only in passing. Lyr and I peek into the living room and wave at our moms. Chǔ Auntie smiles and waves back, but Mom just nods and keeps giving instructions to the parent volunteers seated around her.

"Awesome. Looks like they've got it covered."

We leave our luggage with one of the other volunteers and head over to the Student Center building, where there's a big room Carmen College has helpfully labeled "the Multi-Purpose Room." Campers have called it the Flex ever since one of the parents who's also an interior designer described it as a "flexible room.'" Squee uses the Flex for a bunch of different activities, including the big dance. Although the tables for check-in are set up, the room keys aren't here. And there aren't any counselors or CITs in sight.

"Do you think they're still eating lunch?" Lyr asks.

I snort. "I bet Emerson is. He never stops eating. Let's go check it out."

It's Emerson's first year as a CIT, so he came to camp a couple of days ago for orientation. I wonder if he knows which group of campers he's been assigned to. It had better not be my group, or I'm going to insist that Mom reassign him. He bosses me around enough at home.

We head up a flight of stairs to the cafeteria, which is right above the Flex. Sure enough, Emerson is at a corner table with a bunch of other guys, a slice of pizza in his hand. He looks up as we come in and immediately checks the time on his phone.

"Hey!" he calls loudly. "You're early. Check-in doesn't start for another hour. Go back to your room and wait until it's time."

The boy next to him shakes his head. "We're supposed to be nice to the campers, dude."

Emerson scoffs. "Cooper. They aren't normal campers. That's my sister and her friend, Assistant Director Chǔ's daughter."

The boy catches my eye and quirks his brow. That's Cooper Han? I didn't recognize him, either. What happened to the skinny guy with bad skin? I scan the faces around the table, feeling my cheeks warm. High schoolers can really change a lot in a year.

'I shrink a little as the group of guys watches us approach and force myself to just focus on my brother. "We can't go back to our room, *Emmy*. If you'd paid attention at Orientation instead of staring at the girls, you'd know why."

The other boys laugh, and one says, "Oooh, burn."

Emerson scowls. Lyr clears her throat and says lightly, "We're trying to get our room keys. They're not on the tables down in the Flex. Do any of you happen to have them?"

There's a round of "nopes" and headshaking around the table. Then someone behind me says, "They were in the

lobby last time I saw. One of the staff was sorting the envelopes." The voice is unfamiliar, with an accent I can't quite
place.

A cobalt-blue Hydro Flask appears next to me. It's being
held by a boy in an open long-sleeved white button-down over
his turquoise camp T-shirt. He's definitely new. I wouldn't
forget someone who looks like he belongs in a boy band. His
hair is on the longer side and swoops perfectly over the side
of his face. My breath catches as I try to respond, and I end
up coughing instead. *Get it together*, I tell myself.

"Thanks," Lyr says. "We'll just go back to Agnes."

Confusion flickers across the boy's handsome face. "Um,
it was actually a man. Sorry, but I don't know his name."

There's a burst of laughter from the table. "Agnes isn't a person; it's the name of the dorm. St. Agnes Hall," Emerson says.
"Don't worry, you'll learn our nicknames for everything, H."

"H? Like Hydro Flask?" I blurt. There's another round of
laughter, but now it's directed at me. My face feels like it's
been scorched by the sun.

Hydro Flask Boy grins. "Well, yes, but in my case it's *H* for
Harrison."

"Um, hi," I stammer. "I'm Phee and this is Lyr."

"Hello, Phee and Lyr. Nice to meet you." Harrison's *hello*
sounds more like *haa-lo*, and I wonder if he's British?

I can barely remember what I'm supposed to say. "Nice
to meet you, too," I finally manage, while Lyr just grins and

Emerson shakes his head. I grab Lyr's hand and practically run out of the cafeteria.

On the sidewalk, Lyr bumps my shoulder with hers. "H for Hydro Flask?!" She giggles uncontrollably.

I cover my face with my hands. "I know, I know. So cringe." I take a deep breath and try to shake it off. "Now I'm going to have to avoid him for the next two weeks."

Lyr and I pretend to fan ourselves on the path back to Agnes, giggling the whole way.

In the lobby, Chǔ Auntie hands us each a lanyard. She introduces us to Zhang Uncle, who holds a box of envelopes.

"Chǔ, Chǔ, Chǔ," Zhang Uncle murmurs, flipping through the box of registration cards. "Here you are, Lyrica." He hands Lyr a small manila envelope with her name, room number, group number, and roommate's name printed on it. Inside are an ID card and room key card. Lyr slides them into the plastic pocket on her lanyard and hangs it around her neck.

"Look! We're roomies!" She points to my name on her envelope and mimes surprise.

I press my hand against my heart and exhale dramatically. "Whew. I was really worried." Sometimes it's great that our moms are best friends, just like me and Lyr. They know that we'd be devastated if we weren't rooming together. And that we'd make their lives miserable.

Zhang Uncle finds my envelope, and I immediately scan it for our group number. "Group 13? Since when did we start having a Group 13? I don't want our last year of overnight camp to be full of bad luck."

Chǔ Auntie overhears me and laughs. "Phoenny, we also have a Group 4, so we are equal-opportunity superstitious. Or not superstitious, as the case may be. And we had to create an extra group because a lot of new campers joined us this year. "

Oh, right. I seem to remember Mom saying something about that months ago. I honestly haven't thought about it since. There are new kids every year, but they're usually little and just come to Squee for day camp. I can't think of a time when there were so many that a new group had to be created, though.

Lyr looks as puzzled as I feel. "I don't get it. They're all in overnight camp? Why did you have to make a whole new group? Aren't there enough existing groups?"

Her mom thinks for a moment. "The Committee members that handle registration said a bunch of the new campers are all entering eighth grade in the fall, like you two. Since groups are created according to grade level, we could either have one enormous Group 12 or create a new group. We decided it would be too difficult for the teachers and counselors to manage a very large group, so now we have a Group 13."

I'm the first person to admit that I don't like change, especially after my circle of friends at school broke apart last year. I watched helplessly as they joined other groups without inviting me along, leaving me on the sidelines by myself. I never want to experience that kind of loneliness again. "Well, that sounds okay, as long as the Squad is still together."

There's a long moment of silence before Chǔ Auntie says, "About that . . ."

I give Lyr a look and we both start to talk, but Chǔ Auntie holds up a hand to stop us. "We had to place some of your friends in the other group to even out the numbers. I'm sorry; I know that's not what you were hoping for, but we couldn't keep all eight of you together this year. Five girls in your group asked to remain together, and since they're new, we agreed."

My head spins like an empty spool of thread left on the machine. Squee doesn't take campers older than eighth grade. I'd been imagining my friends and I hanging out day and night, soaking each other up one last time and creating memories we'd never forget. Now we've been separated, and I'll hardly see some of them at all, after not seeing them for most of the school year. One look at Chǔ Auntie's set face tells me nothing I say will change her mind about the groups. It's no use asking my mom, either. I feel the sting of tears.

"Come on," Lyr says, tugging on my arm and breaking me out of my thoughts. "Let's go set up our room."

Numbly, I grab my suitcases. They feel ten times heavier than they did before. Which of the Squad are in Group 13 with me? Which ones aren't? I try to take a deep breath and remind myself that at least Lyr and I are together. I'm not totally on my own.

# CHAPTER TWO

One tiny perk of being the kids of the camp directors is that we get to ride the elevator. But only before anyone else arrives. Lyr and I manage to cram ourselves, our suitcases, and her keyboard into the tiny space.

"What's our room number again?" Lyr asks.

I look down at my registration card. "Room 320. Top floor, coming up." I hit the button for the third floor and wait for the door to close. The elevator is old and slow, but still better than lugging all our stuff up all those stairs. As clumsy as I am, I'd probably drop and smash my sewing machine.

The main staircase and the elevator are next to each other, at the intersection of the two wings of the building. I lead Lyr down the right-hand hallway, where we finally find our room all the way at the end, next to the emergency exit staircase. It feels like we've walked a long way. The bathrooms are where we came from, opposite the elevator and stairwell. So that means we'll be trekking from our room to the bathroom in the morning, then back to our room to get dressed, and then all the way to the stairwell again to get out of the building. I make a face. Exercise is not my thing.

"This is great!" Lyr says. "It's so nice and quiet at this end of the building. Not like last year, when we were near the bathroom and could hear all the hair dryers and flushing toilets. Plus, it's right next to the emergency exit!"

"What's so great about that?" I grumble.

She nudges me and holds her key card to the door lock. "Well, for one thing, we'll survive in case Matty and his friend set the dorm on fire. Those electric hoverboards are a hazard."

"Emerson let it slip last year that the alarms on the emergency doors are disabled," I said. "That must be how they sneak out at night after curfew."

As much as I love my brothers, they're trouble. Or they would be if they ever got caught. Being boys gives them some sort of weird immunity. All the Chinese parents who have ever been on the Committee, including our moms, always turn a blind eye to boy campers' shenanigans. And the girls? We always get scolded by the night monitors for staying up too late and chatting too loudly. Don't they realize the boys' rooms are quiet because half of them aren't even there? I follow Lyr as she pushes through the doorway to our home for the next two weeks.

"Do you want to smush the beds together again?" I ask her.

"Absolutely!" she chirps. "How else are we going to stay up and gab all night?"

We leave our suitcases next to the door and each take

hold of one end of the bed on the left. We scoot it toward the middle of the room, and then do the same with the other bed until they're right up against each other. When we started going to overnight camp two years ago, we got our moms to buy us matching bedding. The bright pink-and-purple tie-dyed sheets, pale green cotton blankets, and sunny yellow pillowcases are so cheerful that I can't help but feel better.

Next, Lyr and I unpack our clothes, shoes, and books. We put our baskets of toiletries on top of our dressers and then turn to our extra stuff. Our fun stuff. I set my sewing machine on top of my desk and put the shoebox of spools of thread and various tools in one of the desk drawers. Stacks of fabric go into my bottom dresser drawer, underneath my hoodies. I feel oddly protective of my fabric, even though it hasn't become anything yet.

"Hey, Lyr. Here's your dress for the dance." I shake it out gently and hold it up. She'd asked for a poufy skirt, so I chose a gold brocade that used to be Wàipó's dining room drapes and added a layer of tulle underneath. The bodice is from a cream-colored satin blouse I found in a thrift shop. I'd cut off the original sleeves and the bottom half and used the leftover fabric to make two new flutter sleeves.

Lyr gasps. "Oh, Phee, it's even more amazing in real life!" I'd texted her photos while I was making it, but she'd been so busy with school and piano that she hadn't been able to come over and see it in person.

"You should probably try it on before you say that." I hand the dress to her. "I'll put mine on, too."

We change out of our T-shirts and shorts and admire ourselves in the full-length mirror on the back of the closet door. Lyr sighs happily and twirls, the skirt floating and swirling. "I love it. It's perfect for our last dance at Squee." She glances at me and then grabs my hands. "Wow, you look gorgeous! The boys won't be able to stop staring."

I bite my lip. "Are you sure it's okay? It's not, like, too Chinese or old-fashioned?" Năinai, my grandmother on Dad's side, had given me a box of her old qípáo that she didn't wear anymore. I'd taken two different blue ones and cut them both across at the waist. With the fabric from the bottom sections, I'd made a skirt that was above my knees in the front and curved down to my calves in the back, and attached it to the darker, cerulean-blue top section. Now, instead of having a tight sheath skirt with a thigh-high slit, I had one that flowed in soft waves around my hips and thighs. I could dance in it without worrying about ripping anything or showing too much skin.

"It's more than okay," Lyr reassures me. "The cut of the skirt makes it really different and modern. Besides, you *are* Chinese, so I say go for it!" She hugs me. "When are you going to be on *Project Fashion Junior*?"

I shake my head. "I can't even say hi to a new CIT without losing my cool and you want me to be on a reality TV show?

Anyway, my parents would never let me apply. Not handling curveballs well and having no filter are not things they want the world to see. "

"At least show them this dress. Maybe it will change their minds."

"I doubt it. They're supportive of my making upcycled clothes as long as it's just a hobby. When I talk about fashion designers, they're suddenly a lot less encouraging." I'm overcome with a wave of sadness and sink down on the bed. "I can't believe the Squad isn't all in the same group. It's our last year of camp. Why did all those new campers have to come?"

Lyr sits down beside me and puts her arm around my shoulders. "It's their one and only chance to be campers at Squee. They'll be too old next year, just like us. It'll be okay, Phee. We can still do most of the evening activities with the Squad, including going to the dance."

I nod, but inside I know it won't be the same. The Squad won't be all together in the camp photos, hamming it up for the camera. We'll be on opposite teams for Field Day. We won't be sharing the same experiences during classes and creating inside jokes. I heave myself up, take off my dress, and hang it in the closet. Lyr changes back into her casual clothes, too.

"Help me set up Casey," Lyr says.

She sets the long black padded case on the bed and unzips

it to reveal Casey, her eighty-eight-key digital piano with all the bells and whistles. Literally, there are buttons that play bell and whistle sound effects. She takes it out lovingly and places it gently down on her desk while I plug in the extension cord and power cable. We stack her sheet music and notebooks into one of the desk drawers, and then we're done. Camp hasn't even started, and already I wish we never had to leave.

I look around. Everything is in its place, but it still feels like something is missing. Then it hits me. "We forgot the pandas!" Did I pack mine? Frantically, I rummage through my dresser drawers and check my empty suitcases. Just when I'm about to panic, I remember my backpack, which I'd tossed in the corner next to my desk. Sure enough, I find Bao Bao jammed in behind some books. I fluff her up, give her a hug, and rest her against my pillow.

Lyr reaches into her pillowcase, pulls out Bei Bei and props him up against her pillow so the two pandas are sitting next to each other. I take a deep breath. Other kids might think we're too old for stuffies, but Bao Bao and Bei Bei are special. I made them.

Two years ago, when Lyr and I were in fifth grade, our families had taken a trip to Washington, DC, together over spring break. We'd visited the pandas at the Smithsonian National Zoo, including Bei Bei. There were lots of adorable baby photos of him with Bao Bao, too, and I was inspired to try and make panda stuffies when I got home.

That was my first big sewing project, where I designed and cut out everything myself. I tweaked a teddy bear pattern I found online and decided to appliqué the black patches over the panda's shoulders instead of trying to cut and sew together shaped pieces. I used a black velvet with a burned-out floral pattern from one of Mom's old cocktail dresses for Bao Bao and plain black felted wool from an old sweater for Bei Bei. For the white parts, I bought a quarter yard of satin brocade at Van's Fabrics on Beach Street in Chinatown for each panda. Bao Bao's has a pattern of phoenixes and clouds, while Bei Bei's has dragons and waves, to represent her yin to his yang. I made a bunch of newbie sewing mistakes and had to pull out stitches more than once, but I finally succeeded in making my first stuffies and I'm super proud of them.

"I remember when you gave Bei Bei to me, to celebrate our first year of overnight camp," Lyr says. "Now it's our last year." She digs out a small grocery bag from her backpack. "And I brought something to kick it off right!" With a flourish, she pulls out two bottles of soda. Coke, the original kind made with real sugar and packaged in glass bottles. My favorite. Mom refuses to allow soda in the house, and things that are usually off-limits always seem extra special.

I'm touched by Lyr's thoughtfulness. "You're the *best* friend," I tell her, taking a bottle.

She laughs. "I'm *your* best friend, and don't you forget it!"

As if I could. Lyr is the warp to my weft, the thread that runs through my life and gives me strength. Together, we make whole cloth.

"Here's to camp!" I say, her lightheartedness buoying me. "Our last summer at Squee is going to be spectacular," I vow. "One we'll never forget."

"Hear, hear!"

We clink the tops of our bottles together and take long swigs. Suddenly, I feel as fizzy as the soda.

# CHAPTER THREE

Lyr looks at me. "Are you thinking what I'm thinking?"

"If it involves glitter pens, dry-erase markers, and stickers, then yes."

When we were tiny day campers, we'd been envious of the older girls in overnight camp, who got to do fun things like decorate their dorm room doors and go to the dance. Now we're the big girls, and we come prepared.

Lyr grabs the pens from her desk while I fish around in my backpack for markers and stickers. "I found someone on Etsy who makes really cute zodiac animal stickers, so I got the tiger ones for the Squad. There might even be enough for everyone in Group 13."

"I hope you got ox ones for yourself!" She grins when I show her that I did.

Lunar New Year was in the middle of February the year we were born, so according to the Chinese lunar calendar, my birthday was still in the year of the ox. Mom likes to tease me that it's why I'm stubborn, bad at communicating, and dislike change.

In the hall, I write "So excited to Squee with everyone!" on the dry-erase board attached to the door, while Lyr draws kawaii food and musical instruments on the paper name tag taped above our room number.

"Ready for the stickers, Lyr?" I ask. When she doesn't answer, I turn to find her across the hall, studying our neighbors' door tag. "What's up? Are you decorating Squad doors now?"

Lyr taps the paper. "Look. No wonder they wanted to be together. I think they're twins. "

I step next to her and read the door tag aloud. "McKenna and Teagan. Oh, so they're not Squad. They're new." Their English last names aren't printed, but underneath their English names are their Chinese names. Immediately, I see that two of the characters in their names are the same. "Both girls, same last name, same first character of their given names. Yep, all signs point to them being siblings," I reason. "And if they're both going into eighth grade, then you're probably right— they're twins. That's cool. I wonder if they're identical?"

"Hi, I'm McKenna," a voice says.

"And I'm Teagan," a slightly deeper voice adds. "We're not twins."

Startled, I spin around to find a tall girl in a coral T-shirt and ivory capri pants, holding the handle of a glossy rainbow-colored suitcase. Next to her is a shorter girl in a lilac sleeveless shirt and faded jeans. My first thought is about how much I love their clothes. My second thought is, wait, they're not twins?

"Hi," Lyr and I say together, and then we introduce ourselves.

"So you're not twins?" I ask. "You're sisters?"

The two girls glance at each other. "Not really," the girl in coral responds mysteriously.

I don't know what to make of her answer, because either you're sisters or you're not, right? And if they're not, then why do their Chinese names indicate that they're related to each other? I can't quite wrap my head around it—it feels like I'm trying to sew together a bunch of pattern pieces without knowing what the final product is supposed to look like.

"Oh, so you're cousins?" Lyr says. She smiles, clearly happy that she's figured out the mystery. "That's awesome that you came to camp together!"

Part of me can't help but think that it's not awesome. If these two girls hadn't come to Squee, then maybe the whole Squad could've all been in the same group again.

The girl in lilac raises her eyebrows. "What gave it away? McKenna and I are curious."

I point to the door tag. "Your Chinese names are on here."

McKenna, the girl in the coral shirt, looks confused. "What does it have to do with our Chinese names?"

I'm a little surprised, because how Chinese people traditionally name their kids is something I've known since I was small. Mom and Dad had explained why Emerson and Matty's Chinese names were so similar. "Oh, that's easy.

20

Because you both have the same two characters in your names. My brothers and my tángdì have that, too."

McKenna's eyebrows draw together slightly. "Your brothers and who have what?"

"Um, my tángdì? My younger boy cousin on my dad's side. His English name is Kyle. He has the same last name as us, obviously, and all three of them have the same first character in their given names. It's *qí*, not the one that means 'flag' but the one that means 'that.' It's from some ancient poem or something."

Teagan crosses her arms. "It doesn't matter to me what his name is. I don't speak Chinese."

"We're named that way for other reasons," McKenna adds, but she doesn't elaborate. Both girls look annoyed now, their mouths pressed together like they're holding back more that they want to say.

Embarrassment tightens my chest, and I bite my lip. "I'm sorry. I guess I just assumed you could speak some Mandarin since you have Chinese names."

There's a long pause that gets more and more awkward the longer it drags on. Why can't I seem to say the right thing when I meet someone new today? I don't remember it being this hard before. I should just let Lyr do all the talking for me.

As if she read my mind, Lyr pipes up, "We're all in Group 13 together. If you need anything, feel free to ask us. We've been coming to Squee since we were six."

Another pause. "Thanks." McKenna motions to the door. "Um, should we unpack now?"

"Oh, right, sorry!" Lyr chirps. "We'll let you get to it. Feel free to move the furniture and let us know if you want help!" She tugs my arm, and I realize that I'm blocking the door. I move aside silently, my face burning.

McKenna and Teagan go into their room and shut the door, leaving me and Lyr in the hallway staring after them.

How did that conversation unravel into such a messy tangle of yarn?

"Come on." Lyr tugs my arm again, pulling me toward the door next to McKenna and Teagan's. "Let's see who else is in our group."

I'm not sure I should be greeting anyone else right now, but my curiosity wins out. "Delaney and Piper, Group 13," I read. "Two more new girls." I'm about to move on but do a double take. "Lyr, they have the same two characters as the ones in McKenna and Teagan's Chinese names. What do you think that means?"

Her face lights up. "Maybe they're all cousins! No wonder they wanted to all be in the same group. I wish I had cousins close to my age like that."

One of Dad's favorite sayings is "Once is an accident, twice is a coincidence, three times is a pattern." There are not three, but four new girls in our group with the same last name and first name character. While it could just be that their parents decided to send all their kids to the same camp, it feels more complicated than that somehow.

The room next to ours belongs to Maisie and Fei Hong. "Yay! Maze and Fei Fei are in Group 13 with us!" Lyr squeals.

Maze's humor and Fei Fei's enthusiasm never fail to lift my spirits. "I bet you we'll hear Fei Fei before we see her," I joke.

Lyr squeezes my shoulder. "That's better."

"What's better?"

"You're smiling again." She smiles back at me and urges me farther down the hall. "Who's behind door number three?"

"Lina and Ava, also Group 13. Awesome," I say. "Lina's with us. We'll have the best candids for the camp memory book. I don't recognize her roomie's name, though."

"That makes five new girls in our group so far. And five of the Squad, which makes ten girls," Lyr calculates. "That does seem like a lot. No wonder the Committee decided to create a new group."

"And no wonder all of them wanted to stick together. Ava's related, too. She has the same two Chinese name characters. It's like a cousin reunion or something." I sigh. "I wish our moms took our Squad reunion request just as seriously."

"Speaking of the Squad, let's find the rest of their rooms and see if anyone else is in our group."

"Look, the next room has counselors in it." I read the info on the door tag. "We got Sarina! I love her! Her roomie is Bora, the counselor for Group 12 this year. Look, Bora wrote her Korean name next to her Chinese one. That's so cool that she has both."

"Here are the CITs," Lyr says. "We have Gemma, and Group 12 has SuRong. I'm not sure I know either of them? The rest of the rooms from here to the stairs are probably Group 12 girls."

I nod. "Queena and Kirrily are in Group 12, according to this tag. So that just leaves Danielle."

"She's supposed to be in this room." Lyr stands in front of the room next to the counselors'. "But her name is crossed out. Is she not coming? I wonder what happened?"

"Kir will probably know. Ugh, I'm bummed that Kir and Q aren't with us and Dani might not be at camp at all. What's the big deal about having two more girls in our group? They totally could've kept the Squad together."

# CHAPTER FOUR

Lyr tries to cheer me up. "At least Maze, Fei Fei, and Lina are with us. And there will probably be other campers in our group, too."

"Yeah, but they're boys."

"Not all boys are like your brothers," Lyr reminds me. "Although, I wouldn't mind if they're like Emerson . . ." She trails off, turning pink.

"Ewww." I wrinkle my nose. "No crushing on my brother allowed."

The sound of voices in the hall saves her from having to respond. Girls of different ages and in other groups chatter excitedly as they find their rooms, meet roommates, and greet friends they haven't seen in months. Lyr and I are lucky that we see each other a lot, even though we live in different towns and don't go to the same school. We meet up with the other Squad members several times a year and text constantly, but some campers don't see their friends except at Squee. Lyr and I say hi to several we know, but soon I drag her back to our room, where it's quieter and we can chat, keeping our door open so we can hear when our friends arrive.

McKenna and Teagan's door is open, too. They're probably listening for their cousins.

McKenna's voice drifts across the hall. "I had no idea what to pack, did you? What do you bring to a place like this?" I can't make out what Teagan says, but it sounds like she's agreeing with McKenna.

Something about the way she says "a place like this" rubs me the wrong way. I look around the room. So the painted cinder-block walls and faded industrial carpet have seen better days, but their shabbiness is comforting. This is Squee. It's a happy place, *my* happy place. She doesn't know anything about it yet, but she'll see soon enough.

"I wish my mom had listened when I said I didn't want to come," McKenna says. There's a telltale crinkling sound of someone lying down on the bare vinyl-covered mattress, and I wonder why they haven't made their beds yet. It's like she's in denial that she has to stay here.

"I know what you mean." Teagan's voice is flat. "We've been here barely an hour, and it's already hard. I don't think I can take two weeks of this."

I feel a little flicker of hope—maybe if McKenna and Teagan get homesick and ask to leave soon, I can talk Mom into letting Kir and Q switch into Group 13 with us.

I mention this to Lyr, who doesn't seem as excited about the idea as I am. She puts down the pencil and notebook where she was trying to compose a song. "I wonder why

McKenna doesn't want to be here?" she says softly. Looks like I'm not the only one eavesdropping.

"The name thing bugged you, too, right?" McKenna's asking Teagan. "And mixing Chinese words into her speech, practically forcing me to ask what it means. To think I could be in Italy right now, practicing my Italian instead of learning Chinese words I'll probably never use."

My mouth drops open. I did *not* force her to do anything! I said tángdì because it's so much easier than saying "younger male cousin on my father's side." I wasn't trying to show off, either—lots of campers at Squee mix Mandarin into their conversations. It's not just that Mandarin words can be more precise than English ones, but it's also fun to blend them together. If I did it at school, no one would understand me. But at Squee, it's like having a special camp language. And no one makes a fuss about not knowing a particular word—if you can't figure it out from the rest of the sentence, you just say so. There've been plenty of times when I didn't know what a Mandarin phrase meant, but it's never bothered me.

Lyr pats my hand, trying to soothe me. But I'm past that point. I stand, ready to march across the hall and tell McKenna and Teagan that if they don't want to be here, I'm happy to have Mom call their parents to come and pick them up.

Lyr grabs the hand she was patting, keeping me in place. "Don't let them get to you, Phee. They're new, and it's the first day. They just sound insecure. It's not personal."

I'm not sure I believe her, but I hear another voice that stops me. And then I'm pulling Lyr to her feet. "Fei Fei's here. Let's go."

# CHAPTER FIVE

I was right—I can hear Maze and Fei Fei before I see them. Their voices echo in the main stairwell and their laughs bounce down the hallway. I have good friends at Squee, amazing friends. I don't need to make friends with new campers, especially ones that think I'm annoying. Well, the feeling is mutual. This is my last year at Squee, and I want to spend it only with the Squad.

Lyr and I stop in front of Maze and Fei Fei's door and strike a pose just as they step onto the third-floor hallway and spot us. They squeal, we squeal, and then the four of us run toward each other like a scene out of a sappy romance movie, hair streaming out behind us, arms outstretched, before we collide in slow motion and wrap ourselves around each other in a giant group hug. For a moment, I let myself sink into their embrace and believe that nothing has changed, and this is going to be the best camp year of them all.

Fei Fei starts jumping up and down and we're forced to jump with her, but it's awkward with our arms around each other and someone steps on my toes and I'm pretty sure I stomp on someone else's, but nobody complains—we just all dissolve into laughter.

"You guys have the room right next to ours!" I tell them. "We'll help you move the furniture." I grab Maze's giant duffel bag and start to drag it down the hall. It weighs a ton. Lyr catches hold of the strap and helps me. Maybe Maze's dad actually made her bring textbooks.

Fei Fei says, "Yesss! Did you hear that, Maze? We're roomies again!" She grabs the handles of her suitcases and rolls them along, easily catching up to us.

"I knew that already," Maze replies. "Our room numbers are on our registration cards, and I saw yours."

"Well, I didn't see yours. You should've said something!" Fei Fei mock-pouts.

"I wanted to get there first so I could snag the better closet," Maze deadpans.

"What?" Fei Fei sputters. "That's so rude!" Then she sees Maze's face and says, "Ohhh, you think you're so funny."

"Speaking of rude," I say, "Lyr and I have things to tell you. But it'll have to wait until we get inside your room."

"So mysterious and serious, Phee!" Fei Fei grins. "This must be some dirt!"

"Oh, it is," I assure her. "It's, like, next-level dirt."

As we approach their door, Fei Fei smiles and waves. I look to see who she's waving at and catch sight of McKenna and Teagan. They're peering around the doorframe at us. "Hi!" Fei Fei says. "I'm Fei—"

The new girls slam their door shut before she even finishes

her sentence. Fei Fei turns to me. "What was that all about?"

Maze unlocks their door, and I usher them all inside before closing it . . . quietly. "They're the 'rude' I was talking about." I fill Maze and Fei Fei in on meeting McKenna and Teagan, and then what we overheard. "McKenna complained about my using Mandarin," I tell them. "At a Chinese heritage camp!"

"Well," Maze says slowly, "that wasn't cool. But if Teagan doesn't speak Mandarin or any of the other dialects, then she must not have to go to Chinese school. Honestly, that makes me a little jealous. Are they the only new girls in our group?"

Lyr shakes her head. "No, there are five of them. My mom said they all requested to be together."

"They're all cousins, too," I add. "I hope the other three are more friendly." I explain to Maze and Fei Fei about the new girls' Chinese names.

"McKenna and Teagan weren't *unfriendly*." Lyr looks at me sympathetically. "Like I told you earlier, they seem insecure. They also don't want to be here, so maybe they took it out on you a little bit."

I shrug. "Whatever. If they don't want to be part of the group, the five of us can do our own thing." After all the drama with my friend group at school last year, I learned that you can't force people to be friends with you, no matter how hard you try.

"Five of us?" Fei Fei's eyes widen. "But that means the Squad isn't all together!"

"No, we're not. Kir and Q are in Group 12. Dani is supposed to be, too, but it looks like she might not be coming to camp at all. Did either of you get a text from her?" I ask.

Maze and Fei Fei shake their heads. "She's been pretty quiet on the Squad text thread lately, now that I think about it," Maze says.

Just then, there's a knock on the door, and Fei Fei flings it open. Lina appears, grinning. "Leeee-naaa!!" Fei Fei envelops the smaller girl in a bear hug, lifting her off her feet and carrying her into the room. The rest of us jump up and hug her, too.

Maze and Fei Fei decide to put their beds in an "L" shape in one corner with the heads together, leaving a large space in the middle of the room. Fei Fei pulls out a large fleece picnic blanket printed with palm fronds in different shades of blue and green and spreads it over the floor.

After we settle down on the blanket, I bring Lina up to speed on McKenna and Teagan. Her forehead furrows. "That's weird, especially if they're related to my roommate, Ava. She seems really excited to be here."

"You met her already?" Fei Fei asks. "Come on, spill the tea!"

Lina takes a moment to consider the question. She's super thoughtful like that, always trying to be diplomatic. "She seems sweet. Shy, too. Maybe a little sheltered. Both of her moms came upstairs with her, and one was helping her unpack while the other was setting up all this computer equipment. When I left, she'd started connecting a laptop to a large separate monitor."

"They know this is a heritage camp, right?" I say. "Not one of those academic camps for overachieving Asians. There's no need for a computer or a big monitor."

Lina shrugs. "I didn't get a chance to ask yet—maybe she's a coder?"

"Or a gamer!" Fei Fei suggests. "That would be cool!"

Maze's eyes gleam. "I hope she has a streaming account. I've been bingeing the last season of *The Great British Bake Off*, and I'm dying to watch the season finale."

Despite the picnic blanket, I shift uncomfortably on the hard floor. Fei Fei and Maze are already talking like Ava is one of the Squad, even though they haven't even met her yet. I don't want them to drift away from the Squad like my old school friends did from our group.

"There's no need for a sewing machine, either," Lyr says with a laugh, "but you brought yours." She sees my frown and adds, "And I brought my keyboard, because I can't seem to live without Casey. Also, I want to try and compose something for the New England Conservatory's music contest while I'm here."

"Okay, that's a good reason to bring your keyboard. But your sewing machine?" Maze says to me.

"Are you making us clothes?" Fei Fei claps excitedly.

"Lyr texted me pics of the T-shirt you made her with the piano keys on it. I want one with a palm tree design!" Maze and Lina chime in with the objects they want on their shirts. Not surprisingly, Maze wants cupcakes and Lina wants cameras.

Their enthusiasm warms me. "I'd be happy to make you all shirts if there's time. I brought it just in case we need to whip up costumes for the Variety Show or CIT Dress-Up."

Lyr nudges her shoulder against mine. "Phee made us the most gorgeous dresses for the dance. Wait until you see them!"

Fei Fei pouts. "Forget the T-shirt. I want a new dress for the dance, too! I brought the hot pink one I wore to my school's glow party, but now I think it makes me look too much like a flamingo."

"You could never look like a flamingo," Maze says reassuringly. "Your nose is more pug than beak."

We burst out laughing, even Fei Fei. "Hey!" she says between giggles. "I love our Chinese noses. We should do something for the Variety Show where we can all pretend we're pugs!"

Lina rubs the tip of her nose. "I wish my wàipó liked my nose. When I was little, I used to hate whenever she came over because she would pinch it to try and make it grow taller. It hurt!"

"My grandma did that, too," I say, "until I got mad and told her I liked my other grandmother, my nǎinai, better because she didn't do that to me."

"I wish I could express my anger like you do, Phee," Lina says. "Sometimes I think things only change when someone gets mad about it."

I shake my head. Getting mad at my ex-besties at school hadn't changed anything. They still left me. "I get angry about lots of things, but the other side has to be willing to listen for things to change."

"Both sides have to listen," Maze corrects me. "My social studies teacher has this big poster on her wall with a quote by Jane Goodall: LASTING CHANGE IS A SERIES OF COMPROMISES."

This conversation is getting too intense for me, so I joke, "And . . . now you know why I hate change."

My friends laugh while I take a deep breath. "The worst change," I say, "is that this is our last year as campers. Lyr and I want to make it spectacular. What do you say?"

"Let's do it!" We cheer and bump fists and hug each other. Lyr's optimism is definitely rubbing off on me. Now the question is *how* are we going to make it spectacular?

# CHAPTER SIX

We chat for a little bit longer, until Maze's phone chimes and she looks at the screen. "It's Q," she announces. "Her flight was delayed, but she's in the lobby now and wants help carrying her luggage up the stairs."

Fei Fei rolls her eyes but grins. "Queena living up to her name, as usual!"

We pop into Lina's room to meet Ava, and I vow not to say anything besides "hi." I've already botched two introductions today—I don't need another . . . Besides, Lina has to live with her.

Ava turns out to be just as tiny as Lina, but with a cute pixie haircut. Despite the heat, she's dressed all in black, except for the design on her T-shirt. She says hi to us shyly.

"Oh my god!" Fei Fei exclaims, startling the other girl. "Is that Captain Yeoh from *Rise of the Alien Wombats* on your shirt?"

"You play?" Ava asks, and suddenly she's not shy anymore. "Who's your favorite character to play? What level are you on? Have you gotten to planet Uluru yet?" She stops herself and blushes. "Sorry, I haven't met another *RotAW* player my age in person before." She pronounces the acronym like a word, just like we do with the camp acronym.

Fei Fei laughs. "I love *RotAW*, but I'm not very good. Will you show me how to get past the underwater level later? I keep running out of air."

"Sure," Ava says. "I brought an extra controller, so we can even play together."

"Awesome! We should definitely do that!"

Lina tells Ava that we're going to help Q with her luggage but that we'll see her during the all-group meetup in a half hour.

"There's a big living room off the lobby," I tell her, feeling helpful. "There'll be posters on the walls with the group numbers on them. Just find the one for Group 13, and we'll meet you there." She smiles and I smile back, relieved that I didn't stick my foot in my mouth again.

Heavy suitcases seem to be the theme of the day because Q doesn't even pretend to be able to lift hers. Lyr and I carry one together, while Maze easily lifts the other one by herself. "Where did you get those biceps?" I ask Maze.

"I've been working at the market after school this past year helping my dad restock the shelves. Those bags of rice are heavy! When I started, I had to drag them across the floor. Now I just heave them up onto my shoulder." She flexes and the rest of us with skinny arms admire her muscles. By the time we reach Q's room, my arms feel like wet wool—limp and heavy.

We find Kirrily asleep on one of the beds in her and Q's room'. At least we're all on the same floor and can easily hang out together at night.

Fei Fei flings herself across Kir's still form and hugs her. "Kir-Kir!" she sings. "Get up—we're all here!"

Kir opens her eyes and yawns. "I'll get up if you get off me, Fei Fei."

Fei Fei laughs and rolls off. "Why didn't you text us when you got here?"

"I had a race this morning," she says, pushing her pink-streaked hair out of her face and propping herself up on the mattress.

"Wow, you ran a marathon this morning, before camp?" I marvel. I can't even run the length of two hallways without falling over. Clumsy in conversations and physical activities, that's me.

"It was just a half," she murmurs, standing up and giving me a sleepy hug. "I thought I'd nap before all the chaos started." She turns to hug everyone else. "I'm really bummed that we're not in the same group this year. What happened?"

Quickly, I explain about the new girls and how they wanted to stay together, thereby breaking up the Squad.

Q makes a face. "If my mom was the director, I would've made her keep us all together."

Everybody laughs except me. It's true—Q is more commanding than the rest of us. Her family nickname is Xiǎo

Xiōng, which sounds similar to *Little Bear* in Mandarin but really means "Little Fierce One."

I don't feel like talking about Mom or the new girls anymore, so I ask, "Where's Dani? Have you heard from her?"

Danielle Guo is the eighth and final member of the Squad. Kir's smile disappears. "Dani's wàipó got sick suddenly, so she had to pull out of camp. She texted me yesterday to say she's going to California to help her mom take care of her. She didn't put it on the group text because she was too sad."

"Oh no, that's awful!" Lyr cries. "We should send her lots of photos so it feels like she's with us."

We all agree that that's a great idea. Then Q puts us to work helping her and Kir set up their room. Like Maze and Fei Fei, they want their beds in an L shape in the corner. Kir unrolls an exercise mat on one side of the open floor space, while Q pulls out a bunch of metal tubes and fuchsia fabric. Once assembled, it turns out to be a cute butterfly chair.

"You brought your own throne this year," Maze observes. "And the rest of us are supposed to sit on the mat at your feet?"

"There shall be no sitting," Q says haughtily. She lowers herself into the chair and holds up a hairbrush like a scepter. "All my loyal subjects must kneel before me."

"Good luck with that," Maze snorts. Meanwhile, Fei Fei throws herself down in front of Q and does an old-fashioned kowtow, the kind that shows respect to the emperor, knocking her forehead on the floor three times. Even Q can't help laughing.

"You may rise," Q decrees. "It is time to meet the rest of my court."

I check my phone. She's right—it's time to meet the rest of our groups. Fashionably late, the way Q always is.

We troop down the stairs, across the lobby, and through the ornate carved wooden doors to the living room. The college buildings are still full of fancy woodwork, stained-glass windows, and vintage velvet sofas in the common spaces. Fei Fei describes it as "Gothic Shabby Chic." I love it.

The seven of us swoop through the large room, Q leading the way. This year, we're at the top of the food chain. The youngest campers, who are going into fifth grade and are in Groups 6 and 7, fall silent and stare at us as we pass. Last year, most of them were day campers and gathered in the Flex on Monday mornings. This is their first year of overnight camp, and they look a little nervous. Except for Matty, who waves wildly and calls out, "Hi, Phee! Hi, Lyrica!"

Without breaking stride, I turn to my little brother and throw him a hang-loose hand gesture. Lyr waves back at him, and the other girls smile at him in that *oh, aren't you adorable* way. The posters on the walls end at Group 12, the oldest group. Scratch that—Groups 12 *and* 13 are now the oldest groups. Our posters are at the far end of the room, taped up on either side of a dreary old oil painting of the first headmistress of the college. Sister Martha Finchley glares down at us disapprovingly, sandwiched between Chinese dragons on the Group 12 poster and plump pandas on the Group 13 poster.

"Hi, Sarina!" I greet our female counselor. "Did you pick the pandas? Tài kěaile!" The Mandarin for *too cute* pops out of my mouth without thinking. McKenna gives me a look from beside Sarina, but I don't apologize.

Sarina puts down her clipboard and hugs me. "Phee! So good to see you. Yeah, we ran out of zodiac animals to use, and I love pandas, so it was kind of a no-brainer." She greets Lyr and the rest of the Squad and gives them hugs or high fives. She looks at the new girls, who have formed a tight circle on the floor in front of her. "Why don't you all scoot back and make the circle bigger so we all fit?"

"It's okay," I tell her. "We'll sit on the couches." I make my way around McKenna and Teagan and a girl I haven't met yet and plop down in the middle of a threadbare navy velveteen sofa. Way more comfortable than the floor. Lyr, Maze, Lina, and Fei Fei squish in on either side of me. Kir gives a peace sign, and Queena waves regally before they turn away and join Group 12. My heart sinks to see them go.

There's a gust of air as the emergency exit door behind the sofa opens and a group of boys lopes in, holding Chinese yo-yos under their arms or in their hands. "Sorry," the tallest guy says to Sarina, "we were practicing out back and lost track of time." Several boys trot off to join other groups without acknowledging us. I'm not paying attention to them, anyway.

I stare at the tall boy and then catch Lyr's eye. *Whoa.* Win Lai really bulked up over the past year. He's always been tall, but now his chest and arms stretch the seams of his T-shirt. What do they feed people in college? Win sits down on the love seat next to Sarina. He's our male counselor? Being in Group 13 might not be so bad after all.

A sharp rap on the top of my head breaks me out of my thoughts. I flinch and swivel around to discover Emerson smirking at me, yo-yo sticks in his hand. I take a swing at him, but he easily catches my fist with his other hand. "You know the rules, Phee. No fistfighting." He lets go of me, ruffles my hair, and saunters away.

He's so dead. Now I'm glad that my room is next to the emergency exit staircase. I'm going to sneak down to his room and steal all his underwear. Or spray perfume all over his clothes and bed. The Squad will help me. Except that when I glance at them, they're all staring after my brother, and not in the same *you're adorable* way they looked at Matty. More like they adore him. And is it my imagination or does one of the new girls look a little starry-eyed, too? I swat Lyr. "Stop it. You keep saying we're like sisters, so doesn't that make him your brother?"

"Nope," she says. "It most definitely does not."

Lina adds her two cents. "There's nothing brotherly about it."

"Don't worry, I'm not crushing on your brother," a voice behind me says.

"Neither am I," another voice chimes in.

Brandon Qiu and Howie Lin circle around and plop down on the sofa across from us, and my breath catches as Harrison plants himself in the middle, directly opposite me with that tousled hair and perfect features. He nods. "Hey there, Phee. Guess we both found Agnes."

Add fascinating accent to the list. I swallow and find my voice. "You're our CIT?" I'm not sure how to feel about that. I was planning to just admire Harrison from afar. The thought of being so close to him practically 24-7 makes me feel all kinds of awkward.

"Is that a problem?" He raises an eyebrow.

"What? No, of course not."

Out of the corner of my eye, I see McKenna watching us, a slight frown on her face.

Maze pokes me in the side. "You didn't tell us that you've already met our CIT."

Harrison leans across the coffee table and shakes her hand. "Hello, I'm Harrison. Now you've met me, too."

Maze, the most unflappable of all the Squad, trembles like a bowl of grass jelly. Oh, boy. He's got a charming smile all right.

Sarina clears her throat and says loudly, "Good idea, Harrison. Let's begin the introductions. Here comes our other CIT now."

A teenaged girl sits down on the floor next to McKenna. A small section of her hair is dyed green, and she tucks it behind her ear before glancing around, nodding with familiarity when she reaches the Squad. I don't recognize her, but Fei Fei sucks in her breath so loudly that I turn to see if she's okay. Instead of saying anything, she blushes furiously.

Hmm. Interesting. Fei Fei has always fallen for boys in the past, but maybe that's changed. Our green-haired CIT definitely has an effect on her. Just like a certain Hydro Flask Boy has on me.

# CHAPTER SEVEN

"Okay," Sarina says. "Let's introduce ourselves. Tell us your English name, your Chinese name, where you live, how long you've been coming to camp, and your favorite animal. I'll start. I'm Sarina Chiang, one of your counselors. My Chinese name is Wèi Shānlì. I started coming to camp as soon as I turned six and could join Group 1, and my favorite animal is the panda, if you haven't already guessed from our group's mascot." She points to the poster on the wall, then at Win. "Let's have all the counselors go first."

"I'm a lifer, too," Win begins. "Just can't stay away, like some of you, am I right?" He grins at me, and my mouth goes dry. "My full name is Winson—like 'Winston' but without the 't.' My parents are first-generation Chinese American, and when they had me after having three daughters, they considered it a win." He makes a face. "So stereotypical, you know? But now Win is my nickname and you can call me that if you want to. My last name is Lai, Chinese name is Lài Yǔxuān, and I love the Bruins, so I'm going to say bears are my favorite animal." He sits back and nods at Harrison. "Your turn, dude."

"Thanks, bro," Harrison says. "I'm Harrison Ko, and this is my first time at Squee."

Emerson or the other CITs must have taught him to call camp Squee. It sounds way cooler in his accent.

"You can probably tell that I'm not from Boston," Harrison continues. "I'm a Hong Konger. Born and lived there my whole life up until a couple of weeks ago when we moved here for my dad's new job. I guess that makes me a first-generation immigrant." He catches my eye again. "Met Emerson on a football pitch, he told me about an opening for a CIT, and here I am. What else? Right, my Chinese name in Mandarin is Gāo Hóngshān, although I'm more used to the Cantonese pronunciation, and I like falcons."

Emerson is responsible for Harrison being at camp? I guess I won't wreak revenge on my brother after all.

The girl with the lock of green hair clears her throat. "Hey, everyone, I'm Gemma Lee. Good to see a bunch of you again." My jaw drops—the last time I saw Gemma was four years ago, when she was twelve and I was a day camper. She had glasses and braces back then, so it's no wonder I didn't recognize her. "I've been coming to Squee since I was seven, but only every other year because I spent alternating summers with my dad in Denver. My Chinese name is Lǐ Jiāyí, and my pet iguana is my favorite animal."

Fei Fei barely suppresses a little squeal. She loves everything tropical, which includes iguanas. Although given her reaction earlier, she's not as excited about a pet iguana as she is about its owner.

Sarina taps one of the new girls sitting around her and asks her to introduce herself next, then tells the rest of us to go in order, clockwise.

The girl says her name is Piper Bennett, it's her first time at camp, and her favorite animals are owls. Before the next person can say anything, Howie points out, "You forgot to say your Chinese name." I find myself leaning forward to better hear Piper's answer. Will she mention that she's related to the other new girls?

"It's Jiāng Báiguǒ," she says in a voice barely above a whisper. Her pronunciation of *Jiāng* isn't quite right, but her tones are correct.

"Are you half?" Howie's face lights up. "Because I'm a halfie, too, although it's my dad who's Chinese, so my English and Chinese last names are the same."

A range of emotions wash across Piper's face before she looks down and lets her hair cover her. She shakes her head silently. I'm as perplexed as Howie looks. He opens his mouth again, probably to ask how she can have a Western last name but not be biracial, but Win cuts him off. "All right, now Delaney, yeah?" he says.

"Hi, I'm Delaney Detarando," she says, playing with one of her braids. "My Chinese name is Jiāng Báilì, which means 'river white jasmine,' and I'm also new to camp." Her Mandarin pronunciation is pretty good. "I have a pet guinea pig, two gerbils, and four hamsters, so you can tell that rodents are my fave." Delaney smiles, showing both freckles and dimples. She's so cute that everybody smiles back at her, except for Howie, who still looks confused. I don't blame him, because how can Piper and Delaney be cousins on their dads' side if their English names are different?

Win gives Howie a pointed *don't do it* stare. Howie gets the message and stays quiet, but I get the feeling that won't last.

McKenna is next. She inhales deeply before speaking. "I'm McKenna Fitzgerald, Jiāng Báiyù in Chinese, I think sharks are cool, and it's my only time at camp." She turns to Teagan, and I see her mouth, "Thank god." Sarina and Win glance at each other but don't respond. They're trained to deal with reluctant campers, and now they know what the Squad knows—McKenna is very, very, reluctant.

Howie squirms in his seat, and I realize that McKenna also has a different English last name than Piper and Delaney. This is getting more and more mysterious.

"I'm Teagan," McKenna's roomie says. "Teagan Kennedy. My Chinese name is Jiāng Báiguī, I'm new like McKenna, Delaney, and Piper. I don't really like animals." She looks around defensively. "I guess tigers are okay."

"Fair point," Sarina says. She looks around the group. "If animals aren't your jam, that's fine. Just tell us something else about yourself. Whatever you want."

"I like praying mantises," Ava offers. "They're technically

animals, even though most people don't think of insects that way."

Beside her, McKenna and Teagan snort softly. I'm put off by their reaction until I realize that I don't think of insects as being animals, either. Mosquitoes, moths, and stinkbugs are all pests in my book. Especially the moths that eat fabric.

"Praying mantises eat moths, right?" Brandon says. I stare at him, wondering if my dislike of moths shows on my face.

Ava nods enthusiastically. "Yeah, they're carnivorous. They eat lots of other insects, too. Some of the larger mantis species will even hunt and eat frogs and lizards."

"That's seriously cool." Brandon gives Ava a thumbs-up, and she turns pink and stops talking.

The silence drags on until Teagan pokes her and says, "Tell them your name," in an exasperated voice.

"Oh, I'm Ava Dentzer," she squeaks, before introducing herself in Mandarin. "Wǒ jiào Jiāng Báilián." Unlike her friends, she speaks fluently and flawlessly.

Maze nudges me. "Chinese school," she says sympathetically.

"I don't get it," Howie bursts out, hands clutching his head. "Why are all your Chinese names practically the same, but your English last names are totally different?" He looks at Win. "I'm sorry, but I like things to make sense, and this just . . . doesn't."

Unable to help ourselves, everyone besides the new girls

turn to look at them. McKenna glares back, Teagan rolls her eyes, Piper ducks her head again, Delaney's dimples disappear, and Ava looks startled. I wonder how Win and Sarina are going to respond, but Howie's question has caught them off-balance. Personally, I'm dying to hear what McKenna or Teagan have to say, because it's pretty clear to me now that the five of them aren't actually cousins, and I have no idea why they'd lie about it. But neither of them opens their mouths.

"It makes perfect sense," Gemma finally asserts. "You just don't know the context. And, in this case, it's a personal matter, so you don't get to demand an explanation."

Now everyone looks disconcerted, even the new girls. Piper whispers something to Delaney, who murmurs, "Oh, maybe." Then they eye Gemma with something that looks like curiosity. Howie crosses his arms and slumps into the sofa. Relieved that Gemma's handled the situation, Sarina quickly motions to us on the sofa.

"Hey, you folks in the Squad, how about introducing yourselves now?"

I shrink back against the cushions. We normally just use "the Squad" among ourselves, and it sounds childish coming out of the counselor's mouth. Especially in front of Win and Harrison.

At the end of the sofa, Lina starts and I tune out a little bit because I know what my friends are going to say. Lina likes meerkats, Lyr likes gazelles, and then it's my turn to speak.

"Hi, I'm Phee, and this is my seventh year at Squee, too. My Chinese name is Fāng Xiǎofèng, and I like birds." Harrison raises his eyebrows, and I remember belatedly that his favorite animals are falcons, which are . . . birds.

McKenna fake-whispers, "Try-hard," to Teagan, who smirks. My face burns, and I look down at the faded carpet. I actually do like birds. I'm not saying it just to, what, flirt with Harrison? I mean, Piper likes owls. They're birds, too. And no one thought she was trying to make a move on him.

Lyr nudges me. "You actually have a favorite bird." I narrow my eyes at her and shake my head a fraction. *I don't want to go there.*

But Harrison overhears. "What is it, then?"

I pick at a slub in the velveteen covering the sofa. "The phoenix, but—"

"That's not a real animal!" McKenna blurts. She turns pink when everyone looks at her. "I mean, if I knew we could name mythological creatures, I would've said something else."

"It's not a test," Sarina says gently. "You can change your answer if you want."

McKenna shakes her head and stares straight ahead. I wonder what mythological creature she would've said. Basilisks, maybe? Gorgons?

"Go ahead, Phoenny," Win urges. "What were you going to say?"

I know he's just being nice and giving me a chance to finish my sentence, but now it feels like everyone's prying. "It's not important. I was just going to say that it's my name, so it's weird to say it's my favorite animal, too." I turn quickly to Fei Fei so she can introduce herself, but Harrison leans forward again, stopping her.

"Your name is Phoenix in English and in Chinese?" he asks. "Here I thought Phee was short for Fiona."

"Fiona?" I make a face. "Like the girl ogre in *Shrek*?"

"Not like that at all." He looks amused.

Fei Fei introduces herself and tells everyone her English name is the same as her Chinese name and she likes blue morpho butterflies.

I risk a glance at Harrison, and he mouths, "You're much prettier."

I flush and look away.

Maze and Howie take their turns, but I barely hear them. The one thing I register about Brandon is that he wants to be called "Bran," which makes Win laugh and ask, "Like Raisin Bran?" Brandon—no, Bran—shakes his head but 'doesn't reveal why he wants to be called that nickname.

Then, for the remaining fifteen minutes, Sarina and Win talk about Squee and some of the special activities that have become camp traditions. They get everyone excited about the Carnival, CIT Dress-Up Contest, Dance, Bingo Night, Field Day, Variety Show, and, of course, Showcase. They explain how we're responsible for waking up on our own and getting breakfast in the cafeteria, then meeting them here under our Group 13 poster by 8:00 a.m. The group stays together until classes are over in the afternoon and then gets back together after dinner for evening activities. I've heard it all before.

What haven't I *ever* heard before? *A boy telling me he thinks I'm pretty.* Especially older ones who look like pop stars. I have no idea how to react, so I just stare at the carpet until dinnertime.

# CHAPTER EIGHT

Win and Sarina want us to eat dinner together the first night. After filling our plates with pasta and salad, we sit at a long rectangular table. Naturally, the Squad sits together. The new girls choose the other end, leaving the middle seats for the four counselors, Howie, and Bran.

Sarina tries to get a conversation going by asking about what we're all looking forward to at camp, but it's hard to hear everyone and the discussion soon fizzles out. The Squad and I chat, but I'm distracted. Harrison is just nice to everyone, right? He introduced himself to Maze and shook her hand. He smiled at Delaney. He said, "You're much prettier," to me, but how much of a compliment is that, really? I should hope I'm prettier than an ogre!

The five of us finish eating quickly and stand up to leave. "Hold on a second," Sarina says. "Icebreakers are going to be a little different this year. Instead of meeting in the living room, we're going to gather in the hall outside our rooms."

"We'll join them up on the third floor later, okay?" Win tells Bran, Howie, and Harrison.

"Why the change?" I ask Sarina.

"Just something new we're trying this year," she says lightly. "See you all there at seven thirty."

Promptly at 7:30, we step out of Q and Kir's room and into the hall. Q drags her chair to where Group 12 is gathered and settles into it rather than on the floor with everyone else. Kir tries to sit in her lap but is promptly shoved off, making her whole group laugh. Their counselor shakes her head but lets Q stay on her throne. I'm glad her group is getting along, even though it makes my heart ache just a little bit to see my friends having fun without me.

I take a seat and lean back against my room door. Lyr, Fei Fei, Maze, and Lina sit in a line to my left. Sarina and Gemma wind their way through Group 12 with the guys behind them, who are lugging several large crates. Bran and Howie plop down next to Lina, while Harrison and Win sit in the middle of the hallway. Sarina is on my right, Gemma is on McKenna's left, and I realize we've done it again. Just like at dinner, the new girls are separated from the returning campers. The counselors are like a few stitches trying to hold two pieces of fabric together.

"I love your hair, Gemma," Fei Fei says, a breathless quality in her voice. "You look amazing."

Gemma grins and is about to reply when Sarina raises her hands. "Okay, Group 13! Let's get started on the first hall meeting!"

Lyr and I look at each other with raised eyebrows. Hall meeting? What happened to icebreakers?

"We're starting a new tradition, yeah?" Win chimes in. "Every couple of days we're going to meet and do what we're calling Snaps, Squawks, and S'ups. The schedule will depend on that evening's camp activity and if we think the group needs it. It'll give us a chance to check in with each other and make sure we're all cool. Cool?"

Delaney raises a hand and then lowers it quickly when Win nods at her. "Um, I think I know what 'Snaps' are, but what are 'Squawks' and 'S'ups'?"

"Excellent question!" Win booms, making us all jump. "Harrison, why don't you explain it to us?"

"Sure," Harrison says, unfazed. "Snaps are compliments, about something you liked doing at camp or someone who did something nice. After you finish giving a compliment, we all snap our fingers." He demonstrates, using both hands.

I envy his ambidexterity the same way I envy Lyr being able to play complicated piano pieces with her nondominant hand. That would be so helpful when I'm sewing or crafting.

"Squawks are the opposite of Snaps—they're basically complaints, but, like, constructive ones," he continues. "You can't just say mean things. And S'ups are questions—things you want to know about other people in the group." He looks directly at me as he finishes talking, like there are things he wants to know. About me.

"What's up with that?" I blurt, and then hunch my shoulders. I don't know why I can't control my mouth around this boy.

But Harrison just laughs. "Exactly! That's where 'S'up' came from."

A few others murmur, "Ohh," which makes me feel slightly less mortified.

"I want you all to know that this is a safe space," Sarina says. "We don't tell people outside our group anything that is shared inside this circle. If you don't want to share a Squawk or answer a S'up, that's okay, too. But everybody has to share a Snap, even if it's a small thing like getting your favorite chocolate chip muffin at breakfast. We'll do themes sometimes to make it easier."

"What happens in hall meeting stays in hall meeting," Win intones dramatically.

Sarina shakes her head at him, but she's smiling. "Tonight, we're going to do a mix of games and sharing. Let's start with Giant Jenga. Win says he's a champion, but I bet one of us can beat him."

Win rubs his hands together. "I accept the challenge." He opens one of the crates and dumps out the large wooden blocks.

At first, we're all tentative, carefully studying the tower and gingerly pulling out our chosen pieces. The game proceeds excruciatingly slowly, and no one is really talking except for the counselors, who taunt each other good-naturedly. Then Lyr has the genius idea to get her keyboard and play music to set the mood. When Howie takes too long tapping on each of the blocks, she plays the *Jeopardy!* game show tune to hurry him along. When Ava successfully pulls out a tricky block, she plays "Happy" by Pharrell Williams. And when it's Win's turn, she plays the suspenseful music from the movie *Jaws*.

McKenna steps up for her turn. As she circles the tower, Lyr plays another thrilling, spine-tingling song. It's familiar, but I can't place it. McKenna clearly recognizes it, though, because she bobs her head along to the beat and waits for the crescendo before pulling her chosen block out with a flourish just as the music reaches its peak. We all clap while McKenna does a graceful pirouette.

Bran snaps his fingers. "I got it, I got it! *Sharknado!*" There's a pause before we realize Lyr was playing the theme song in honor of McKenna's favorite animal, and then everyone cracks up, because that was the wackiest shark movie ever. McKenna laughs, too, and our laughter fills the room with warmth.

I'm gently wiggling a block from the bottom of the tower when the music changes, and I realize it's that Smash Mouth song—the one from *Shrek*, about believing in love after seeing Fiona's face. I turn to glare at Lyr, forgetting to let go of the block, and the tower collapses with a loud crash. I can't help but giggle, because she's my best friend after all, and also because Sarina gives me two fun-size bags of Swedish Fish as a consolation prize. Everyone else gets Sour Patch Kids.

"Quick," Win says. "Everyone share a Snap about someone else in the group. The person named goes next until we've mentioned everyone. I'll start. I loved the music during Jenga. Snaps to Lyrica!"

We all snap our fingers, and Lyr grins. "Snaps to Fei Fei for bringing a picnic blanket and making sitting on the floor more comfortable!"

Fei Fei curtsies as we snap. "Snaps to Ava for bringing an extra game controller and offering to play *Rise of the Alien Wombats* with me."

Ava looks startled and her cheeks turn pink, but she smiles and gives Snaps to Lina for helping her set up her computer equipment. Lina compliments Maze for carrying Q's heavy suitcase, Maze winks at me and says it was nice of me to knock the Jenga tower down so Win could keep his title as c"hamp," and then it's my turn and I draw a blank.

I feel like someone's tied a gag around my mouth. I try to say something, anything, but all that comes out is "Uhhh." The rest of the Squad have been named already. Whatever I could say about Harrison would be too cringey, and I honestly can't think of any compliments for the remaining campers. For instance, did Teagan do anything nice for anyone today? If so, I didn't notice. Finally, I make a helpless gesture with my hands and notice the candy I'm holding. "Right! Yes, Snaps to Sarina for knowing my favorite candy," I say in a rush, relieved when people start snapping their fingers.

Sarina bows, and the compliment sharing goes on, from Sarina to Delaney to Piper to McKenna, who chooses to give Harrison Snaps "for his fashion sense." Harrison smiles and hams it up, putting one hand in his pocket, the other on his hip, and tossing his hair like a runway model.

I try not to look at him the way my friends were looking at Emerson earlier, but it's hard. Really hard. Especially when his eyes flicker to meet mine. Quickly, I shift my gaze to the floor and don't look up until Harrison praises Bran for putting away the Chinese yo-yos. Bran compliments Howie, Howie actually admires Gemma for "putting up with his questions about Chinese names," and Gemma says she appreciates Teagan helping to collect plates after dinner.

It's Teagan's turn now, and only Win is left. After a pause, she smirks. "Snaps to Win for the ability to end every other sentence with a question."

"It's a true skill, don't you think?" he jokes.

I laugh along with the rest of the group, grateful to have survived the first round of Snaps.

For the remaining time, we split into smaller groups and play different board and card games. I lose to Lina at Connect Four and go over to watch Maze, Lyr, Delaney, and Teagan playing Ramen Fury. Teagan and Maze keep stealing each other's ingredients and putting chili peppers in each other's bowls, gleefully trash-talking the entire time.

A roar draws me over to where people are playing Fastrack, where two players face off over a small board. Each one uses an elastic band to shoot little wooden discs through a slot in the middle of the board. Evidently, Howie had been beating everyone, but then McKenna crushed him, despite never having played before. As I watch, she proceeds to defeat every opponent after that with her impressive aim and quick fingers.

Piper, Fei Fei, Win, and I start a game of Exploding Kittens, and my pulse speeds up as Harrison joins us. The rules are complicated, so I settle myself by trying to figure out the best strategy.

"Yes!" I shout as Harrison draws an Exploding Kitten card. "I win!"

When hall meeting is over, Sarina and Winson hand out little goody bags. There are a half dozen mini bags of Swedish Fish in addition to other assorted candy in mine. "I'm going to give you Snaps every night!" I tell her.

She laughs. "I guess I'll have to send someone out to get more candy fish. I gave you all I had left." She moves on.

Harrison must've overheard, because he comes over and holds out his hand, palm up. "I didn't get any Swedish Fish," he whines. "They're my favorite, too."

I'm dubious. "You're just saying that. Do you even have Swedish Fish in Hong Kong?"

He puts his hands together and begs, "Please? I'm really sad my kitten got blown up. Don't be an ogre."

How can I say no to that? I give him a couple of bags. Behind him, Fei Fei and Maze pretend to swoon and make smooching lips. They're not even trying to be subtle, and my face feels like it's on fire. I say a hasty good night to everyone and duck into my room. I don't leave to wash up until I'm sure all the guys have gone back down to theirs.

Lyr and I stay up for hours after lights-out, whispering in the dark and listening to Mando-pop, each of us with one earbud in. She knows me so well that she doesn't ask how I feel about Harrison. Which is good because I have no idea.

# CHAPTER NINE

Kirrily wakes us up early at camp because she's always ravenous after her morning training runs. I'm still groggy when we roll into the cafeteria, but it's nice to have the place to ourselves. Queena insists that we all get coffee, saying that we need to learn to drink it if we're going to survive high school. It still tastes terrible after adding several packets of sugar, so I go back for orange juice.

"How do you like your group?" I ask Q and Kir. "I still can't believe that we're not all together."

"Remember Sarah and Betina?" Kir says. "The last time they came to camp was a few years ago. They said they wanted to come to overnight camp to get away from their parents." We nod, and Fei Fei does the *I agree* hand signal. "It's good to see them again."

Q sips her coffee and puts it down quickly. "The other three girls are new. Dani was supposed to room with one of them. Kara's mom didn't want her to be alone in a room, so they crammed another set of furniture into Chelsea and Yiyi's room and made it a triple." She frowns. "They're kind of quiet."

Maze rolls her eyes. "Probably because they're afraid of

you. Let me guess—you commanded them to share their candy with you as a tithe to the crown."

"I was just kidding!" Q insists. "Besides, our counselor stopped them."

"Who are the boys?" Fei Fei asks around a mouthful of cantaloupe.

Kir thinks for a moment. "Jesse, Andrew, Parker, and a new guy, William. He has an accent. Different than the typical Chinese accent, though."

"Like our new CIT," Lina observes. "Is William from Hong Kong?"

"I don't know." Q shrugs.

Lina looks up from her phone. "According to the camp roster, they have the same last name. Plus, they're both new and speak with accents. I bet they're brothers."

"Speaking of our new CIT, he obviously likes you, Phee." Lyr grins, and I poke her in the arm.

"He's just being nice," I say, although last night it had felt like something more. "He's in high school! There's no way he likes me like that."

Lina keeps tapping on her phone. "So my mom gave me access to the whole camp database because I'm helping her with the camp memory book," she reveals. "Harrison might be in high school, but he's fourteen."

"What? That can't be right. I know for a fact that CITs have to be sixteen, or Emerson would've been one two years ago."

"I should be horrified that you're looking at his personal info, but I also kind of want to know more," Lyr admits.

"It's probably all on his social media accounts, too," Lina says. "This is just faster."

Maze peers at Lina's phone. "His birthday is in September. He's almost fifteen. And Phee is already thirteen because her birthday was in January." She looks at me speculatively. "So he's, like, a year and three months older than you. No big deal." She goes back to eating her coffee cake muffin like she didn't just drop a bombshell.

"His application says he's going into eleventh grade," Lina confirms. "That's the only thing the form says is required—it doesn't actually say you have to be sixteen. He must've skipped a couple of grades and whoever reviewed his application didn't do the math."

"Do *not* tell my mom," I say. "She hates loopholes."

A year and three months. It doesn't sound like a lot. But there's a huge difference between an almost eighth grader and an almost junior in high school, isn't there? I've never had a boyfriend, so I have no clue. Then again, Emerson is sixteen, and I swear he's more immature than I am.

Kir puts down her fork and snaps her fingers in front of my face. "Earth to Phoenny! Come back from Planet H and tell us all about him. Q and I missed all the good stuff, remember?"

Fei Fei puts her head on my shoulder. "I was there, and I still want to hear about it. You disappeared after hall meeting."

"There's nothing to tell," I protest. "He told me not to be an ogre. That's all."

"That's *not* all," Fei Fei says, throwing a bit of her toast crust at me. "He practically begged for your candy. And you gave it to him!"

"He was sad he lost." I know it's a pathetic excuse as soon as it comes out of my mouth.

"He was flirting." Fei Fei bats her eyelashes dramatically. "And so were you, kind of. Wouldn't a summer romance make camp spectacular? We need to help you work on your game!"

"No, no, and NO." Oh my god. I love my friends, but this is too much. "I am perfectly okay with not having any 'game'!' I seriously doubt he likes me like that. He's a CIT—it's literally his job to be friendly to everyone." I push my plate of scrambled eggs away. "Can we *please* talk about something else?"

"I heard you think he looks like Xiaojun from WayV," Q says, completely ignoring my plea. I glare at Lyr, and she looks mildly embarrassed for telling Queena. "I see it, but I think he looks more like Wang Yibo when he was in UNIQ. Do you think he can sing like them?"

"Whoever he looks like, here he comes." Lyr points to the cafeteria entrance with her chin.

"Good morning!" Fei Fei trills. She waves enthusiastically.

Why isn't there anything to hide behind? I take a gulp of orange juice and turn to greet him.

Harrison looks at me—I mean us—and waves. Today,

he's layered the turquoise staff T-shirt over a black one and rolled the sleeves up together to create a black band around his biceps. Black cargo pants complete his outfit. As he approaches, I notice swirly turquoise designs around the heels of his Vans and wonder if they're custom-made.

Fei Fei points to an empty chair at our table, and he nods. He's going to sit with us! But then Ava appears from behind him and waves to Fei Fei, too. "We'll be right there," she calls.

As Harrison turns to see who just spoke, McKenna and Teagan swoop in and link their arms through his. Teagan has on a pink T-shirt and black shorts—a classic color combination. The front of her shirt says "Salty" in cursive. McKenna is wearing a simple white tank top and a denim skirt. Her top is anything but basic, though. It's stitched to look like a corset and emphasizes her curves. A pair of colorful espadrilles complete her outfit. My heart sinks as Harrison bestows his smile on them and leads them to the food counter.

I turn back to my plate, not wanting to watch any more. To my chagrin, Kir and Fei Fei have a clear view of the food area and narrate their every move.

"He's putting strawberries on their plates for them."

"McKenna just stumbled, and he caught her arm. Pretty sure she faked it."

"Teagan is pulling him to another table!"

Of course he'd go sit with them. They radiate fun and

style, just like him. But Ava steers their little group toward our table and sits down next to Lina. Delaney, Piper, and McKenna follow suit. There's an awkward moment when we all realize that there are twelve seats at this particular table and only room for one more person.

"No problem," Harrison says quickly. "Cooper's right over there. See you all later." Is it my imagination or does he glance at McKenna as he walks past?

"Definitely more like a young Wang Yibo," Q says once he's out of earshot.

Delaney tilts her head. "Who's that?"

Lina has a photo of the singer-actor-dancer up on her phone in a flash and shows it to the new girls, while Lyr opens her music app and plays UNIQ's "Best Friend."

"You listen to Chinese music?" McKenna asks. "Why?"

I feel my hackles rise. "Millions of people listen to K-pop. Why not C-pop?"

"That's not what I meant," she says. "I just didn't know it was a thing."

I'm too dumbfounded to respond. She didn't think modern Chinese music existed?

Lyr stays calm, as always. "It's true—it's not as popular as K-pop here. I guess you kind of have to search it out. UNIQ's an older band, too. One of our day camp counselors introduced them to us a while ago. Now we all listen to it, especially the newer bands."

"Some of us listen to it against our will," Maze says drily, while Fei Fei gives her a *who, me?* innocent look. Maze turns to Teagan. "Love the shirt, by the way. At the risk of making you even saltier, can I ask a question?"

I brace myself when Teagan nods. Her shoulders are stiff, though.

"Why didn't you all just say you're cousins when Howie brought up your Chinese names yesterday?" Maze asks. "It's such a simple explanation."

"Because they're not," I blurt. "How can they be? Real cousins with the same Chinese last name would have fathers who are brothers, but all their English last names are different, which means their dads aren't related."

"We're right here." Teagan's voice is irritated. "So you can stop talking about us like we're not."

For a moment, I'm embarrassed by my outburst. But I'm determined to unravel this mystery. "Fine. But why did you lie to us about being cousins?" I shake my head. "What are you hiding?"

"Phee." Lina is shocked, but I don't understand why. Isn't she angry that the new girls lied? How am I supposed to simply trust them and let them into our circle when they won't even answer a basic question about how they know each other?

McKenna's voice is hard. "We didn't lie. You both just assumed we were cousins, and we didn't correct you. And you heard Gemma yesterday—it's a personal matter. Why are you still asking?"

"Whoa, whoa, whoa," Piper says, holding her hands out. She looks around at her friends. "Didn't we talk about this last night? Didn't we decide that we were going to tell them?"

"That was before I got called a liar," McKenna says. She pushes her plate away and sits back.

I take a deep breath. "I'm sorry I said that. We've had new campers before, but not five at once who all wanted to be put in the same group. And who won't tell us why. Can you understand how that makes us feel?"

McKenna doesn't respond. Ava looks at me and then at Piper. "We did agree. I think it makes sense to tell them, especially because Lina already guessed when she met my moms."

Lina knew and didn't tell us? I feel a pang. Somehow that's worse than just the new girls keeping something secret. Squad shouldn't keep secrets from Squad.

Piper and Delaney nod at Ava. Teagan mutters, "Fine." McKenna shrugs.

Ava meets my eyes. "Okay. Our Chinese names are similar because we are all from the same orphanage. We were part of the same travel group, meaning we were adopted at the same time, and our families did some sightseeing together before returning to the States with us. So we're not blood-related, but we consider ourselves to be like cousins, especially since we all live in New England and see each other pretty regularly."

There's a pause while the Squad absorbs what she said. Then I feel like laughing. That's it? That's the big secret?

Fei Fei actually snorts. "Well, that's kind of a letdown, to be honest. I was hoping you were a secret group of kid super-heroes, or immortal aliens like in *Eternals*."

"Oh, didn't I mention I'm also a superhero who slays alien wombats?" Ava says, and she and Fei Fei crack up.

There's an awkward moment when some chuckle and others, like McKenna and Teagan, don't smile. Then we start eating and chatting again, but I've lost my appetite. I understand now why the new girls wanted to be in the same camp group—they've been together even longer than the Squad. But I don't get why they made it such a big deal. Should I think this is a bigger deal? Do I need to change how we interact? Do I need to stop mixing Chinese words into conversations and talking about C-pop? It seems like I run the risk of upsetting them with anything I might say about Chinese culture. It's impossible to not talk about Chinese culture at a cultural heritage camp, though.

How has camp become so nerve-racking? It's always been my safe space. The place where I can relax and just be me. I look around the table and feel like I'm back in seventh grade, watching my school friend group slowly break apart, choosing new friends, forming new relationships. Will Lyr eventually abandon me, too?

After breakfast, a gaggle of younger campers crowd

around the lobby wall where the Committee has posted each group's schedules. They whisper and move aside when Q and the rest of us approach.

"Phoenny!" Matty steps forward and pulls on my arm. "How do we tell what activity we're doing for the Showcase performance? Please don't say I'm going to have to sing." Matty hates singing as much as I hate exercise.

"Easy," I tell him. "It's always the first class of the day. It's also printed in bold." I point to the first-class block on his schedule. "Look, you have music class first." I squint at the tiny Chinese characters. "Drums. So that's what you'll be doing for the performance."

"Yessss!" Matty pumps his fist in the air. "We're playing drums, not singing some kiddie song in Chinese! Let's go tell the other guys!" He high-fives a kid wearing bright blue hearing aids, and they sprint away.

"Achievement unlocked," Fei Fei comments. She and Ava glance at each other and smile.

"Phee!" Lyr calls. "Look at this!"

"Lyr, your million-dollar piano-playing finger is covering the class name." She drops her hand. I read the words, but they don't make sense. "Wǔshù? We've got martial arts first?" I turn to Lyr's pale face, feeling the color drain out of mine as well. "But the oldest group always learns a traditional dance from Tāng Auntie and performs it for the Showcase."Both of us have been looking forward to it for years. For Lyr, it's about the dance and the music, while I've been yearning to wear the beautiful costumes. Also, the dance steps are simple enough that even I probably won't mess up too much.

"We've got her for first period," Q says. "And martial arts for third."

Sure enough, Group 12 has Chinese dance first. Another dream dashed. My throat closes and tears prick my eyes, so I spin around before anyone can see but end up bumping into the person behind me. A person with wedge-heeled espadrilles.

McKenna says, "What's your problem?" Or maybe she says, "What's the problem?" but it doesn't matter because the answer to both questions is the same. Instead of replying, I step around her and into the living room, making a beeline for the navy velveteen sofa.

The rest of the Squad joins me. Lyr puts her arm around my shoulders and squeezes. "I'm disappointed, too," she says. "But we'll find other ways to make our Showcase performance fun. Don't the women in historical Chinese dramas do martial arts in their beautiful robes? Maybe Tāng Auntie will let us borrow some costumes for our wǔshù routine."

"Or maybe you can make some for us!" Fei Fei suggests brightly. The others chime in, telling me how I'm awesome at sewing and that I'd be great at costume design, too.

"Thanks. I'll be fine. It was just too much to process all at once, you know?" I wipe my eyes and smile at my friends.

"Let's talk about something else. Who's got a story?"

Kir rolls her eyes. "Parker has gone from annoying to totally obnoxious. Last night he said I shouldn't eat any more candy because my thighs are already 'huge.' What a jerk."

We all gasp. "I hope you chewed him out," I say.

"Better." She smiles. "I challenged him to a race around campus this afternoon after classes."

We hoot. Parker is going to get smoked, as Howie would say.

A voice cuts in from across the room. "What's the joke? I could use a laugh."

Fei Fei squeaks as Harrison appears and drops a plastic crate onto the floor next to her with a loud thump. His hair sticks out in different directions, and his shirts are rumpled. Somehow it makes him look both younger and more attractive at the same time. Mentally, I shake myself. I need to focus on my friends, not this boy.

Kir tells Harrison about her race with Parker this afternoon. "The joke is that he doesn't know I'm a competitive runner."

Fei Fei grabs Kir's arm and raises it in the air. "Cross-country state champ!"

Harrison lets out a low whistle. "Hóu jǐng." He bumps fists with Kir. We look at him quizzically until he says, "Oh, it means 'great' or 'awesome' in Cantonese. I think the Mandarin pronunciation would be *hǎo zhèng*, but no one ever says it that way."

"Your brother and Parker are roomies, right?" Q says. "Tell William not to pick up any bad habits from Parker."

Harrison chuckles. "Win wasn't kidding when he said the Squad knows everything that goes on here. Thanks, I'll pass the advice on to Wills. Not sure he'll listen to me, though." He looks at his phone and plops down between me and Lina. He smells like sandalwood and spearmint, earthy and fresh all at once. "Showtime."

Right on cue, campers and counselors stream into the room, chattering and laughing. McKenna spots Harrison next to me, and her eyes narrow. I narrow my eyes right back at her. He sat by me after all, not the other way around.

# CHAPTER TEN

Cold air blasts us as we file into the atrium of the Performing Arts Center. It sends a zap of energy through me like ice-blue embroidery thread. The teacher isn't there yet, so Sarina and Win go looking for him, leaving Harrison and Gemma in charge. We all plop down on the floor to wait, except for McKenna, who can't sit on the floor in her short skirt. She wanders around the space for a few minutes before approaching the CITs.

"Harrison," she says in a voice as sweet and sticky as spider silk, "could you find a chair for me?"

Harrison looks at her and then scans the room, as if a chair will magically appear. "This is my first time here, too. I've no idea where they'd be." His eyes come to rest on me. "Hey, Phee? Do you know where to find some chairs?"

"They're in a storage room back there on the right," I tell him, pointing to the doors that Sarina and Win disappeared through. "But it's locked, because all the musical instruments for camp are stored there, too. Only the music teacher and the directors have keys."

Harrison shrugs at McKenna. "Sorry."

McKenna looks at me as if the locked room is my fault. "Are we doing martial arts in a lobby?"

"The gyms are being used for dance and sports. The classrooms are too small and have too much furniture. This atrium is spacious and air-conditioned. But if you're really unhappy, I'll ask the teacher to move the class outside," Gemma responds.

"That'll be fun," Maze says. "It's gotta be at least eighty degrees already."

Without responding, McKenna goes over to stand next to Teagan.

The counselors reappear with an older man following them. Win gets us all on our feet in a large semicircle and Sarina introduces the teacher to us as Gāo Shīfu, or Master Gao. He's from Taiwan and doesn't speak any English, so she and Win will translate. First, we go around the circle and introduce ourselves with both our English and Chinese names, with different levels of fluency. Howie doesn't wig out about the new girls' names again, so maybe he knows they're adopted now, too, and we can all move on.

Gāo Shīfu nods at each person, but when I say "Phoenny Fāng. Fāng Xiǎofèng," he walks right up to me and sticks out his hand.

"Ah, Fāng Xiǎofèng! Wǒ hěn gāo xìng de rènshì nǐ. Nǐ māma shì wǒ de lǎo péngyǒu."

It figures that the teacher is Mom's old friend and says so in front of everyone else. I shake his hand politely and murmur back in Mandarin that I'm happy to meet him, too. Hopefully, his friendship with Mom will make him go easy on me when he sees how clumsy I am.

My ears perk up when Harrison says his Chinese name.

"Goū Hǔngsaān," he says, not in Mandarin but in Cantonese. His name sounds like go hoong sahn, and I wonder what the characters are and what they mean. It almost sounds like they took Harrison and translated the sounds into Cantonese.

After introductions, Gāo Shīfu says something to Sarina, then points to McKenna. The counselor's voice carries across the atrium. "Gāo Shīfu would like you to go back and change into appropriate clothes and shoes before joining the class."

McKenna is shocked. "What's wrong with what I'm wearing?"

"Camp dress policy is pretty relaxed. But not for martial arts. No open-toed shoes, no high heels. It's for your own safety. Gāo Shīfu doesn't want you to twist your ankles," Sarina answers evenly. "Also, he's afraid your skirt might be too constricting for some of the movements. Shorts or athletic pants and sneakers would be best."

"No one told me," McKenna says. "It's not like I've been to camp or taken martial arts before."

Sarina raises an eyebrow. "It's in all the emails sent to

parents before camp starts, with recommended packing lists and guidelines."

"Not everyone takes martial arts, though, right?" McKenna presses. "I didn't know we were."

"Class schedules were also sent to parents last week," Sarina says, a touch of frustration in her voice. "I'm sorry that I didn't notice what you were wearing when the group met this morning, or I would've reminded you of the dress policy. If you want, I can see if the teacher will make an exception for you today so you don't have to go all the way back and change."

When McKenna nods, Sarina switches to Mandarin and asks Gāo Shīfu. He agrees to her skirt, but not her shoes.

"I thought you were worried about safety," McKenna says when she hears she has to do class barefoot. "I could step on something sharp and cut my feet!"

"Just sit out this time, yeah?" Win suggests. He looks at his watch. "We need to start class."

"There's nowhere to sit!"

Harrison has found a dust mop. "How about if I sweep the floor first? I'll make sure there's nothing sharp."

McKenna's face goes from annoyed to appreciative in an instant. "That's so sweet of you."

He tips an imaginary hat. "At your service."

Everyone scatters while Harrison quickly runs the mop back and forth. He served her food at breakfast; now he's cleaning for her. I shake my head. CITs aren't servants. I'm not sure who I'm more irritated with—McKenna or Harrison.

Floor swept, Gāo Shīfu arranges us in rows facing him, Sarina, and Win. I'm at the end of the front row with most of the Squad when Harrison comes and stands next to me. Great. I'm even clumsier when I'm nervous.

We learn a few basic stances and practice them over and over again. The counselors stay at the front while Gāo Shīfu walks up and down the rows, evaluating our form., He shows us the stance again, and then moves our arms and legs into the proper positions. Lyr and I had martial arts classes when we were day campers, but that was a long time ago. I wobble and almost fall when dropping into the crossed legs stance, and I catch Harrison grinning at me. He's as steady as a soccer player would be. I make a face, and he chuckles.

Gāo Shīfu watches Howie for a while and grunts, "Hén hǎo." He asks Howie how long he's been studying wǔshù and leads him to the front of the room. Then he notices that we've stopped practicing and gestures to Win to lead us through all the stances again.

"And a star is born," Harrison says.

"What?"

"Howie. He's quite good. No wonder Gāo Shīfu placed him in front. The parents won't be able to take their eyes off him during the performance."

Is he right? I watch Howie do the routine perfectly again.

Hmm. Maybe Group 13 won't have a dismal performance for the Showcase after all. Putting on a decent show isn't what will make our last year of camp spectacular, but at least it'll end on a high note. I remember what Lyr said about borrowing costumes, and my spirits lift a little. Maybe I can talk to Gāo Shīfu about it later, after I've checked with Tāng Auntie that she actually has costumes that could be used for wǔshù.

After another half hour of practicing stances, my legs are like jelly. I mention it to Lyr and she says, "My legs are like tofu!" and we giggle at her making an American cliché into a phrase that you'd probably never say in Mandarin.

Our second class is Traditional Crafts with Sūn Lǎoshī, who has been teaching it for years. She talks a little about the history of Chinese rice dough art before setting us loose to make our own figurines. I don't know what to make, which is strange. I'm usually bursting with ideas when it comes to creating art. Another unwelcome change, I think.

"Phoenny-ah?" Sūn Lǎoshī's voice cuts through my thoughts. "What are you planning to make with all those little balls?"

I glance down at the table, where I've mindlessly rolled half a dozen small balls of black dough and twice as many balls of white dough. "Um, pandas?"

The teacher clucks in disapproval. "Didn't you do that last year? And maybe the year before that, too. Try something different this year, okay?"

Even though I know I didn't make pandas for two years in a row, I don't want to contradict her. Instead, embarrassment washes over me. "Okay, how about chess pieces?"

Sūn Lǎoshī shakes her head. "Something with more color! You wear such colorful clothes—I know you can think beyond black and white."

My cheeks burn even hotter. I look down at my sleeveless baby-doll tunic, the three ruffled tiers from different patterned blouses Năinai didn't want anymore. "Okay," I say again. "More color."

Sūn Lǎoshī moves on, praising Lyr's calico cat and Fei Fei's tropical fish before going over to the table where Harrison, Bran, and Howie are working. To my right, in a low voice so the teacher doesn't hear, Teagan says, "I hate crafts. What's the point of making something that I can buy in Chinatown? Handmade stuff is overrated."

"It's not personal," Lyr murmurs in my ear. "None of them know that you make clothes and art."

I muster a grateful smile. McKenna's clear dislike of me, Teagan's snarkiness, wǔshù instead of dance, and now the teacher's criticism—it's suddenly all too much. For the second time this morning, I blink back tears and reach for some of the other rice dough colors.

My hand bumps into another, and I look up, startled, only to find myself staring into Harrison's eyes. They're filled with concern. "Everything okay?" he asks softly.

I swallow and change the subject. "Making snakes?"

He looks at the green dough in his hand. "I ought to. I was bitten by a bamboo viper a few years ago. One of the most venomous snakes in HK. It might be satisfying to make one and take revenge on it."

"Have a car run over it," Maze suggests.

"Make an iguana eating it," Fei Fei offers.

"I think falcons are their natural predators," Lina says.

His eyes gleam. "See? Falcons are hóu jǐng." He takes some red and black dough and returns to his table. I manage to focus and make a brown ox with white horns and a tiger. I hope its orange and black stripes are colorful enough for the teacher.

Sūn Lǎoshī admires them. "Zodiac animals. Good. Very traditional." She hands out short bamboo skewers and blocks of Styrofoam. I push a skewer partway into each of my figures and then stick the other end into the foam, so it holds the skewer upright. This way, the dough dries more evenly.

The new girls all made the same thing—pink roses. They also made animals, except for Teagan, who made a 3D poop emoji. It's not until I notice that McKenna's gray shapes are actually sharks and not seals that I realize they each made their favorite animals. I wish I'd thought of that—except I don't have the skill to make a multicolored Chinese phoenix. Yet. Maybe I'll practice in class tomorrow.

We put our dough figurines on a table in the back of the

room labeled with our group number. I write my name on a small sticker and attach it to the side of the foam block. Bran sets his down next to mine, and I gasp.

"Nice, right?" he chuckles. "I've been watching *Game of Thrones.*" He's made a row of decapitated heads, with faces contorted in fear or agony. One of them even has a tiny purple tongue lolling out of its mouth.

"They're so . . . lifelike," I finally say.

"Thanks. When I get home, I'm going to make Winterfell out of Legos and then set these guys in front. It's going to be awesome." He grins and I smile back, because I've just figured out why he wants to be called Bran.

I look for Harrison's creations, but don't spot any. Maybe he didn't want to keep them. Counselors and CITs don't have to display their work in the gallery part of the Showcase on the last day of camp.

It must be nice to not have that pressure to perform.

Traditional Chinese Dance, our third class, is taught by Tāng Auntie, a good friend of both my and Lyr's moms. She announces that we're going to learn ribbon dancing.

"I know I'm super uncoordinated," I say to Lyr as the counselors and CITs start handing out the ribbons, "but I'd still rather dance in the Showcase than do wǔshù." She gives me a sympathetic hug.

"Ladies, your bouquets." Harrison bows and holds out a fistful of ribbons. Each ribbon is bunched up at the top of a wooden dowel and secured with a rubber band. They do kind of look like flowers. Lyr giggles and takes a bright gold ribbon. I choose the indigo one and thank Harrison.

"I live to serve," he says, reminding me that he said something similar to McKenna during martial arts class. He scans the room to see who else needs a ribbon, but Sarina and Win have already handed them out to the remaining campers. He looks down at the one in his hand. "Guess this one is mine. 'Hot pink it is."

"It's actually fuchsia," I say. "Hot pink would be a little more neon."

"Are you always this specific when it comes to colors?" he asks. "Is Lyrica's ribbon yellow?"

"Um, no. It's clearly gold." I'm honestly getting a little annoyed. I hate it when people describe colors too simply. There are so many shades—call them what they are!

Harrison just grins, which makes me feel like . . . an ogre.

At Tāng Auntie's signal, Sarina starts the music.

Maze says, "This is going to be great," in a voice that suggests it will be anything but.

She's right. We're terrible at ribbon dancing. Either we can't twirl our wrists without tangling the ribbon or we can't keep our arms raised high enough to keep the ribbon off the floor. The two exceptions are Fei Fei, who takes a dance elective at her Chinese school, and McKenna, who announces that she's taken ballet lessons since she was three. Somehow, I end up behind McKenna when Tāng Auntie has us run in a large circle, and I accidentally step on her ribbon, yanking her arm down and making her drop it entirely. We both rush to pick it up at the same time, cracking our heads together.

"I'm so sorry!" I rub my forehead ruefully. "I'm such a klutz."

"I noticed." She grabs her ribbon and rejoins the circle without another word.

If I had stepped on any of the Squad's ribbons, we'd be laughing and joking about it. Instead, I stand there, watching the rest of the group spin past me.

# CHAPTER ELEVEN

At lunch, we sit the way we did at dinner last night, with the counselors and CITs across from each other in the middle of the long rectangular table, returning campers on one side and new ones on the other. Stitching Group 13 together is probably more work than they expected, especially if a couple of the pattern pieces don't want to be part of the whole garment.

I'm next to Sarina, so I have a clear view of her phone screen when she opens an app. "You posted videos of us on social media? Since when did Squee get an account?"

My voice carries, and everyone stops eating and pulls out their phones. Even the campers at the tables nearby. Sarina and Win share an amused glance. "All the counselors talked Director Fāng and Assistant Director Chǔ into it. We thought it would be fun for former campers and counselors to see what we're up to and also do some publicity for Squee. Look." She shows the latest post to the group—a clip of three girls during crafts class. McKenna, Teagan, and Delaney twirl around with their rice dough roses held up to their cheeks. "So cute."

"Beautiful," Harrison says to McKenna.

So she's beautiful and I'm just pretty. My insides knot

together as McKenna thanks him sweetly. She sees me watching and smiles a little more widely.

"You're using us as models for Squee?" Delaney sounds both excited and nervous. She touches her top lip unconsciously, tracing a faint scar running from the bottom of her nose to the top of her lip.

I'm not the only one who notices this—Lina does as well.

Win gives Delaney a cheesy grin. "Of course! Group 13 is the best, am I right? Who better to represent Squee?"

Lina tilts her head. "Why does Squee need to do publicity? Aren't there enough campers?"

I would argue that there are too many campers this year, especially rising eighth graders.

Sarina says, "It's always good to attract new people. I think some kids who've been coming to Squee for a long time are choosing other camps. Or maybe their parents are choosing for them. I heard the STEM camps are really popular."

"And sports," Howie pipes up. "Jun Wen and Colson decided to go to soccer camp instead of coming back to Squee."

"No surprise there," a voice snarks. "Who in their right mind pays to mess with Play-Doh and ribbons?" Teagan looks appalled.

"Again, millions of people?" I retort. "Making figures out of dough has been part of Chinese culture for more than eighteen hundred years, since the Han dynasty. Ribbon dancing has been around for a really long time, too. They're both important parts of our history." I wrote a paper on Chinese crafts for social studies last year and followed a bunch of artists who are still making things the traditional way, but with their own modern spin on it. They've inspired me to do the same with my fabric art and upcycling of clothes.

McKenna mutters, "*Your* history," at the same time that Teagan says, "What are you, a history nerd?"

"Hey, now." Win holds up a hand. "No name-calling." His tone is gentle but stern.

I stare at McKenna. "What do you mean, *my* history? Isn't it your history, too? Especially since you were born there?"

"You were born in China?" Howie jumps in. "But you have an English last name? Make this make sense!"

Oh no. I guess he didn't know that McKenna and the other new girls are adopted. I had to open my big mouth. I look around wildly.

Gemma comes to my rescue. "Let's all chill for a moment. It's complicated, so I need you all to just settle down and listen to us." She glances around the table. Piper and Ava give her tiny nods. After a moment, McKenna, Teagan, and Delaney nod, too. "Howie, all their names make sense if you know that they're adopted." She looks first at him, and then at me, Bran, and the Squad. "I am, too. The orphanage gave me the Chinese last name Li, and it was just a coincidence that my adoptive parents' last name is Lee. So I never told anyone at Squee that I was adopted. My parents are divorced, and I guess my mom didn't think it was important to tell the directors or the Committee. There's nowhere to put that kind of information on the application form, anyway."

There's a ripple of surprise from the returning campers, and even from Sarina and Win. Sarina reaches across the table to put her hand over Gemma's. She turns to look at the new girls. "I wish I'd known earlier so Win and I could've been better prepared for these kinds of conversations, but I'm glad we know now. Thank you all for sharing this important part of your identity with us."

I force myself to look directly at McKenna. "I'm sorry that I let it slip that you were born in China. And that I upset you when I said, 'our history.'" I know it's right to apologize even though I'm still not sure why she reacted so negatively.

Gemma must see my confusion because she says, "That's the complicated part, Phee. I personally don't feel a huge connection to China, even though I was born there. My parents also didn't do a lot of the cultural stuff, so when people meet me and assume I should know things or feel connected based on the way I look, it can make me feel bad about myself."

I bite my lip, trying to understand. I wasn't born in China, but in some ways, it feels like home to me. Like the sweater that Wàipó handed down to Mom and then to me, my connection to my culture has also been passed along. What would it be like to not have any of that? What would it be like to not have any of that when everyone assumes you do?

Gemma turns to Teagan and says gently, "I can understand that you don't like Chinese crafts or ribbon dancing, but it's not cool to disrespect people who do."

Teagan looks abashed. "Sorry, but I just don't get how dough and dancing are so important."

"It's art," Harrison says, in a more serious voice than I've heard before. "And art shows us who we are. On a historical level, art tells us what was going on during that time period—in politics, society, culture, government—everything, basically. It's how people have expressed themselves since the beginning."

He definitely skipped a grade. Or two. And he's definitely out of my league.

Piper looks thoughtful. "So what you and Gemma are saying is that making art, like crafts or music or whatever, can connect us to other people, and also to . . . other countries?"

"Yes," Harrison says, smiling.

"And maybe even to our heritages," Gemma adds.

After a moment, Sarina and Win ask if anyone has further questions, and when no one chimes in, they remind us that we can always ask questions as S'ups during hall meetings. Then they start a group debate about the best donuts to use for Carnival tomorrow night, and I feel my shoulders relax.

We leave lunch a little early so McKenna can change her clothes, and then we go to our afternoon classes. In Traditional Sports, Hsu Lǎoshī explains the basics of badminton and has us practice basic racket strokes, standing in a line at the back of the gym. Although it's as repetitive as the wǔshù stances, at least I don't trip over my own feet.

After sports, we go to Chinese music class, where we each take a seat behind a gǔzhēn. I run my finger along the lacquered wood and admire the mother-of-pearl inlay of flowers and vines. It reminds me of the patterns of the fabrics back in my room, and my fingers itch to start a sewing project. Maybe I'll work on Lina's appliqué T-shirt during free time.

Lyr has been curious about what Peng Lǎoshī, the new music teacher, is going to teach us. He's younger than I expected, and his eyes are kind behind his chunky black plastic-framed glasses. He reminds us that the instruments are delicate, so we have to be super careful playing them, and then shows us how to pluck notes on the strings. After seven notes, I realize that he's teaching us the melody to "Twinkle, Twinkle, Little Star." All our previous music teachers have stuck to traditional Chinese tunes. Piper picks it up right away and plays the song all the way through, earning the teacher's nod of approval.

"You're really good," Lyr tells her. "Have you taken gǔzhēn lessons before?"

Piper smiles shyly. "Thanks. No, I haven't played this instrument before, but I've taken guitar lessons for a while. It's kind of like a guitar on its back."

"You're a musician!" Lyr is delighted. "I play piano and keyboard and dabble in other instruments. Are you in a band?"

"I tried to start a garage band last year." Piper makes a face. "But I live in a tiny town in New Hampshire and most of the kids at school are into sports or theater. The music teacher had to partner with the middle school in the next town just to get enough kids to have a band and orchestra. It's been tough trying to find people on my own."

"That's a bummer. If you lived closer, we could jam together."

I feel a twinge, as though someone has grabbed a few of my heart's muscle fibers and twisted them. Why is Lyr buddying up to Piper, anyway? She knows a ton of other musicians from all the programs she's in.

"I brought my guitar," Piper tells Lyr. "Maybe we could play together while we're at camp."

"Let's do it!" Lyr says.

I must have forgotten to trim the thread ends on my tunic, because they're making me itch. It's totally not jealousy.

"*Smile*, Phee." I look up as Sarina aims her phone at me. "Try to look like you're having fun." I smile dutifully and pluck a few notes. "Great. I'm going to post that one, okay?"

Win rushes over, with Gemma and Harrison on his heels. "Wait. Stop. Don't post anything!"

"Why not? What's going on?"

He holds up his phone, and to my shock, Mom's voice comes out of the speaker. "We have trolls, Sarina. We have to stop posting camp photos and videos on social media immediately."

Sarina gasps. "Oh no! Is it bad? Should I delete the posts?"

"It's bad," Mom says grimly. "A parent noticed racist comments on our account and called me. Understandably, they're very upset. We all are. But don't delete anything or close comments right now, until I give further instructions. We're gathering the Committee together to decide how to proceed. In the meantime, please help me contact all the other groups' counselors and tell them to stop posting, too."

Win mutters a bad word under his breath, and Sarina shakes her head in disbelief. "Okay, Director Fāng. We're on it. Is there anything else we can do?"

Mom sighs. "Try to keep things as normal as possible for the campers. Don't tell them about this—I don't want them reading those horrible comments."

Sarina taps me on the shoulder and gestures to the phone, so I speak up. "Mom? It's too late. We already know about the social media account and read the comments. Maybe you should have a discussion with everyone after tonight's all-group activity."

Her sigh is even louder this time. "I don't want to scare or upset the younger campers if they haven't seen the comments."

"Mom. It's camp. Everyone's together all the time. Everyone's going to know about the trolls and the comments in, like, five minutes." I pause and think about Matty. "If you don't want to talk to all the overnight campers at once, at least have the counselors bring it up during the hall meetings tonight. Then the counselors for the younger kids can talk about it more simply and not make it sound as scary."

There's a pause. "That's a good idea, Phee. Thank you. I assume I'm still on speakerphone?" When I make a sound of agreement, she continues. "Sarina, Winson, Gemma, and Harrison—please pass Phee's idea along to the other counselors and CITs. Have all the overnight groups do a quick hall meeting after Movie Night is over."

"Got it," Sarina says. "Anything else?"

"Above all," Mom says, "don't let the campers out of your sight. Keep them safe." She hangs up.

Fear descends on our group like a chilly fog, damp and oppressive. Instinctively, the Squad moves closer to each other. We've all heard about the increase in attacks against Asians. People blame us for all sorts of problems, because of the way we look and the things politicians say about us. Dad said we have to fight against racism by voting for better leaders in government. Mom bought me a personal alarm. I didn't bring it to camp. I never thought I'd need it here.

Peng Lǎoshī tries his best to keep teaching, but we're too distracted. All four counselors are on their phones messaging the other groups' counselors. Finally, the teacher asks us to put our chairs in a circle and he plays soothing music on his gǔzhēn while leading us through a calming breathing exercise.

Win gathers us together outside after class. "I know everybody has questions about the social media issue. But let's try to finish our day normally, like Director Fāng suggested, okay? That will give me, Sarina, Gemma, and Harrison time to find out what the Committee is planning to do."

"You heard Phee and Director Fāng. We'll discuss it at hall meeting tonight," Sarina adds. "Right now, we've got Mandarin class and then it's Counselor Time." Delaney raises her hand, and Sarina smiles at her. "Go ahead and ask; we're not in school."

Delaney blushes and pulls on one of her braids. "I was wondering about Counselor Time—what is that?"

"Oh, that's basically when you have to do anything we say," Win jokes. "Like cleaning bathrooms."

Sarina rolls her eyes. "Don't listen to him. We come up with fun activities for Counselor Time—games, crafts, making snacks, stuff like that. Mostly we hang out as a group, but sometimes we'll split up and give you options for different activities with other groups, or even give you free time. Today, though, we're doing group photos. We like to get you when you're fresh, before the sleep deprivation sets in." She laughs. "It's a tradition."

Delaney is clearly relieved that she won't be scrubbing toilets, but she still seems a little anxious. Behind her, Teagan groans about doing more crafts. Personally, I hope they give us lots of free time so I can work on sewing projects.

The counselors seem like they're back to their usual lighthearted selves, but I notice that they herd us along a little faster than usual and their eyes constantly scan our surroundings.

# CHAPTER TWELVE

We're halfway across campus before Sarina's words sink in. "Mandarin class? Since when do we have Mandarin class at Squee?"

Maze trudges next to me. "Right? Like going to Chinese school isn't painful enough."

"You don't like Chinese school?" a voice asks. I look up to find Delaney walking next to Maze.

"I'd honestly rather work in my dad's market than go spend hours cooped up in a classroom on a Sunday," Maze says. "My Mandarin teacher is the worst."

I snort. "No way. *My* Mandarin teacher is the worst. He gives me, Lyr, and Lina extra homework every time he catches us talking." Beside me, Lyr groans just thinking about it. I remember Delaney saying her Chinese name correctly during introductions yesterday, but I remind myself not to assume anything. "Do you go to Chinese school, too?"

"I used to when I lived in Bangor," Delaney replies. "I actually really liked it. Then my family moved to Portland right before I started middle school. My school offers Mandarin classes starting in seventh grade, so I took it last year. I'm going to take it again this fall."

Lyr, Maze, and I let out little whines of jealousy. "What I would give to learn Mandarin in regular school! I'd have all day Sunday to sew," I say.

"I'd bake." Maze's voice is full of longing.

Lyr plays an imaginary keyboard in the air. "And I'd compose all the songs! Delaney, what do you do with all your free time on Sundays?"

She laughs. "We're all a bunch of homebodies, aren't we? I take care of all my pets—clean their cages, play with them, give them treats—I could do that all day. My gerbils are pretty smart, but I actually want to get a pet rat and build obstacle courses for it."

Delaney and Maze lose me when they start talking about their favorite videos of animals running obstacle courses. There's a giggle behind me, and I look back to see McKenna and Teagan flanking Harrison and chatting with him. I wonder how they learned to be so comfortable around boys— especially older boys. What do they talk about? I'm pretty sure it's not Swedish Fish or ogres. Ogres are like trolls, right? And suddenly I'm thinking about the online trolls again. I walk faster, eager to reach the safety of the classroom building.

Lyr hurries to catch up to me. "What's wrong?" she asks.

"Everything feels out of control," I tell her. "What if the trolls come to Squee? What happens then? Will the Committee shut down camp?"

She links arms with me. "Our moms will figure it out—

they're the most in-control people we know, remember? Try not to worry so much. We've got one more class, then Counselor Time, and then we're free. Don't forget—Kir's going to show Parker who's boss!"

I muster a smile. "That sounds great." I give her a side hug, looping my arm around her waist. "Thanks."

She hugs me back, and we walk in step the rest of the way.

Lyr and I stop dead in the doorway of the classroom, as though we're wedged into it. Are we in some alternate-reality version of Squee? One where our super-serious Chinese school teacher shows up? Unfortunately, it's real *and* a nightmare. Huáng Lǎoshī is busy writing his name in both Pinyin and characters on the whiteboard. He turns and spots us, but we don't get a friendly greeting, just a curt nod and a gesture for us to sit down. We find seats near Lina in the back row.

"I can't believe this," I whisper to Lina. "I need to have a serious talk with my mom. I've told her a million times that he's not good with kids. And the Committee decides to hire him for the first time Mandarin is offered at camp?"

She shakes her head. "Maybe they couldn't find anyone else and they got desperate?"

"Fāng Xiǎofèng! Liào Lina!" Huáng Lǎoshī barks out our Chinese names. "Shàng lái."

Lina's head droops as we both get up and shuffle to the front, where the teacher motions to two empty seats in the first row, right in front of him. We've never gotten homework because this isn't that kind of camp. That better not change.

Huáng Lǎoshī introduces himself and talks about what we'll be learning during camp. He speaks in rapid-fire Mandarin, forgetting or ignoring the fact that not all of our parents speak Mandarin to us at home. Even though Mom and Dad are pretty fluent, they were both born in the US and speak to me and my brothers in English. If it weren't for years of Chinese school, my vocabulary would be limited to phrases like "I brushed my teeth" or "I'd like two orders of shrimp dumplings." Most of the returning campers are like me, except for Fei Fei, whose parents immigrated here just before she was born and don't speak much English.

I hear murmuring but don't want to risk turning around to see who it is and getting scolded by the teacher. "This is not working for me," McKenna says loudly. Huáng Lǎoshī abruptly stops talking and points to her. "What did you say?" he says in Mandarin.

"I'm going to guess that you asked me what I said." McKenna starts. "But I don't know Mandarin, so I haven't understood anything you said so far."

Huáng Lǎoshī is thunderstruck. "You do not speak any Chinese?" he says in English. Then he eyes the class. "How many of you cannot understand what I said?"

McKenna, Teagan, and Piper raise their hands reluctantly.

"Why is this?" Huáng Lǎoshī snaps. "I was told your group

has the oldest campers. You should all have had many years of Chinese school by now."

All the adoptees look distinctly uncomfortable, even Ava and Delaney, who do know some Mandarin. Sarina takes a step forward as if to intervene, but Gemma nods encouragingly at Piper, who sits a little straighter. "We're adopted," she says quietly. "Our parents are white and don't speak Chinese. Some of us have gone to Chinese school or learned a bit in other places, but we're not fluent." She looks down, embarrassed.

Huáng Lǎoshī's eyes are wide, his eyebrows raised in surprise. It's probably the most expressive I've seen him besides when he's annoyed. He recovers quickly, though. "Okay," he says. "This changes my lesson plan. Today, we just learn to introduce ourselves. I will give you a Chinese name if you do not have one. Raise—"

"We all have Chinese names," McKenna interrupts. It's obvious from her tone that she's irritated. But what did she expect at a Chinese heritage camp? Even in my first-grade Spanish class the teacher gave us all Spanish names.

"Actually, I don't," Brandon calls from the back row. "Just because my parents are Chinese American doesn't mean that they automatically gave me and my siblings Chinese names."

"Wait, what?" I swivel around to look at Bran. "Then whose name did you give us during the intros yesterday?"

He smirks. "It's the first name of a character in my favorite martial arts movie."

"So you do have a Chinese name; you just gave it to yourself," I insist.

"Nah, I change it up all the time, depending on my mood and who's asking," Bran says. "My teachers at Chinese school gave up and just call me 'Brandon' now. That's my real name, anyway."

I've been in the same camp group as Bran several times over the years—how did I not realize that he gave different Chinese names each time? Maybe because none of us call each other by them, so aside from the Squad, other people's Chinese names don't stick in my head. It still kind of boggles my mind that he doesn't want a permanent Chinese name. It feels like he's rejecting an important part of his heritage.

"Good, good," the teacher says, and it's clear he's buying time to figure out how to adjust his lesson plans. He scans the room, counting under his breath. Then he looks straight at Lina. "Liào Lina, you partner with her." He points to Ava, behind her. "Turn your desks to face each other."

Oh no. I know what's coming. Huáng Lǎoshī addresses me next. "Fāng Xiǎofèng, turn your desk around, too. You will work with her." He motions to McKenna. Then he points to Maze with one index finger and to Teagan with the other. "You two are partners." Bran and Howie high-five when they get each other. I feel a stab of jealousy when Huáng Lǎoshī pairs Lyr with Piper and they smile at each other. Lastly, Fei Fei is partnered with Delaney.

Everybody except for Ava and McKenna stands up and moves their desks to face their partners. McKenna crosses her arms and glares at the ceiling. "I could've been learning Italian instead."

"But you're Chinese," Lina says, confused.

"I am *not*," McKenna says sharply. "I'm American. I don't have to learn Mandarin just because I was born there. It's not a *requirement*. I can learn whatever language I want to."

"You're right," Maze says softly. "I wish my dad thought that way. I don't want to be forced to learn Mandarin just because I'm ethnically Chinese."

My eyebrows raise. Maze has always complained about going to Chinese school, but she's never talked about it like this. Chinese school is just something we all suffer through without questioning—like a rite of passage so we can claim to be "really Chinese." But are Maze and Brandon and McKenna *less* Chinese because they don't want certain aspects of the culture? Part of me thinks *yes*, but a growing part of me also thinks *of course not*. I massage my temples with my fingers—this whole discussion makes my head hurt.

Huáng Lǎoshī has been ignoring our conversation while he wrote dialogue on the board in characters and Pinyin. Now he reads it out loud and tells us to practice it with our partners. He wasn't kidding; it's basic "Hi, my name is such-and-such. I'm pleased to meet you" stuff.

"Ní hǎo," I say to McKenna. "Wǒ jiào Fāng Xiǎofèng. Wǒ hěn gāoxìng rènshì nǐ."

McKenna stares at me for a long moment before she gives in. "Ní hǎo," she replies. "Wǒ jiào Jiāng Báiyù. Wǒ hěn gāoxìng rènshì nǐ." Her tones are all over the place, her pronunciation is off, and she has to look at the board to remember what to say, but she gets through it. We practice several more times before Huáng Lǎoshī comes over to assess our ability. Well, mostly McKenna's ability, because he already knows mine from all those Sundays.

He listens as McKenna recites her lines. "Repeat after me," he tells her. "Wǒ." She repeats the word for "I," but it comes out more like "whoa" in second tone instead of third. The teacher shakes his head. "Again. Wǒ." Her cheeks grow redder and her forehead furrows each time. When he insists that she "try harder" and say it again, McKenna pushes away from the desk, her chair screeching against the floor, and runs out of class.

The room falls silent, and we all stare at the door. Then Sarina and Gemma go after her. Huáng Lǎoshī looks confused at first and then shrugs, as if McKenna's behavior has nothing to do with him. He tells us to continue practicing. Partnerless, I study the scratches on the top of my desk and wonder what the heck just happened.

After about ten minutes, McKenna comes back with Sarina

and Gemma. She slumps down in her chair without a word. Her eyes are red and puffy. She and I have both been in tears today, and it's only the second day of camp.

When the teacher moves to the students in the back, Teagan asks McKenna if she's okay.

McKenna lets out a huff. "Why are the teachers here so awful?"

"Huáng Lǎoshī can be kind of strict, but he just wants you to learn," Lina says. "Getting the tones right is pretty important."

"He didn't have to humiliate me like that."

Maze chimes in. "Welcome to our world. Lots of Chinese teachers aren't into encouragement. Especially the older generations. They don't believe in coddling you. They're not going to say something nice just to make you feel better."

"That's rude," Teagan says.

"I don't know," Maze says. "They're not trying to be rude—it's just a different culture. I find it refreshing, that kind of honesty. I may get annoyed with my dad when I don't think he's being supportive, but I always know where I stand with him."

McKenna looks incredulous. "Are you saying that our parents aren't honest with us because they're white?"

Maze is taken aback. "No, not at all. I'm just trying to explain what it's like to have traditional Chinese parents or teachers. They have expectations."

"What makes you think our parents don't have expectations of their kids?" McKenna demands. "God, you all think you're so much better than us."

I don't know how this conversation got so out of hand. "We don't think that. I'm sure your parents expect stuff from you," I say. "It's just different for us because we have another culture to deal with, too."

McKenna's eyes blaze. "Could you two *be* any more condescending? What makes you think that I don't have another culture to deal with? I have four, so I think I've got you both beat. All of us adoptees have more differences to cope with than you do. You're whining about living up to your parents' expectations when you have no idea just how easy your life is!" Everybody else stops talking and stares at us.

I feel like I've been slapped. Maze looks shocked, too. Four cultures? How is that even possible? Also, I was not whining. Was I?

Huáng Lǎoshī claps his hands sharply, making me jump. "Okay, that's enough. Turn your desks to face the front and take a seat. Time to do worksheets."

McKenna pops out of her seat without a word and stalks to the desk farthest from the front. As far away from me as she can get. Fine by me. I drag my desk so it faces the board again and drop into the chair.

Huáng Lǎoshī grabs a stack of papers off his desk and hands it to Harrison. "These are for the campers with more Mandarin experience." He shuffles through some folders in his briefcase and pulls out different worksheets. "These are for the younger campers' classes tomorrow, but I think they will work for the beginners in this class, too." He hands one sheet to Win, asking him to go make more copies, and then gives the rest to Gemma to hand out.

I glance up at Harrison as he hands me a worksheet. "Thanks." He nods and keeps moving.

I wonder if he overheard the conversation and what he thinks. Both his parents are ethnically Chinese and he's grown up in Hong Kong, among other people like himself. He's not Chinese American or a descendant of immigrants. He probably doesn't feel like there's a culture gap between himself and his parents. Then there's me and the Squad, all American Born Chinese, ABCs who code-switch between white American culture and whatever version of Chinese culture our parents create in our homes. And then come the adoptees, who I thought only had to navigate white American culture at home and in the larger world, but McKenna made it clear that I was wrong. They must have to deal with Chinese culture, too, now that I think about it, because their faces tell everyone that they're Chinese. But that leaves two other cultures that she said she has to contend with, 'which does sound complicated.

Being Chinese American is like wearing a patched-together coat—half wool overcoat, half padded cotton jacket. It keeps you warm, but it can be rough and scratchy and impossible to take off. Maybe being an adoptee is like that, too.

# CHAPTER THIRTEEN

"Photo time! To the soccer field!" Win raises his arm like a tour guide and leads the way across campus.

Fei Fei sidles up next to the CITs. "These photos won't get posted on the Internet, will they?"

Harrison slings an arm around her shoulders. "Of course not. No need to worry," he says soothingly.

Quick as silk, Fei Fei scoots out from under his arm and closer to Gemma. Harrison looks startled, but he doesn't say anything. That probably doesn't happen to him very much. Their whole interaction lasted barely a few seconds but convinces me that he doesn't like me that way. He flirts with everyone. I'm not special.

"Given what happened this morning, we probably won't even put them in the newsletter to parents," Gemma reassures Fei Fei.

McKenna turns around. "What if I don't want my picture taken?"

Gemma studies her for a moment. "We won't make you, if that's what you're asking. But you won't be in the memory book."

"Oh, the memory book!" Ava exclaims. "That's what made me want to come here. Everybody looked like they were having so much fun doing the activities." She turns to Lina. "I think it was your mom who sent an old copy to my mom when she asked for more info about Squee."

Lina smiles and pats her camera bag. "Probably. My mom is in charge of putting it together, and I help with layout and design. I also take a lot of photos—I like having my group well-represented."

"We're here," Sarina announces from the front of the group. "Everyone grab a seat while we get the T-shirts ready and talk to Liào Auntie."

The metal bleachers are hot from baking in the sun all day, so we just lean against the fence separating them from the field. Despite the heat, I'm glad to be outside, away from the tension that built up in Mandarin class.

Lina looks at McKenna. "If you really don't want to be in the photos, tell me now so I can let my mom know. She's the photographer today and will make sure the other camp photographers and counselors don't take candids of you during whole-camp activities. That makes it a lot easier than photoshopping you out later."

"You'd take me out of *all* the pics? Like, just *erase* me?"

"Well, yes." Lina sounds confused. "We respect your right to privacy. If you don't want to be in the group picture, we assume that applies to all of them."

McKenna presses her lips together. "What about you?" she asks her friends.

They look at each other, shifting from foot to foot. Finally, Teagan shrugs. "I don't have a problem with being in the photos."

Delaney touches the scar above her lips again. She catches my quizzical glance and explains, "I was born with a cleft lip. Sometimes I get self-conscious about it." She smiles when I tell her the truth—that I'd never have noticed if she hadn't called my attention to it. She says that she doesn't mind being in the camp photos, and Piper echoes her.

'Ava looks relieved. "I *want* to be in the memory book. Don't you want to be in the photos with us, McKenna? It won't be the same if you're not in them."

"Okay, fine. I'll be in this amazing memory book," McKenna says.

"Great," Lina replies. "I'll go tell my mom, in case Gemma already told her you wouldn't." She sets off toward Liào Auntie, who's on the field next to a large tripod, talking to our CIT.

Win puts the crate he's been hauling around on a table a few feet away and opens it. He pulls out a stack of T-shirts and I clutch Lyr's hand. The shirts are garnet, a gorgeous dark red. The design on the front is always the current zodiac animal, so this year it's a rabbit. My goal is to collect a whole set of twelve camp shirts, each with a different animal. I'll buy them off Matty if I have to. Once I have the set, I'm going to make a quilt out of them. Three animals across and four down.

"Lyrica," Win calls out at the same time Harrison says, "Phoenny." Lyr and I smile at each other and trot over to the table.

"Thanks," I say to Harrison as he hands me my shirt. I unfold it to see the design and inadvertently gasp, "Ohh."

The rabbit on the staff's turquoise T-shirts is hunkered down in the grass, with a circular border composed of stylized Chinese clouds, SCCWEE's name spelled out, and the year. The whole design mimics traditional Chinese cut-paper techniques.

The campers' shirts are completely different.

I pet the rabbit on my shirt. It's sitting up, alert, looking back at me. Painted in black ink, the rabbit's body is filled with swirls and curlicues to show the details of its legs, feet, and ears. Within the swirls are the numbers for the year and the letters SCCWEE. The brushstrokes are broad and bold, mimicking Chinese paintings. The art is both traditional and modern at the same time.

"Everything all right?" Harrison asks, his voice a bit brusque.

"We've never had a design like this before."

"Is that a good thing?" His eyes are intent on mine.

I say the first thing that pops into my head. "I love it. I might never take it off."

He blinks. The sun reflecting off all the garnet shirts makes his cheeks glow pink.

Lyr taps me on the back. "Phee? You coming?"

I swivel and follow her back to the bleachers. "This is the best shirt Squee has ever had!"

Behind me, Harrison clears his throat and calls out Delaney's name. He and Win continue to hand out the shirts until everyone has one.

"Okay, Group 13!" Sarina calls out. "Put your shirt on and then stand on the bleachers in three even rows of four people each!"

"Where are we supposed to change?" McKenna's eyes flicker between Win and Harrison. Yeah, that would be totally awkward if we had to actually take off our shirts in front of them. Good thing we don't.

"Just put the camp shirt on over your current shirt. We're just wearing them for the photos and then you can take them off."

"No way!" Bran says. "It's way too hot for that." He promptly strips off his T-shirt and yanks the new one on. Howie follows his lead. "See? No changing room needed!" He and Howie break into laughter.

Why are boys our age so juvenile? I slip the shirt on and tie a knot at the hem, so it sits above the ruffles of my tunic. After some hesitation, McKenna and Teagan also layer their camp shirts over what they're wearing. McKenna's is way too small, making the one underneath bunch unattractively. If she didn't have that on, her waist would be exposed. I brace myself for what's coming next.

"I got the wrong shirt," she says a little too loudly. She peels it off and holds it out to Sarina. "I need a different one." She sounds kind of panicked.

Sarina frowns. "If your name is written on the tag, then that's your shirt. There aren't any extras." She points to the empty crates and table.

"I can't wear it. There must be a mistake."

I'm pretty sure McKenna doesn't want to have anything to do with me, but I also know what it's like to care about how your clothes fit you and how they make you look. That's why I started making my own clothes to begin with, because I wasn't happy with the cutesy style all the clothes in my size seemed to have. Bunchy and too tight is definitely not McKenna's style. I take a deep breath and pull off my camp shirt. "I'll trade with you," I offer. "My shirt is your size."

I watch as McKenna's face changes from annoyed to confused to slightly suspicious. "Why would you do that? What do you want from me?"

"I've been thinking about what you said in Mandarin class, and I just want you to have an easier time at camp." I hold out my shirt and try to joke with her the way I do when I'm trying to persuade Matty to do something. "C'mon, let's swap. At least for the photo. If you want, you can have your super-trendy belly shirt back right afterward."

McKenna tilts her head and blinks at me. Then she smirks. I think that means she's pleased, but if there's anything I've learned about her, it's that we don't read each other well. The seconds tick by, and it feels like everyone, even the counselors, are holding their breaths for her answer. "Okay," she says slowly. "Thanks." We trade shirts and put them on. We smile tentatively at each other. The world doesn't explode. I'm as surprised as anyone else.

Sarina claps her hands to get our attention. "All right! Let's get these photos done, campers!"

The four counselors climb up the bleachers to stand behind our group.

Lyr leans toward me and whispers, "That was really nice of you."

"For a second, I think I understood how she felt," I explain.

After Liào Auntie gets enough bleacher photos, Win shouts, "Pyramids!" and ushers us all down to the field. He, Harrison, Sarina, Bran, and Howie get on their hands and knees in a line. "Phoenny, McKenna, Maze, Teagan, get on. Gemma, help them up."

Gemma takes my hand and steadies me as I climb onto Win's and Harrison's backs. She doesn't seem to find the situation awkward at all, which makes me feel better. I'm definitely reading too much into this. Once I've gotten up, she helps McKenna, Maze, and then Teagan, who is on the other end position.

Harrison's shoulder muscles bunch under my right hand, and suddenly I worry that I'm too heavy, or that my knees are too bony, or my fingers are digging into him. How embarrassing would it be if I was the one who made the pyramid collapse?

Win calls out for Delaney, Piper, and Fei Fei to make the third row. "Then Lyr and Lina, and Ava on top. Hurry!"

The girls giggle as they step on us and clamber into position. Ava is so tiny that Gemma just hoists her up to Lyr's and Lina's backs, where she finds her balance. "Quick, take the picture!" Lina shouts to her mom, who starts snapping away.

"I'm going to try and stand up," Ava announces. Gemma holds her ankle while she gets to her feet, and the third and fourth rows wobble as her weight shifts.

Below me, just a literal arm's length away, Harrison starts to groan loudly. "Whose brilliant idea was it to put me and Sarina in the middle?"

Win snorts, Ava shouts, "I'm up!" Liào Auntie takes the shot, and then Bran and Howie crumple and the whole pyramid sways to the right and collapses onto the grass in a pile of arms and legs and laughter. Since I'm on the left end, I miss being crushed and just end up between Win and Harrison. McKenna, however, somehow ends up draped over Harrison's back. Harrison doesn't seem to mind. He peers at her over his shoulder and smiles. "So this is what Americans do for fun, is it?"

She rolls onto the grass beside him. Her teeth gleam. "Are you saying you can't take it?"

He stands up and reaches out a hand to help McKenna get to her feet. "Not a chance. I could do this all day." They walk together toward the bleachers, her hair swaying, his head bent toward hers.

They're perfect for each other. I should be happy McKenna is getting along with someone outside of her circle, but all my emotions are like the hem of her trendy jean shorts—frayed.

# CHAPTER FOURTEEN

As soon as we enter the lobby of Agnes, the counselors remind us to meet in the Flex after dinner for Movie Night. Then the four of them head to the counselors-only lounge at the other end of the first floor. Howie and Bran run off to get their yo-yos, and McKenna leads her friends to a table where they can check out playing cards and various board games. I make a beeline for the living room, the Squad right behind me.

Kir and Q are already waiting for us. I flop down on the sofa next to Kir. "It has been a *day*, and I'm so ready to watch you crush Parker!" I tell her.

She shakes her head. "We have to do it at a different time. The aunties and uncles won't let us race today. Something about not enough supervision."

I remember Mom's words at the end of music class: *Don't let them out of your sight. Keep them safe.* I feel my pulse speed up. "Would online trolls really come to camp to harass us just because we're Chinese American? How does picking on a bunch of kids serve any purpose? We're not even old enough to vote yet."

None of the Squad have an answer.

Lina shakes her head wearily. "I noticed that there were more staff and counselors outside. Looks like the Committee wants to keep campers from roaming too far away from Agnes and the Student Center. I saw a group heading toward the Sports Center, too. No one's walking around on their own."

"I see two options," Q says. "Sit on the blanket in Maze and Fei Fei's room and chat. Or head out and see if the CITs are playing basketball." Her smile is like a little mischievous ray of sunshine.

"The last thing I want to do is to watch you all drool over Emerson." I shudder as my friends laugh. "I vote for the blanket. I might fall asleep on it, though. It hasn't just been a day—it's been a wicked long roller coaster of a day."

"Your Boston is showing," Maze teases. "And no napping! I have an even more *wicked* idea—let's make the boys drool over us!"

Fei Fei bounces in her seat. "I love this already! How are we going to do it?"

"First, we need to steal some eggs."

The moment we step outside, Sarina approaches us. She must be on door duty. "What are you girls doing for free time?"

"We're just going to walk around," Q says innocently. "Why? Do you have any suggestions?"

The counselor nods. "Lots. Besides the yo-yos and board

games, there's a crafting station where you can make brace-lets, key chains, or whistle holders. They've got plastic lanyard, paracord, and embroidery floss, I think." She smiles at me knowingly. "I bet they could use your help, Phee."

I shift my feet. "Um, that does sound fun. Maybe later?" I look up at Sarina. "Wait. Why would we make whistle holders?"

Now it's the counselor who looks uncomfortable. "We'll make an announcement at Movie Night, but it's to offer a safety precaution." She holds up a hand to stop our ques-tions. "We're making some other changes, too, that you'll hear about tonight. For now, it's okay to walk around, but stay inside the flagged areas."

We notice for the first time the wooden stakes and flag bunting that encircle the green space around Agnes. More flags outline the roadway and sidewalk leading to the Student Center. Down the hill to our right, the road has been blocked off with sawhorses and there are two adult staff members standing there. The multicolored triangular flags flutter in the breeze and make the campus look festive, but we know there's nothing to celebrate.

"That's not much of a walk," Q observes.

"Or a run," Kir adds. She bites her lip. "How am I supposed to do my training? I already had to run around the entire campus twice this morning to get my miles in."

Sarina shakes her head. "I don't know the answer to that,

Kirrily. We're not supposed to let campers be outside alone, either. You should talk to the directors about it. Maybe the Squad can be your running buddies? They might allow it if there's a big group of you going together."

Maybe it's stress, but I can't help it—I start laughing uncontrollably. I can't even beat Lyr running the length of a hallway. There's no way I'd be able to keep up with Kir for the bazillion miles she runs every morning. At dawn. After a moment, everybody realizes how ridiculous Sarina's idea is and laughs with me, including Sarina herself, and the tension breaks.

"Okay, that was officially a bad idea," Sarina says, grinning. "Maybe ask around tonight—there might be a counselor or CIT who's also a distance runner. Someone older, maybe a guy—that actually might make the directors feel like it's safe to let you go."

"'Someone older, maybe a guy,'" Lyr repeats, and puts a finger to the corner of her mouth in a flirty way. "Like, say, *Emerson?*"

"Now that is a fantastic idea," Kir says.

Fei Fei pretends to swoon and falls into Maze's arms. I roll my eyes, sure that they're acting like this just to mess with me. Well, mostly sure.

"Quick," Maze says. "We better go get Fei Fei some ice before she overheats. Let's go to the cafeteria."

Her words make us all erupt into laughter again, even

while reminding us of our mission. Because we're supposed to be stealing eggs, not worrying about trolls or thirsting after my brother. We wave goodbye to Sarina and follow the flags to the Student Center.

We cross through the Flex, which is full of day campers playing games before their parents come pick them up. I catch a glimpse of black cargo pants and turquoise-patterned Vans and realize with a start that it's Harrison. He's carrying a large speaker over to where a few other counselors and CITs are setting up for Movie Night and doesn't see me. I hurry the others through the door at the rear of the Flex and lead them up a set of stairs at the back of the building. I tell myself my heart is pounding because he almost caught us.

"So that's where these stairs go," Fei Fei says.

Three of us turn and shush her. We're standing in a hallway that runs between the cafeteria and a bunch of administrative offices. Even though it's summer, people from Carmen College are still working. I can hear them talking on their phones or typing on their computers. This area is usually off-limits to Squee, so campers don't disturb the employees.

Across the hall from the stairwell is a set of double doors that lead to the cafeteria's kitchen. Maze creeps over and peeks through one of the porthole windows. Almost immediately, she ducks down and motions for us to move out of sight of the doors. We all crawl over to the wall next to the doors. My heart pounds.

"There are already a couple of workers in there preparing for dinner," Maze whispers. "We're going to need a distraction." She looks at each of us, thinking. "Fei Fei and Q—you two are the most dramatic. Go into the cafeteria and do something to get the workers out of the kitchen. We only need a few minutes."

Queena looks at Fei Fei, unhappy about being called "dramatic." Fei Fei stares back and just shrugs. Then she gets to her feet and holds out a hand to Q. Arm in arm, they strut silently down the hall, swinging their hips and flipping their hair with exaggerated motions. Maze shakes her head while the rest of us cover our mouths to keep from laughing. "There's at least one in every group," she murmurs, which, strangely, makes me think of McKenna and Teagan. I push the thought away.

"Come on," Lyr whispers, her head pressed against the kitchen door. "The coast is clear." Cautiously, she pushes the door open a crack, just enough for us to slip through. "Kir and I will stay here and be lookouts," she says. "Be quick!"

We sneak across the kitchen, our shoes making little *squick-squick* sounds on the sticky floor. There are three huge stainless-steel doors—one of them has to be the refrigerator. I sidle up to one and pull on the handle, wincing as it makes a noise. It's a walk-in fridge the size of Mom's closet. "Hurry!" I wave Maze and Lina inside so they can check it out, but I hang on to the handle. I've seen enough movies where people get stuck inside fridges like this.

From the food service area of the cafeteria, I hear Q's imperious voice. "Well, it wasn't working for me before." There's the sound of ice from the soda machine falling into a cup. "No, this won't do. These cubes of ice are too small. I need bigger cubes. We're doing an important project, and we need, like, *blocks* of ice, not these pitiful chunks!"

One of the workers explains that they don't have big blocks of ice. His voice is low, and he speaks slowly, clearly trying to keep his patience. I snicker and then jump when Maze and Lina reappear.

"No luck," Maze says. "It's all fruits and veggies."

"Try this one next," Lina says, pointing to another door.

I pull on the handle of the next door, and they slip inside. Right away they push their way back out.

"That one's a freezer!" Lina rubs her arms with both hands.

Maze moves to the third door. "It'd better be this one. I think we're running out of time." She yanks on the handle and disappears, with Lina following.

I stand there, straining to hear what's going on in the cafeteria. Q isn't talking—does that mean the distraction is over? Then I hear Fei Fei in classic meltdown mode.

"Where's the gluten-free bread?!" she whines. "You have baskets and baskets of bread, but no gluten-free stuff? White, whole wheat, sourdough, English muffins, and what's this? Multi-grain honey?" After she says each type of bread, there's a pause, then a swish and a soft thump. Oh my god, she's literally tossing each loaf to the floor! I really hope no counselors or staff members walk in, or Fei Fei might get in serious trouble. But also, my gut hurts from holding back laughter.

Out of nowhere, I remember McKenna saying, "This is not working for me," in Mandarin class and then demanding a larger T-shirt for the group photos. She has the same kind of imperious energy as Fei Fei and Q—so why don't I find her drama as funny?

"We got it!" Maze slips out of the fridge, carrying a large carton of eggs. Beside her, Lina cradles a huge block of butter in her arms. "Let's get out of here."

We scamper out of the kitchen, Fei Fei's shrieks of frustration ringing in our ears. "Finally!" Lyr whispers loudly, and we push through the door to the stairwell. While we wait for Q and Fei Fei, Maze takes a towel out of her backpack and shoves the butter inside. Then she wraps the carton of eggs in the towel and hands it to Kir.

Kir looks at the towel. "How am I supposed to explain this?"

"You're an athlete," Maze replies. "Don't you all carry towels around to wipe off your sweat?"

Before Kir can say anything, Fei Fei and Q bolt into the stairwell and clatter down the stairs, gesturing for us to follow them. We dash after them, not daring to look back to see if we're being chased. We weave through the little kids in the Flex and rush outside, where we stop, look around, and burst into wild laughter.

"That was epic," Q says, wiping her eyes. "What now? Are we egging Parker's room?"

Kir's face lights up. "Yes! Let's totally do that!"

"Nope." Maze slings an arm around Kir's shoulders. "Now we bake!"

We spend the rest of our free time in the kitchen on the third floor. Turns out that Maze's giant duffel bag was so heavy because she'd brought all the ingredients, bowls, and pans, plus an electric mixer and equipment to bake goodies for the entire two weeks. Everything except for the eggs.

I hold up sticks of shortening and a jar of coconut oil. "What are these for?"

"They're butter substitutes," Maze says. "But when I saw the butter in the fridge, I couldn't resist. The real stuff tastes better."

"I love that we're making cupcakes," Lyr says, "but how does that make the boys drool over us? Won't they just be drooling over the treats?"

Kir nods in agreement. "We should prank them instead. Like, use salt instead of sugar in the recipe."

"One of Win's sisters was my CIT when I was a day camper. She told us about a prank they played on the boy counselors," Lyr recalls. "They took all their snacks and food out of the fridge on their floor and filled it with cupcakes instead."

"Lyr," Q groans. "That's not a prank; that's a *gift.*"

"At least they'll love us!" Fei Fei says brightly.

Maze rolls her eyes. "No way am I baking cupcakes that taste bad. Also, I was thinking tormenting them would be more fun. And to do that—"

"We don't let them have any!" Lina pipes up. "And we eat our delicious cupcakes right in front of them and make them drool with jealousy!" She cackles like an evil villain from a movie, something none of us have ever heard her do.

We stare at Lina for a moment, and then, starting with Maze, we all give her Snaps.

# CHAPTER FIFTEEN

We lose track of time decorating the cupcakes, so there's a long line when we finally traipse into the cafeteria for dinner. Q sighs loudly and I wonder if she's going to make another scene, this time for real, when Fei Fei elbows me.

"What was that for?" I ask. She responds by pointing toward the head of the line with her chin. Harrison is waving us over. "Is he serious? He's going to let us all cut in line?"

Lyr chuckles. "Not us, Phee. Just you. Go ahead." She gives me a little push.

"How rude to think he can break up the Squad," Q says. "We shall all grace him with our presence. Come along, friends." She grabs my arm and propels me with her, the other five on our heels. When we reach Harrison, Q glares at the young camper behind him, and he immediately shrinks back to let us all get in line. I feel kind of bad, but Harrison just grins.

"You should get some perks as the oldest campers, I guess," he says. He looks at me closely and suddenly starts laughing. "Phee, what happened to your hair? Are you that stressed out?"

"I . . . What? What's wrong with my hair?" I pat my head,

and a sweet-scented dust cloud floats around my face. Oh no. I whirl around and jab a finger at Lyr. "You said I got all the powdered sugar out! I can't believe you let me walk around looking like—"

"Grandmother Fa in *Mulan*?" Lyr and the Squad dissolve into a fit of giggles. "I'm sorry, Phee, but we couldn't resist! You just look way too cute with gray hair."

"I agree," Harrison says from behind me. "Hó oĭ" he adds, before repeating himself in Mandarin. "Kě'ai."

I turn around again to face him, even though I can feel myself blushing. He told me I was pretty yesterday, and now he's saying I'm cute. In Mandarin, to make sure that I'd understand him. "I . . . um, thanks," I falter, and then mentally shake myself. *Get a grip.* "I mean, thanks a lot for pointing out my sugar addiction."

Over Harrison's shoulder, Emerson looks back at me in line. He faces forward again quickly, but not before I spot his scowl. He made that face at me yesterday when Lyr and I were trying to get our room keys. What is his problem with Harrison? He's the one who got him to apply for CIT after all.

Harrison, the Squad, and I make small talk as the line shuffles forward. He asks what we were doing with powdered sugar, and Maze just shrugs mysteriously. Fei Fei tells him we were powdering a wig for Q to wear for our Variety Show skit. When he asks what our skit is about, Lina says that Q is playing Marie Antoinette, at which point Q cries,

"Let them eat cake!" and we all start laughing again. I can tell that Harrison doesn't know if we're kidding or not, which just makes me laugh harder.

We load our plates with pasta and sauce and salad. I stop to get an apple, but Harrison's arm is longer and his hand quicker. He grabs one out of the basket above the salad bar. "Here," he says, putting it on my tray. I'm about to thank him when he leans closer to me. "Phee? I want you to know that I didn't have anything to do with choosing the movie tonight. Okay?" He looks into my eyes, but I'm confused and stare down at my feet. Why is he telling me this?

"Okay," I say slowly. "What movie is it?" But when I look up, he's already gone.

I'm still wondering about Harrison's cryptic statement as he and Win lead Group 13 into the Flex after dinner. Mom and Chŭ Auntie came up with Movie Night several years ago, after campers and counselors complained that they needed a low-key activity after the first full day of classes. Everyone is still getting used to being at camp and meeting new people. For a lot of the younger campers, Squee is the first time they've been away from home, and they get homesick. And starting new classes, even if they're non-academic and not graded, can be stressful for kids who are expected to be high achievers in everything they do. I have to hand it to our moms—Movie Night is a great way to decompress and bond with our groupmates.

We each take carpet squares from the stack by the door and follow Win and Harrison to the back of the room, where we create a row behind Group 12. They leave us to go help fill little bags of popcorn.

"I feel like I'm in preschool again," Ava giggles as she puts her square down and sits on it.

Lina smiles. "They do use them for the littlest day campers."

Piper, on the other side of Ava, leans forward to address Lyr. "Thanks for telling us to bring pillows and blankets. It's way cozier this way—almost like a sleepover."

"It is, isn't it?" Lyr nudges me. "We even have the interrupting younger sibling!"

I look up and see Matty headed our way. He squats in the space behind me. "What's up, Matty?" I ask.

"I'm freezing, Phee." He shivers dramatically and rubs his bare arms. "Can I use your blanket?"

The staff keeps the air-conditioning set to arctic temperatures in the Flex. I feel bad for not telling him to bring a pillow and a blanket. Or to wear a hoodie, at the very least. Matty is a newbie, too, I remind myself. And my own little brother. I sigh. "Of course. Here, take it." I hand him the quilted throw I made from all the leftover remnants from my sewing projects.

"Thanks, Phee! You're the best jiějie ever!" He blows me a kiss and scampers back to his seat, which makes the Squad coo.

I roll my eyes. "Trust me, he's only that sweet when he wants something."

"Speaking of sweet, someone's got a secret admirer!" Piper pretends to faint.

McKenna shushes her, but the smirk on her face tells me she's glad I overheard. "It's not even a real rose," she says, pulling her knees up to her chin and wrapping her arms around her legs.

"A red Play-Doh rose is still a rose," Teagan says. "We all know what it means."

Delaney giggles. "Who do you think it's from?"

"You found it in your room?" Ava asks. "Who else has keys to our rooms?" She looks at me and Lyr.

I take a moment to think. "Actually, a lot of people. There are master keys that can open all the doors. All the counselors and CITs have them in case of an emergency. The Committee keep a few at the front desk for the parent volunteers to use when they're on hall monitor duty so they can go in and check for hazards like lit candles or curling irons that are still on." Hmm. I make a mental note to hide my travel iron better so it doesn't get confiscated. "Oh, and our moms, of course."

Ava nods, but Delaney arches an eyebrow. "Why do your moms have master keys?"

I forgot that new campers wouldn't know about my and Lyr's relationship to Squee. I usually don't need to mention it because everyone has been here forever and just knows.

Lyr smiles at Delaney like it's no big deal. "They're the directors. Director Fāng is Phee's mom, and my mom is the assistant director."

Teagan lets out a bark of laughter. McKenna wrinkles her nose and says, "That explains a lot." An awkward silence descends on the whole group.

Piper's the first to speak. "So pretty much anyone could've gotten ahold of a master key and left the rose for McKenna."

"Anyone who's also making rice dough figures in crafts class," Ava adds. "I think Group 12 is, but we'd have to check the schedules in the lobby to be sure."

Bran and Howie, who have been surprisingly quiet, look at all of us from the end of the row. "Wasn't me," Bran offers.

"Or me," Howie says. He glances at McKenna and hastily adds, "Not that I don't like you; I just don't *like* like you."

"Oh my god, I don't *like* like you, either," McKenna exclaims, her ears turning red.

The counselors signal for everyone to be quiet and Win and Sarina stand in front of the screen. They explain what Sarina told us earlier, about the flags, the whistles, and not roaming around the campus alone. They stress that these are just precautions, and that the Committee believes that camp is still a safe place, but that everyone is taking the online trolls' comments seriously.

One of the kids from Group 9 raises his hand. "Isn't it

against the law to say racist things? Are you going to call the police?"

Win's voice is somber. "Those are really good questions. Unfortunately, except in very specific circumstances, hate speech is not illegal. The trolls have said horrible things, but they didn't make any threats against us. 'They did post on a social media platform that's run by a private company, so the company could freeze the trolls' accounts if they wanted to." Win shakes his head. "But they don't do enough to ensure users' safety. That's why we're going to take care of this ourselves."

"How are you going to do that?" a girl from Group 11 challenges.

"Let's just say that some of us are really, really good at computers." Cooper' cracks his knuckles. "Like, hacker-level good."

Sarina jumps in. "And the directors are reaching out to organizations like Stop AAPI Hate and local community groups to see if they have advice on how to deal with the trolls. We'll keep you posted. But now it's time for the movie!"

The room dims, and the screen lights up. Sarina and Gemma appear with small bags of popcorn for the whole group, and we scoot closer together to make room for them.

The logo for a famous studio appears, and I feel my shoulders relax. It's an animated kid movie. What was Harrison so worked up about? But the opening scene, a drawing of an old leatherbound book, almost makes me choke on a piece of popcorn. The book is titled *Shrek Forever After*. The page turns, and the voice of the narrator begins to read the book. "Once upon a time a long time ago, a king and queen had a beautiful daughter named Fiona."

Lyr and Fei Fei both elbow me, one on each side, and I grab their hands for support. This is unbelievable. Who chose this movie? If Harrison's telling the truth, it wasn't him. Mom and Chǔ Auntie don't get involved—they just tell the counselors that it has to be appropriate for the youngest overnight campers. *The counselors.* I look to my left at Sarina and Gemma, but they're both on their phones, not paying attention to the movie at all. I look at the end of the row to my right. Win has moved up a row and is quietly chatting with Bora. Harrison's eyes drill right into mine. His mouth and waving hands say, "Not me."

I want to believe him, so I nod quickly and then turn back to the screen. Before long, Shrek has signed a contract with the evil Rumpelstiltskin so that he can have one more day as a "real ogre," free of his responsibilities to Princess Fiona and their three kids. Maybe it really is a coincidence, and the universe is trying to tell me something about Harrison. I wish I knew what it was. Does Harrison really want to be the Shrek to my "Fi," or is he the Shrek in this scenario that just wants to go his own way?

Halfway through the movie, Maze opens the box she's

been hiding under her blanket and takes out two cupcakes. She hands them to Kir and Q and then gives two more to Sarina and Gemma, who are thrilled. Then she takes one for herself and passes the box down the row. Each of us takes a cupcake.

Delaney whispers, "What's this?" when Lyr hands her the box.

"Go ahead, take one," Lyr urges. "We made some for the five of you." That was the other part of Maze's plan—to "sweeten" our relationship with the new girls by giving them cupcakes. There are exactly fourteen cupcakes, so McKenna ends up taking the last one. Bran, Howie, Harrison, and Win stare at Maze in distress, but she just shrugs. McKenna glances down our row, too, and I raise my cupcake as if toasting her with a drink. She looks at the cupcake in her hand and lifts it slightly in my direction, too.

Lina and Maze were right. The guys around us—in our group, in Group 12, even some of the day campers' counselors and CITs who are sitting behind us—watch us as we eat our delicious, made-from-scratch treats. Their pained expressions *are* kind of funny. I glance at Harrison only to see McKenna give him her cupcake. Did she not understand that we were purposefully leaving the boys out? She leans around Bran and Howie, ignoring their begging, and holds the cupcake out to him. It's such an obvious display of her crush on him that I expect him to refuse. Because how can he give me compliments and make me feel special while accepting attention from another girl?

Easily, I guess, because he takes the cupcake from McKenna with the same confident grin that he gave her during group photos this afternoon. He thanks her and devours it in a few big bites.

The rest of my cupcake tastes like paste.

# CHAPTER SIXTEEN

After the movie, the counselors round up their groups and usher us back to Agnes for hall meetings. "I feel like a lot has happened today," Sarina begins.

Talk about an understatement. We're gathered in the hall, showered and in our pajamas. I'm wrapped in my lilac plush robe with the hood up so all I can see are my toes as I lean forward and hug my knees.

Win says, "So Sarina and I thought we'd keep tonight's hall meeting kind of free-form. Snaps would be great; Squawks and S'ups are fine, too. Basically, anything you want to discuss, yeah? First, though, we want to follow up about the online troll issue."

"Most of you saw the racist comments on our social media posts this afternoon." Sarina's voice is disgusted. "And you just heard about the safety precautions we've put in place. Do any of you have questions or comments?"

Ava raises her hand shyly. "I have a S'up. What's up with Cooper talking about computers and hackers? And is he taking apprentices? I have some coding skills."

"Texting Coop right now." Win types furiously on his phone for a moment. "I bet he'll say yes. He and some of the other counselors who study computer science are trying to figure out the real identities of the trolls. They can always use more help."

"But how will learning who they really are help us?" Lina wants to know. "You and Sarina already said that they haven't done anything against the law."

"True, but we could find out what they look like, where they live, and what their jobs are," Sarina says. "If they live in California and don't have much money, then they're probably not going to fly all the way here to bother us. But if they live in the Boston area, it would be good to show their photo to all the staff so we can keep a lookout for them."

"We could also teach them that harassing people online has consequences, right? Lots of companies would be upset to find out that one of their employees is trolling kids at a summer camp. Like, what does that say about a person?" Win makes an "L" with his hand and presses it to his forehead. Lyr and I laugh at his old-fashioned gesture for "loser."

"Is it time for Squawks yet?" McKenna asks without waiting for an answer. "The Mandarin teacher made me feel bad about not understanding Mandarin. He was mean and kept picking on my pronunciation." There are murmurs of assent from Teagan and Piper. "I hate when Chinese people see my face and just expect me to know Mandarin and all the cultural stuff." She crosses her arms.

"I'm sorry about that, McKenna," Win says. "We should've

stepped in sooner. I admit that we were caught off guard because we only found out at lunch today that the five of you are adoptees. Just like Howie, we assumed your Western last names meant that you were multiracial. It didn't occur to us that you could be adopted, and that exposes some biases on our end'. It's not an excuse, though. We'll be on alert during classes to prevent more situations like today's."

Gemma bites her lip. "I feel partly responsible, too, and I'm sorry. I figured out from your Chinese names yesterday that you're adoptees, but I didn't tell anyone—not the directors, the Committee, not even Sarina and Win. I felt that you could tell them yourself if you thought they should know. Plus, I never want to be treated differently because I'm adopted, and I assumed you'd feel the same way. Seeing your experience today reminded me of my first time at Squee and feeling like everyone but me belonged to some secret club of Chinese people. That's partly why I went to a heritage camp specifically for adoptees when I spent summers with my dad." She reaches for McKenna's hand and squeezes it. "I promise to be a better advocate for you in the future."

McKenna tilts her head, considering the CIT's words. "I guess I can understand why you didn't tell everyone that we're adopted. I don't always want people to know, either." She casts a fierce look around the group. "Not that I'm ashamed of it, because I'm not. But it's personal, and I don't always want to answer questions about it."

I find myself nodding. I'm proud of being Chinese American, but I get tired of people asking me about what it feels like, too. Or they think I'll know the best Chinese restaurants in town, or what day Lunar New Year falls on, or once, what Taoism is all about. And when I say I have no idea, they always get this *you're a disappointment to your culture* expression on their faces.

"I'll ask Director Fāng to talk to the Education Subcommittee and make sure that Huáng Lǎoshī is prepared to teach campers of all language levels in his classes from now on. And to be more empathetic to the feelings of kids who might not have as much exposure to the language as he thinks," Sarina says gently. "This is the first time Squee has offered a Mandarin class, and it seems like the Committee and Huáng Lǎoshī didn't anticipate how complicated it would be. I'm sure there are second- and third-generation campers who don't speak Mandarin at home and don't go to Chinese school, either." She makes a note on the clipboard in her lap.

Win regards McKenna, Teagan, Ava, Delaney, and Piper. "Are there other teachers that you would like us to inform that you're adopted? Or anything else you'd like them to know? This is the first time we've had any adoptees at camp—sorry, Gemma—I mean adoptees that we know are adopted, and clearly Squee has a lot to learn."

Piper shakes her head. "Being adopted doesn't affect how

we learn music or play sports, so I don't think the other teachers need to know."

"I agree with Piper," Delaney says, "but it would be nice if people didn't just *assume* that we know a lot about the culture when they're talking to us. Our parents aren't from this culture, either."

Huh. That's kind of like what I was just thinking, but different. I never thought about what it's like to have other *Chinese* people assume I know things and not have parents or grandparents I can turn to and ask when I don't know the answer.

"That's a good point," Sarina says, making another note on her clipboard. "What I'm hearing tonight is that we've made lots of assumptions that turned out to be wrong, and that it's made camp hard for you. Again, we're sorry and we all promise to do better. Right?" She looks at all of us who aren't adopted, and we nod. "Okay, I think we have time for a couple more questions or comments. Anyone?"

"I have a S'up," Maze volunteers. "Gemma, you said that there are heritage camps just for adoptees?" Gemma nods, her lock of green hair bobbing around her face. "If they exist, why didn't you all go to one of those camps instead of coming here and having to deal with people who don't understand?" she asks McKenna, Teagan, Delaney, Ava, and Piper in her usual blunt way.

Ava smiles and shakes her head. "We wanted to, but there

aren't any around here. Well," Ava amends, "not any that are for our age. Most of them are for little kids. The ones that have programs for older adoptees are out west, like in Colorado, and our parents didn't want to send us that far away."

"That's the one I went to," Gemma says. "I hope you get to go someday."

Ava smiles. "Me too. Anyway, I saw an ad for Squee in my Chinese school's newsletter and showed it to my parents. It sounded like so much fun and they're both really big on culture-keeping, so here I am." She turns to her friends. "I really wanted you all to be here with me, so I had my moms contact your parents about signing you up." She takes a deep breath. "McKenna, I'm sorry that being here meant you couldn't visit your grandmother in Italy, but I think you could have fun if you gave it a chance."

Piper puts her arm around Ava and gives her a hug, but McKenna looks away. So that's why she's here, even though she doesn't want to be. And why she'd rather be in Italy, learning Italian. A tiny light bulb flashes on in my head. Italian culture must be one of the four cultures McKenna said she had to deal with. And if I had to guess from her dad's last name, Fitzgerald, then the final culture in her world might be Irish.

Gemma looks sympathetic. "I love Squee, but I understand that it can be hard to join a community where everyone else has known each other for a long time. I hope you all hang in there and give us a chance like Ava said. This place helped me feel comfortable in my own skin in a different way. I'll also talk to Win and Sarina about some of the things we did at the Colorado heritage camp to make everyone feel included."

"Thanks for explaining, Ava, and for sharing, Gemma." Sarina acknowledges them both with a smile. "Everybody, please keep telling us how we can make camp better for everyone. Okay, let's end on a happy note! Anyone have a quick Snap to share?"

There's a pause, and then Teagan says with a smirk, "Snaps for secret admirers."

McKenna does a little shoulder wiggle and glances toward Harrison. I'd almost forgotten about the rice dough rose she found in her room this afternoon. Did he leave it for her? I train my eyes on my toes and refuse to look at anyone, but I can feel the glances shooting around the group like a shower of sewing pins.

"Okay! Let's snap for whoever they are, yeah?" Win says brightly, but there's an edge of concern in his voice. After a moment, the rest of us start snapping, too.

Lyr and I lie awake the whole night dissecting everything Harrison's said to me since camp began and comparing it to his flirtatiousness with McKenna. Not only did I wonder if he likes me that way, but I started to question why I like him.

"He's new, smart, handsome, funny, and has a great accent," Lyr had ticked off on her fingers. "Plus, he gives you compliments and seems to care what you think. What's not to like?

"I don't know. All of that is great, but then I see the way he treats McKenna, and it makes me doubt myself. He has longer conversations with her than with me. My dad would say that there's not enough evidence to prove that Harrison *like* likes me."

I wake up the next morning feeling down about everything—Harrison, McKenna, my last time as a camper, the trolls and their horrible comments—so I retreat into the circle of my friends. I don't know if Lyr fills the Squad in or if they figure it out on their own, but they immediately support me. Maze and Fei Fei physically shield me from McKenna and Harrison by making sure I get the spots as far away from them as possible in classes and at lunch. Whenever it seems like Harrison is coming over to talk to me, Lyr or Lina whisk me off to get more rice dough or switch to another ribbon color or even go to the restroom. Anything so I can avoid him and another confusing conversation.

After lunch, in Traditional Sports, Hsu Lǎoshī stops drilling us on racket strokes and just lets us loose to play. I make Lyr, Maze, and Fei Fei wait until Harrison and Gemma have staked out a court before choosing the one farthest away from them. Much to my surprise, I'm fairly decent at badminton. Maybe sewing and crafting has improved my hand-eye coordination? It also helps that the racket and birdie are lightweight, so I don't need a lot of arm strength, and the court is small, so there's not a lot of running.

I flick my racket down and the birdie flies over the net and hits the floor behind Maze, but inside the lines. I actually scored a point! "Did you see that?" I crow. "This is great! Why haven't we done this at camp before?"

"They tried having some of the younger campers do badminton a couple of years ago," Lyr answers. "I remember my mom saying it didn't go so well—the boys kept smacking each other with the rackets."

We both look over at Howie and Bran, who have stopped even pretending to play badminton and are using the rackets in an imaginary swordfight instead. "Still true," I say.

"But we're having fun," Lyr replies. "And it's kind of nice to do something different."

I serve again, and the birdie sails over to Fei Fei, who swings wildly, smashing the birdie and sending it straight into the net, where it sticks in one of the holes. We crack up because we have no idea what the rules are for when that happens.

Hsu Lǎoshī is busy giving Piper and Teagan some pointers, so Maze strides up to the net and whacks the birdie through it. We track its arc as it soars over the court and smacks Win in the head just as he happens to walk by. He rubs his head and shakes his fist in mock anger, while we hold our sides, shrieking with laughter.

It is the best part of the day so far.

Entering the living room of Agnes, I'm relieved to find a bunch of overnight campers and their counselors milling about. It'll be easy to fly under the radar with so many people around.

"We're going to hand out the whistles, okay?" Win announces. "And if you didn't make a holder for your whistle yesterday, we brought all the stuff so you can make one today. The Committee wants everyone to wear their whistle at all times, got it?" Howie starts to say something, but Win cuts him off. "No, you don't have to wear it when you're showering or sleeping. Does that answer your question, Howie?"

Howie nods but then says, "I have another question. Is this it for Counselor Time today? We're just getting the whistles?"

Sarina comes back from a different corner of the room with a plastic bag filled with multicolored objects. "Once you get your whistle, you are free to leave. We'll meet up again after dinner for hall meeting. Just remember to stay inside the flagged areas, and if you want to play sports in the gym, grab a buddy and have a counselor or staff person walk you to the building." She opens the bag and holds it out. "All right, form a line and come on up."

"This is going to be a disaster," Maze mutters. "They should give out earplugs, too."

When it's my turn, I pick a black whistle. All the other colors seem too cheerful.

"Hey, look," Lyr says. "We've already got whistle holders." She picks up the hook part of her lanyard and clips her whistle to it using the little metal keyring attached to its back. The whistle dangles in front of her ID badge, ready for anything.

"That's genius," Fei Fei says, and we all copy Lyr, attaching our whistles to the lanyards already around our necks. "Let's go find Q and Kir."

Lyr texts Queena, who tells her that she and Kir are on the second floor, outside Parker's room. When we arrive, Kir is excited. The Group 12 counselors are letting her and Parker run their race today, as long as they wear their whistles and stay within sight of someone at all times. She and Parker argue about the route they're going to run.

An unfamiliar boy with messy hair slouches against the wall, staring down at his phone. His wrinkled gray shirt is printed with a logo that reads "Hong Kong Football Association" in a circle around a dragon and the letters "HKFA." That must be Harrison's brother, William. The boy looks up as we approach, with a face that is a younger, chubbier version of his brother's. But where Harrison is cheerful and charming, William appears sulky and annoyed. I would look that way if I had to room with Parker, too.

It feels weird to just stand there without acknowledging him, so I say, "Hi, I'm Phoenny, and this is Lyr, Maze, Fei Fei, and Lina," gesturing to each of the girls in turn. "We're the rest of Kir and Q's Squad."

William lifts his chin the way that boys do to signal they've seen each other. "Right," he says, and then turns back to his phone.

It seems like he doesn't want to be here. He'd be a much better match for McKenna than Harrison.

Jesse and Andrew come out of the room across the hall, holding up a tablet. "We have the perfect route—down the hill to the classroom building, across the front of the building, and then back up through the parking lot to the finish line in front of the Student Center." Jesse traces the path with his finger. "It's longer than the field, which Parker wanted, but shorter than the full loop around campus, which Kirrily wanted. Plus, there are grown-ups already stationed at the corners of the classroom building."

Andrew says, "The real bonus is that the finish line is in front of the cafeteria, and we'll be first to get in for dinner."

Parker sneers. "Look at her—she's first in line for every meal. Her thighs are twice the size of mine."

"I'm just fine. And if you really were a sprinter, your thighs would be bigger," Kir snaps. "You ready to get beaten?"

Parker is about to launch himself at Kir, when someone comes up behind me and steps between them. "Hey, hey, what's all this?" Harrison asks, holding his arms up to keep Parker from throttling Kir, who stands there calmly. His eyes meet mine. "Phee?"

I resist the urge to look away. "Parker just body-shamed

Kir again and couldn't handle her comeback," I explain.

"That's not okay, Parker. You owe Kir an apology," Harrison says.

But Parker isn't fazed. "I'm not apologizing for stating the truth. And I'm not going to lose."

Harrison turns to Jesse. "Does the course you suggested favor one racer over another?"

Jesse shakes his head. "It's a compromise."

"Good. Now, you two go settle this on the course, and no taking shortcuts or tripping one another." He points Kir and Parker toward the stairs, then addresses Jesse and Andrew. "Is someone going to be watching them along the whole route?"

Andrew shakes his head. "Not the whole way, but most of it. Jesse will be at the starting line, and we'll both be at the finish. The first turn is at a roadblock guarded by staff, but the road past the classroom building is a little curved, so they'll be out of sight until they reach the next roadblock at the parking lot. We'll be able to see them run up the hill to the Student Center from there."

Harrison frowns. "Hey, Wills?" He beckons to his brother, who peels himself off the wall and comes over. "Could you do me a favor and go watch the race from in front of the classroom building and make sure nothing happens?"

William's mouth tightens. "Parker's not a cheat."

"It's not that," Harrison says. "It's a safety issue. I know the road to the classroom building is inside the flags, but we still need eyes on both Parker and Kir for the whole race. What if one of them trips and gets injured or something?" He doesn't mention the online trolls, but the whole Squad is thinking it. Harrison looks around. "Take someone with you. Bran or Howie or one of the other girls in your group."

"Why not ask one of these girls?" William jerks his head toward us.

"Pretty sure they want to be at the finish line to see their friend win," Harrison says with a small smile.

"Why don't you keep an eye on the race yourself?" William either really doesn't care about Parker or he doesn't want to do what his brother says.

"I trust you lot to handle it," Harrison says. "I've got some stuff I have to take care of." He looks at his brother, who hasn't moved. "Can you help me out here, Wills?"

William scowls and stalks off with Jesse and Andrew.

Harrison gives a dramatic sigh. "Brothers, right?" He shrugs and waves back at us as he walks down the hall, disappearing into the room at the end.

My stomach does a flip. "That was weird. He acted like normal. Like he hasn't been trying to talk to me all day and I haven't been avoiding him."

"Phee," Lyr says in a serious tone. "He's in the room right beneath ours!"

"Oh no, do you think he heard us talking last night?" That

would actually be bad. And incredibly embarrassing.

"No, that's not what I meant. We were too quiet for anyone to overhear. I'm talking about being *right next to the emergency exit stairs.* You could go visit him without any of the night monitors seeing you!"

I almost choke on my own spit. "Lyr! I'm not going to visit a boy in his own room at night!"

She turns pink. "I didn't mean *that,* either. I know you've been avoiding him today, but wasn't it because the rest of the group was around? You could slip downstairs and talk to him in private when his roommate isn't there. Ask him what's really going on inside his head."

I think about this for a moment. Mom and Dad are always saying that there would be fewer problems between people if they just talked to each other honestly. "That sounds terrifying. Won't I be revealing that I like him? What if he doesn't like me back?"

"Then you can stop stressing about it and move on," Fei Fei says. "But, Phee, he just *singled you out* back there. He asked *you* what was going on. Not any of the rest of us. He made sure you knew that he didn't pick the movie because it shows Shrek not wanting to be with Fiona, at least in the beginning. He's totally interested,"

I shake my head. "That's one way to look at it. Shrek also spent a lot of the movie trying to get Fiona to fall for him again. What if Harrison says he didn't pick the movie because he doesn't want me to get the wrong idea—that he doesn't want me to fall for him? I'd rather not make a fool of myself. If he likes me, he's going to have to show me in a clearer way."

Fei Fei tries to talk me out of waiting for a sign from Harrison, but I tell her to zip it. "Why don't *you* show Gemma you're interested?"

Her face turns bright red. "You all know?" She looks around at the rest of the Squad.

"Gemma is amazing," Maze replies. "What's stopping you from letting her know?"

"Because," Fei Fei says haltingly. "Because she's our CIT. And she's sixteen. And I don't know if she likes me like that." She shoots me a glance and sighs. "Okay, I get it. I want her to give me a sign, just like you want Harrison to give you a sign. I guess we'll both just have to wait and see what happens."

I hug her, hard. "Come on, we better get outside so we can watch Kir whip Parker."

# CHAPTER SEVENTEEN

Outside, Kir and Parker are in the crosswalk in front of the dorm, a little crowd of campers forming around them. Parker is doing elaborate stretches while Kir just shakes her head.

"This is the starting line," Jesse tells them. "The finish line is the first edge of the crosswalk in front of the Student Center. Bran, Howie, and William are already in position to monitor the road past the classroom building, all the way to the parking lot. Andrew is over at the cafeteria, stringing up a ribbon across the finish line."

"That's my cue," Lina says, patting her camera. "Gotta get a great shot of Kir breaking the ribbon."

"No way is that happening," Parker boasts. "You're going to be putting a photo of me winning in the memory book."

"Sure," Lina replies. "You keep thinking that."

"All right, is everybody finally here?" Jesse opens his stopwatch app and poises his index finger above the start button. "Queena, do you want to do the honors?"

Queena steps up to the line with the air of royalty. She raises her right arm as though she's holding a flag. "On your mark . . . get set . . . GO!" She whips her arm down, and Kir and Parker take off.

The first stretch is straight downhill, and Parker pulls into the lead quickly. He's taller than Kir, and his stride is longer. But he's a sprinter, so hopefully he'll run out of energy soon. Kir is only a few strides behind him, but she appears to be losing ground as they turn the corner toward the classroom building and we lose sight of them. The two parent volunteers at the roadblock pump their fists and shout encouragement—"Jiāyóu!"

We all hurry over to the Student Center, where Andrew has taped a red crepe-paper party streamer across the road. He's at one end of the long parking lot, watching the other end where the runners would appear from the classroom building. Jesse watches the finish line in case it's a close race. Lina hovers near the crosswalk, pacing back and forth, trying to get a view of anyone coming up the parking lot. A bunch of other kids linger just past the finish line.

The Squad and I head in that direction, standing in the grass just beyond the streamer so Kir can see us as she comes up the hill. There are a few cars in the lot, which probably belong to the cafeteria workers, but since it's summer, the lot is mostly empty.

"I see them!" Andrew shouts. "Parker's still in the lead, but Kir is right behind him!"

Q makes a face. "Parker is going to be even more insufferable if he wins." She cups her hands around her mouth and starts screaming, "Come on, Kir! You can do it! Go, go, go!"

Soon all six of us are cheering Kir on. Bran appears next to us, panting from his dash back up the hill to watch the finish. William is nowhere to be seen, and Howie must be following the racers up the hill through the parking lot.

Parker is clearly winded, holding his side as he struggles up the hill. Kirrily, on the other hand, makes it look effortless, slowly increasing her stride and pace. As she closes in on Parker, she yells, "Passing! On your left!" and blows past him halfway up the hill. Fei Fei and Q are screaming themselves hoarse. Kir's face erupts into a grin as she hears them, and she steps on the gas, sprinting up the rest of the hill, turning left at the top, and breaking the streamer as she crosses the finish line. We surround her immediately, trying to hug her and jump up and down and cheer at the same time, Lina snapping photos nonstop.

"That was amazing!" Q shrieks, very un-queenlike, and hugs her roommate again. "You passed him going uphill!"

Kir laughs. "That hill is a baby slope. I've been training on Heartbreak Hill for years."

We turn to watch Parker jog across the finish line, gasping for breath. Kir walks over to him, and the rest of us follow. She holds out her hand. "You got chicked," she says good-naturedly. "Good race, Parker."

He actually swats her hand away. "That wasn't a fair race. The course was designed to favor a distance runner. It was rigged so you'd win. I want a rematch on a different course."

"You want to race again? Fine. But the truth is that this body, the one you keep making fun of, beat you. And it'll beat you in a rematch, too. Because you know what? This body is a freaking state champion."

"Mic drop!" Andrew calls, and gives Kir a high five.

Parker glares at Kir, Jesse, and Andrew and stomps away.

"Way to be a good sport!" Kir calls after him, and the crowd laughs.

Back upstairs, the Squad gathers on Fei Fei's picnic blanket while I pop next door to grab some snacks to share. As I turn to leave, I spot something different on my desk—a bit of green that wasn't there this morning. My heart flutters in my chest like a silk banner in the wind.

It's a dough figurine. Of a tiny green girl ogre. But instead of having red hair like Princess Fiona, she has black hair, like me.

I think I just got my sign.

# CHAPTER EIGHTEEN

My heart beats fast as we enter the cafeteria for dinner. The Squad has been dissecting the meaning of the ogre figurine since I found it. Everyone agrees that Harrison must have made it, especially since he didn't put any of his work from craft class on the side tables to dry along with ours. And he's the one who thought my nickname was short for Fiona, the one who I have a running joke about being an ogre with. Who else could it be?

Fei Fei, of course, thinks it's incredibly romantic and grudgingly acknowledged that whatever I'm doing seems to be working just fine. I have no idea what I'm doing, but I'm glad she and the Squad promise not to interfere and to let things play out naturally between me and Harrison, if there is such a thing as being natural when you're in middle school.

So we sit by ourselves, without trying to find Harrison or invite him over. If he sees the empty chair, he's welcome to join us. I'm definitely not going to drag him over to my table like Teagan tried to do at breakfast yesterday. But I find myself looking up every time someone walks into the cafeteria.

Emerson strides in with some of the other CITs, and my stomach clenches while my eyes search for a certain head of boy-band-worthy hair. My brother spots me and breaks away from his crew to come over. I feel all my friends' heads swivel to focus their attention on him and sigh inwardly. Is that what I look like when Harrison is around? How embarrassing.

"What do you want?" I ask impatiently. He's blocking my view of the door. Thankfully, Emerson leans down and I can see around him. But then he says in a low voice, "Hey, I hear you and H are hitting it off. Is that true?"

My face flames. "What? Where'd you hear that?"

"Look, guys talk," Emerson says. "Just be careful, okay?" He makes a move to ruffle my hair, and I block him with my arms.

"What do you mean, 'be careful'?' You can't just tell me that and walk away." I'm suddenly angry and afraid and embarrassed all at once. "You're friends with him. You told him to become a CIT. What do you know that I don't?"

Emerson studies me. "He's fun to hang out with and a great midfielder. But he talks like he's a player. Victor is his roomie and told us that H is a couple of years younger than us. Maybe he's trying to put on a good show because we're older. But I was fourteen not that long ago, and guys that age have no idea what they're doing. You're my sister. I don't want you to get hurt. I'm supposed to keep an eye out for you, but I'm with Group 8 most of the day." He sees the look on my face and holds up his hands. "I know you can take care of yourself. Like Dad says, 'More data—'"

"Is always a good thing," I finish for him. "That's why you've been scowling when you see me with Harrison?" Emerson nods. My anger toward my brother dissolves, but now I'm mad at Harrison. Because the data I do have shows that he flirts with me, McKenna, and god knows who else. He gives little romantic gifts to more than one girl. Conclusion? He's a player. "You're right," I tell Emerson. "I'll be on the lookout."

"We all will!" Fei Fei pipes up.

Lyr adds, "We've got Phee's back, don't worry."

Emerson looks around the table at each of my friends and smiles at them. "Thanks, that does make me feel better. Phoenny's lucky to have friends like you."

The collective swoon from the Squad is enough to make me lose my dinner. But Emerson is right—I'm super lucky to have such good friends, even if they're all crushing on my brother.

Later, at hall meeting, Win asks, "I had a good day today, did you?" He scans the group, and his eyes land on Maze. "Well, except for losing some brain cells to a birdie." Maze grins unapologetically.

Win says, "Before we start giving Snaps, Sarina and I will give an update on the online troll issue."

Sarina's voice is hard. "Today, someone with a different username posted a threat." I gasp and look up along with others from the group. "The Committee talked to our camp lawyer as well as the Asian American community groups I mentioned last night, and they decided that the threat is too vague for the police to get involved."

"What did the threat say?" Bran asks.

Win's forehead furrows. "It said, 'You should be scared.' There's no mention of why the troll thinks we should be scared, and more importantly, they don't state that they intend to harm anyone at camp. Even if the police had time to investigate every time someone posted something like that online, they probably wouldn't. And to be honest? I don't want them to come to Squee and interrogate everyone. It would be really stressful for all of us and take time away from what we should be doing, which is having fun."

Gemma nods. "There's a poet named Toi Derricotte who wrote a famous line: 'Joy is an act of resistance.' Basically, the trolls are trying to take away our power by frightening us. But if we continue to do things that make us happy, we are actually fighting back against the trolls."

We all spontaneously snap our fingers for Win and Gemma. Fight back by having fun? I can do that.

"Also," Sarina says, "we're taking a couple of additional safety measures. The doors to Agnes Hall and the other buildings we use for classes will be locked at all times. Counselors have key cards to get into any building, and your key cards will open the doors to Agnes. Parent volunteers will form groups to patrol the campus. I know it sounds scary, but it's not any more than colleges already do to maintain safety on campus."

Win adds, in a tough-guy voice, "Any trolls are going to have to get past me and Harrison first, got it?" They bump fists.

"Snaps to Win and Harrison for keeping us troll-free," Gemma says drily, and the mood lightens a tiny bit as we snap our fingers.

"I want to give Snaps to Phee," Harrison says, catching me off guard. I've been ducking him all day—what could he possibly compliment me on? "For her energy and enthusiasm for badminton today. I could tell she made playing a lot more fun for her team." He gazes at me while he and the others snap, and I search his face, wondering if this is just more flirting.

Gemma clears her throat. "Phee? Do you have Snaps for anyone?"

I wipe my forehead, as if I can clear away the fog in my brain. What else happened today? "Um, Snaps to Lina for taking amazing photos of Kir winning the race."

Lina beams. "Snaps to Teagan for helping me with my camera settings for the race photos."

"It's just math," Teagan murmurs. She looks down quickly and gestures with her hand, as if brushing away the compliment.

Huh. I don't even remember seeing Teagan at the race. I must've been really out of it today. In my head, I can hear Mom talking about "being present," and I promise myself to stay more in the moment, starting now. This is the last time I'll be a Squee camper, and I want to remember every second.

# CHAPTER NINETEEN

The next day, Tāng Auntie asks the counselors to hand out fans instead of ribbons. The large fans are made of light and dark pink feathers, which Fei Fei can't stop cooing over. She flutters the fan next to her cheek while batting her eyelashes, making us laugh.

When Tāng Auntie says she's going to teach us part of the "Jasmine Flower" dance and that there are a lot of ballet-like steps to it, McKenna looks interested. She follows the teacher's steps precisely, and when Tāng Auntie tells her "Very good!" her face lights up. Her smile is genuine when the teacher asks her to do a few solo steps while the rest of the group slowly revolves in a circle behind her. She is graceful and glowing, and my feelings are a jumble of clashing colors and materials. A thin yellow thread of happiness that McKenna is finally having fun at camp. A rough charcoal-gray ribbon of irritation, because why should someone who's been rude and critical deserve to have a good time? And finally, a thick ogre-green cord of jealousy for her agility. As McKenna's spirits lift, mine sink.

In Traditional Sports, Hsu Lǎoshī teaches us to play Chinese jiànzi. It's like hacky sack, but instead of a little ball filled with pellets, the jiànzi is a weighted disc with feathers sprouting out of the top. Along with the counselors, we're separated into two groups and told to keep the jiànzi in the air using any body part except our arms and hands. Most people kick it or use their knees, but Hsu Lǎoshī and Win demonstrate moves using their foreheads and backs.

Every time someone in my circle kicks the jiànzi to me, I miss. My feet just don't want to connect. I have to drop the thing right over my foot just to manage to kick it to someone else. Even then, my kick is so weak that Lyr has to rush toward me so she can punt the jiànzi before it hits the ground. If I was playing with just the Squad, it would be fine. But Bran, Howie, and Harrison are in my group, too, and I can tell that they're getting impatient with my lack of coordination. Instead of being able to laugh it off like I usually do at Squee, I feel judged and humiliated. To make it worse, Harrison has barely looked my way at all today. Maybe I went too far avoiding him yesterday and he's mad? Or he's upset because I haven't said anything about the ogre figurine? What about the rose that he gave McKenna?

Maze kicks the jiànzi to me, and without thinking, I head-butt it. The feathered weight sails across the circle straight at Bran, who is caught off guard and misses it. He picks it up and grins at me. "Go, Phee! Release your inner ogre!"

Startled, I glance at Harrison, who looks equally surprised. Our eyes meet briefly before his slide away. A million questions spin through my mind. Did he tell Bran about our inside joke about me being an ogre? Did Bran pick the Shrek movie? Was it *Bran* who left me the ogre figurine and not Harrison? It can't be. Bran and I have been at camp together since we were six. He's practically another brother. If he liked me that way, he would say so.

The spinning doesn't stop by the time classes end. When Sarina says that Counselor Time is canceled today because they have a lot to do to get ready for Carnival tonight, my shoulders droop with relief. I assume that the Squad will hang out like we always have, but when we meet up with Q and Kir, they have other plans.

"SuRong's a runner, too," Kir says. "The Committee got us access to the exercise room so we can train on the treadmills. I want to try and get ten miles in before dinner, so I better get changed."

Q points to Maze. "You have a ton of butter and eggs. I have a craving for gooey butter cake, and you mentioned there was a recipe you wanted to try. I feel like we could help each other out."

"You mean you'll supervise and eat the results." Maze laughs. "At your service, my queen."

"Oh, can I take photos for the memory book?" Lina asks. "And be the royal taste tester?"

"Save us some," Fei Fei demands. "Ava and I are going to work up an appetite playing *Rise of the Alien Wombats*." She heads across the hall while the others make their way to the kitchen.

"Let's hang out in our room," I tell Lyr. "You can work on your NEC music contest piece, and I'll work on a sewing project."

"That sounds great. I came up with some ideas for my piece during music class today." As we walk toward our room, the strains of a guitar float out into the hallway. "Oh, that must be Piper!" Lyr stops and knocks on the door.

The guitar music pauses, and Piper opens the door. "Oh, hi! I'm so sorry, am I playing too loud? Is it bothering you?"

"No, no," Lyr reassures her. "It's all good. Are you playing T-Swift's 'Mad Woman'? I love that song." She looks wistful.

Piper's eyes sparkle, and she throws the door wide open. "Do you want to join me? It's not a super-challenging piano part, though."

"I'd love to! I haven't had a lot of piano and guitar duets." Lyr looks back at me as if she's just remembered that I'm there. "You don't mind, do you, Phee? It's going to be hard to find a time to jam with Piper once camp is over."

"Of course not," I say, keeping my voice casual. "The sound of my sewing machine was just going to bother you, anyway."

Lyr tells Piper that she'll be right back, and we cross the hall to our room. She grabs Casey and heads out with a cheerful "See you later!"

It's sweltering outside, but the room is suddenly freezing.

Maze must've felt bad about not giving cupcakes to the guys, because she brings the gooey butter cake to dinner and gives everyone in Group 13 a slice. Lina shows off the T-shirt I made for her during free time. The camera appliqués were easier than I thought they would be—black and white rectangles and circles for the camera bodies, and blue circles for the lenses. I added a couple of pink hearts for cuteness. It was good to get lost in a project again.

After dinner, we head downstairs. Dozens of balloons in bright primary colors surround the doorway to the Flex. Fei Fei claps. "They made a balloon arch this year! No wonder they canceled Counselor Time!"

Parker, William, Andrew, and Jesse are standing in a clump by the door, as if they haven't decided if they're going in or not. "Hey," Andrew addresses me. "Who are your new friends?"

I turn my head to find that the new girls of Group 13 have followed us. I wave them forward, and the Squad pulls back to let them through. "McKenna, Teagan, Piper, Delaney, and Ava, this is Andrew, Jesse, Parker, and William." They exchange greetings, and William seems more friendly than yesterday. In fact, his eyes are locked on McKenna. Piper notices, too, and we share little *oh-ho, what's happening here?* smiles.

The boys walk into the Flex with the girls, when Parker

approaches Kir and mumbles something. Shock crosses Kir's face, which quickly turns to amusement. "Not on your life," she snorts.

Parker's face darkens, and he sneers, "You won't find anyone else."

Kir shrugs. "I'm not looking, anyway."

Parker stomps off after his friends, leaving us to stare at Kir. "What was that about?" Fei Fei asks.

"Get this—he asked me to the dance." Kir rolls her eyes. "But he didn't actually *ask*; he just came up and said, 'Go to the dance with me,' like he was giving me an order. Of course I turned him down."

Q taps her chin thoughtfully. "I should try that—command someone to be my date."

Maze says, "I'm pretty sure they wouldn't be called a date. A servant, maybe."

"That works, too."

Laughing hysterically, we link arms and stride into the Flex.

We follow Maze to the ball toss game, where we each get a cup with three Ping-Pong balls in it. We throw the balls at pyramids made of upside-down plastic cups. It's not as satisfying as hurling a softball into a stack of metal milk cans, but it helps me focus and be present. Maze knocks them all down with her first ball and gets a bag of gummy bears as a prize. The rest of us get a single small Tootsie Roll for our efforts.

We visit each booth, spinning a prize wheel, playing limbo, tossing rings, and sticking fake tattoos to our hands. Gemma is at the face-painting station, and she lets me use the paints to decorate my friends' cheeks with the Asian snack foods they love. Gemma admires the bottle of Yakult on Kir's face and asks for one, too. When I'm done, she says, "You're such a great artist, Phoenny! You want to take over this station?"

"Thanks, I'm good." I smile as she gives each of us a handful of Hershey's Kisses.

"Wait," Lyr says as I turn away. "You have to paint something on your own face, too."

It's hard to paint my own face, but Gemma has a mirror. I consider doing a simple kawaii mochi, but I did that for Queena. Ever since she was seven and read *Jasmine Toguchi, Mochi Queen*, she's been obsessed with everything mochi-related. She's the Squad's Mochi Queen. I settle on a cup of taro boba tea, because it's delicious and the perfect shade of pastel lilac. Fei Fei claps and Lyr smiles and then we're off to bob for donuts.

Harrison and two other CITs are tying up powdered donuts to a curtain rod. The sight of him reminds me that he gave McKenna a rose. And the next day, gave me an ogre. A rose is definitely more romantic than a hideous green giant that eats people. A rose is a gift, and an ogre is a joke. My stomach lurches and my heart pounds. Somehow, "being present" also means being hyperaware of Harrison's every move. Lyr pulls me with her, though, and soon I'm staring at a powdered donut hanging from a string. Lyr, Fei Fei, and Maze kneel next to me, nose-to-nose with their own donuts. Lina snaps photos while the others watch and make bets.

"Hey, ladies," Harrison greets us, but I can't meet his eyes. "Ready to play? Okay, ready . . . set . . . go!"

The four of us try to eat our donuts without using our hands. It's so much harder than it sounds—my donut swings and spins, evading my open mouth. It bumps against my nose, and the powdered sugar makes me sneeze. I hear Harrison chuckle and the Squad laughing. Fei Fei finishes her donut in five big bites, and everyone cheers. She takes her prize—a box of Pocky—and bows to the crowd.

I should stick around to root for the rest of the Squad, but I need air. I need to get the powdered sugar off my face. I need to not feel this way. "Restroom," I murmur to Lyr, and start for the door.

"Phee," Harrison calls after me. "Hang on a minute."

I stop but don't turn around. He steps in front of me and holds out his hand. "You forgot your consolation prize."

I stare down at the tiny box of Nerds in his palm. That's me. I'm the nerd, the consolation prize if things don't work out between him and McKenna. I look him in the eye and say, "Keep it. I don't do second place." Not for him, not for anyone.

Then I walk away.

Carnival runs late and we're all tired, so Win and Sarina ask us to do a quick round of Snaps instead of having a real hall meeting. Lina gives me Snaps for making the T-shirt for her.

"Snaps to Maze for sharing her amazing butter cake with all of us," I say.

Eventually, it's McKenna's turn. "I'm giving Snaps for dates to the dance," she says coyly.

"Like, the *concept* of having a date for the dance, or your actual date?" Maze probes.

"Yes," she says, and her eyes flicker to where Harrison is sitting and staring at the carpet.

Everyone except Harrison notices, even Sarina and Winson, because their eyebrows shoot up to their hairlines. Teagan, Delaney, Piper, and Ava start snapping, and the rest of us slowly join them. I feel the sadness and rage build inside me. I was right about being in second place—Harrison has already asked McKenna to the dance. I'm glad I said what I said to him after the donut-bobbing game.

I push back my hood to feel the night breeze blowing through the hall window, and Lyr slips her hand into mine like a satin ribbon tethering me to the earth.

# CHAPTER TWENTY

Thursday, we only have classes in the morning because the afternoon is devoted to Field Day. We have a water balloon fight and discover that Delaney has incredible aim. Maze's buff arms win the tug-of-war for our group. Bran and Howie are so in sync for the three-legged race that they easily beat the rest of us in Group 13, but they also beat everyone in Group 12. Groups 12 and 13 are pitted against each other for the 100-yard dash, making Parker's wish for a sprint rematch come true, even though he and Kir are on the same team. Kir still smokes him.

For the CIT Dress-Up Contest that night, we rummage through our clothes and make Gemma put on Lyr's red cardigan, McKenna's denim miniskirt, and Delaney's purple leggings to look like Meilin from *Turning Red*. Then I poach Emerson's orange T-shirt and pin a cutout Lina made of the 4*Town logo on it for Harrison. The irony of him dressing as a character in a boy band isn't lost on the Squad. Fei Fei accidentally calls him Wang Yibo, and he gives her a weird look. He wears his own jeans, and when he struts onstage and lip-synchs the song from the movie, more than a few campers squeal. But Emerson actually wins first place. His campers used toilet paper tubes, chopsticks, and old sheets and T-shirts to make him look like a Tusken Raider from *Star Wars*.

Since Carnival, Harrison has been civil to me but nothing more. He greets the Squad as a group, sits with the other CITs at breakfast, and talks to me only if necessary. He hasn't mentioned the ogre figurine at all, and there's no way I'm bringing it up now. Instead, he hangs out with the counselors during classes and walks with Gemma between buildings. Even though Emerson was right about Harrison being a player, having proof that I wasn't really special to him makes my heart ache a little. I know it's better this way, but I still miss bantering with him.

In crafts class the next day, Harrison and Gemma hand out paper, scissors, and glue sticks while Sūn Lǎoshī explains how to fold a red envelope. As we work, she tells us how lucky we are to go to the museum tomorrow.

"We're going to a *museum* for our field trip?" McKenna makes a face. "What about going to the beach? Or to an amusement park? I mean, it's *summer.*"

"There are a lot of examples of traditional Chinese folk crafts and other art at the Peabody Essex Museum," Sarina explains. It's the end of the week, and everybody's patience is as thin as chiffon. Though I have to agree with McKenna about how fun it would be to go to an amusement park with the Squad. "This *is* a cultural camp," Sarina continues.

"Activities and field trips are designed to try to keep the focus on connecting us to our Chinese heritage."

"Why should I make a connection to a country that didn't want me?" McKenna mutters under her breath. Teagan and Piper nod in agreement.

Sūn Lǎoshī's hands stop folding paper. She reaches across the table and pats McKenna's hand. "Why do you say this? That China did not want you?"

"Because it's true." McKenna stares at the teacher's hand covering hers. "I was adopted by an American family, so obviously China would rather send me away than keep me."

"Kělián de háizi," the teacher says with sympathy. *Poor child*, I translate in my head, not wanting to interrupt the moment. "I understand why you feel this way. There are many complicated reasons why Chinese parents give up their children for adoption, including government policies, poverty, and cultural beliefs. Please believe me when I say that, as a society, Chinese people love their children. They want to keep them, but sometimes they feel there is no other choice than to give them up." She pats McKenna's hand again. "You have suffered much. I am sorry."

McKenna's face is unreadable, but tears streak Gemma's. Sarina hands her a box of tissues. She takes one and passes the box to the other girls, some of whom take one. Gemma wipes her face and thanks Sūn Lǎoshī. She turns back to Sarina. "Maybe we can make the field trip to the museum optional? It can be really hard to be around so many cultural objects. They are reminders of what we have lost."

"We'll talk to Director Fāng right now," Sarina says. "I'm sure it won't be a problem—since it's a Saturday, the counselors and CITs for the day campers will be free to supervise anyone who doesn't want to go." She nods at Win, and they both head out into the hallway.

Lyr rubs Piper's arm, and Fei Fei scoots closer to Ava. Harrison glances at Gemma, who is quietly making sure McKenna is okay. He clears his throat and asks, "Sūn Lǎoshī, perhaps you can tell us what we'll be doing in class next week?"

"Yes, of course. We are going to learn calligraphy and Chinese brush painting," Sūn Lǎoshī says happily. She reaches under one of the tables and pulls out a cardboard box. "Look, these are all the brushes that we are going to be using." She takes out a handful of brushes and lays them out on the table. We gather around to examine them. Many have bamboo handles, but some of the larger paintbrushes have carved and lacquered wood handles. One has a gorgeous blue-green enamel handle with birds on it. The brush parts range from tiny and pointy to large fan-shaped ones. Some of the bristles are dark brown and soft, while others are white and coarse. One even has three brush heads set in a flat row, attached to a central handle. They're all beautiful.

Piper picks up one of the largest brushes, which is easily

over a foot long. The bristles are a rich brown-black and are cut into a blunt tip.

Sūn Lǎoshī smiles. "That is called the Beijing grab brush because it is so big that you have to hold it in a different way. It's used for writing large-size calligraphy or painting big broad strokes for lotus leaves. Some people also use it to paint abstracts or Zen-style landscapes."

Piper strokes the bristles, which are longer than her hand. Then she turns the brush upside down and runs it over her cheeks and nose. "Or maybe it'd be good for putting on blush and powder," she says with a grin.

"What's this one made of?" Harrison's voice makes me jump. When did he come around the table and stand right beside me? He's holding the cloisonné enamel brush gently in his hand.

"Ah, that one is truly special," the teacher says. "The handle is enamel inlay, with a phoenix pattern. The brush part is láng háo. It is a special edition made by a teacher I once had."

Sūn Lǎoshī reaches into the box again and takes out different colors of ink sticks, smooth black inkstones, and carved wooden brush rests. I want to touch and play with it all. Next week is going to be super fun.

"Láng háo and phoenixes," Harrison muses. "It's like a magic wand." He touches the tip of the brush lightly and then surprises me by twirling it over my nose playfully. The silky bristles tickle and make me sneeze. He chuckles. "Oops."

So now he's flirting with me again. Happiness rushes through me, like warm velvet. "Why, what does *láng háo* mean?" I ask. I barely finish speaking before sneezing again.

Lyr murmurs, "Bless you." She looks at me strangely. Maybe one of the brush hairs got stuck inside my nose. I fumble for my backpack to get a tissue.

"*Láng* in this case means 'wolf.' The brush is made of wolf fur."

"Actually, it's not the wolf that's related to dogs," Sūn Láoshī corrects. "It's what Chinese people call the yellow-tailed wolf, which is actually a weasel."

Weasel fur? "Oh no!" I sneeze again. "Are weasels the same as ferrets? I'm allergic to ferrets!"

Lina looks up from her phone. "Weasels and ferrets are in the same family and genus!"

The itchy feeling inside my nose gets worse. "Sarina!"

She bursts into the room and rushes to my side. "What's wrong, Phee?"

Lyr answers for me because I'm too busy sneezing. "She's having a reaction to the brush because she's allergic to weasels."

Win appears with a handful of tissues. I grab them gratefully and blow my nose. "Are you severely allergic? Do you have asthma? Do we need to give you a shot of epinephrine?"

I shake my head. "I just need—*achoo*—an antihistamine from the nurse. Before my eyes swell up."

"I'll take her," Lyr and Harrison say at the same time. Harrison looks straight at Sarina and Win. "It's my fault. I touched her face with the brush. I should be the one to escort her." He watches as I rub my eyes. "If her eyes swell shut, I can carry her."

Carry me? My breath hitches.

"Go," Sarina tells Harrison. "It's better if a counselor is with her, anyway. I'll call the nurse and tell her you're on your way. Win, call Director Fāng again and let her know what's going on."

Harrison grabs my backpack and guides me out the door. I turn back to see Sūn Lǎoshī and the Squad looking stricken, so I give them a thumbs-up. "I'll be fine," I say, but it comes out sounding more like *Ahbeebine* because my nose is so stuffy.

Outside, Harrison pulls my arm across his shoulders and wraps his arm around my back as we rush across campus. I feel a little jolt of electricity at the close contact. He's really taking this seriously. I try to tell him that my legs work fine, but honestly, it feels good to be held. The word "player" pops into my head in Emerson's voice, and I push it away.

"God, Phee, I am so sorry. I had no idea you were allergic," Harrison says in a hoarse voice.

"Who said anything about allergies?" I tease. "I'm actually changing into my ogre form."

His laugh is strained, but at least he doesn't look so miserable.

The camp "nurse" is actually a parent volunteer who is a doctor in real life, and the nurse's office is just another dorm room in Agnes Hall. Harrison sits me down on the edge of the bed being used an examination table before letting me go.

"Hi, Dr. Ung," I wheeze. "I just need an antihistamine. The same thing happened before when I played with my friend's pet ferret."

She looks bewildered until Harrison explains about the weasel hair calligraphy brush, then hands me two pills and a small paper cup of water. She takes out her stethoscope. "Let's have a listen, just in case."

I swallow the pills and breathe deeply as she listens to my lungs. She takes out a penlight and shines it inside my mouth and in each eye. "You seem a little short of breath," she observes.

"We practically ran here," I tell her. "Ask him."

Dr. Ung looks at Harrison, and he nods. She turns back to me. "No history of asthma? Your chest doesn't feel tight? No coughing or pain?" I shake my head after each question. "Okay, good. I'm sure you're going to be fine, but just in case, I want you to stick around for a half hour until the antihistamine kicks in and the itchiness goes away."

I sigh. I love Dr. Ung, but I really don't want to sit here with her staring at me for thirty minutes. "Um, can I go out back? I promise not to pet any animals and to check back in when the time is up."

The doctor smiles. "All right, but you still need a buddy. Go with her," she tells Harrison.

I lead him down the stairs to an emergency exit door past the recycling bins. We sit down at one of the picnic tables in the grassy area behind Agnes. It's nice and shady here.

"You're really okay?" He puts a hand on his chest. "My heart is still pounding."

"Yeah, I'll be fine. At least now I know to stay away from weasels, too'."

Harrison winces. "I'm so, so sorry." He opens his backpack, finds a pack of tissues, and sets it on the table in front of me. Then he takes out a sealed bottle of water that he must've grabbed from the nurse's office and unscrews the cap for me. "Here, drink more water."

I smile. It's such a Chinese thing to do. I swallow a few mouthfuls and set down the bottle. "Thanks." For the first time in a while, I look straight into his eyes. "So you're going to the dance with McKenna?"

# CHAPTER TWENTY-ONE

"Wh-what?" he stammers. "No! Why would I do that? Who told you that? Is that why you've been avoiding me since Carnival?"

I consider his questions. "I was angry with you that night, and I admit I've been staying away from you."

"Why?" He looks genuinely hurt and confused.

"I've been keeping my distance because Emerson told me to." A dark cloud comes down over his face. "Wait. Hear me out. Emerson was just watching out for me. He said you've been talking with the guys like you're a player. At Movie Night, McKenna and her friends were gushing about the rose you gave her. Everything else supported what Emerson said. I was mad because you were playing me. I don't want to be your backup plan. That's why I walked away."

"What?!" he practically roars, and I sit back. He takes a deep breath and rolls his shoulders. "Sorry. I . . . It's just . . . Look. None of that is true. I am not a player, and I'm not playing you. Seriously. I don't know why they're saying it, but I did not give McKenna a rose." He stops and looks at me anxiously. "I did make the ogre for you—you knew it was from me, right?"

"Who else?" I say softly. "You're the only one who finds my ogre-ishness funny."

He looks relieved and annoyed at the same time. "Why would you believe I gave McKenna a rose? How would I even go buy one? I'm stuck here on campus, same as you." He frowns. "And I did *not* ask her to the dance."

"It wasn't a real rose. It was made out of red rice dough. And whoever made it left it in her room for her to find, the same way you left the ogre for me. You were using the red dough in class, and you were there when McKenna and her friends all made pink roses. McKenna looked at you when Teagan gave Snaps to 'secret admirers' at hall meeting that night. Everything pointed to you. She also looked at you last night when she gave Snaps for having a date to the dance. The Squad and I all thought she meant you were her date."

Harrison groans. "Well, that explains a lot. I have no idea who gave her the rose or asked her to the dance, but it wasn't me. The morning after Carnival, though, Sarina and Win took me aside and said I needed to watch my behavior. They pointed to a section in the handbook about how relationships between staff and campers are against the rules. I thought they were telling me to stay away from you, and I was hurt because I figured you told them about the ogre and complained about me. I decided it was better to keep my distance from all of you and just talk to Gemma." He studies me intently. "But now I realize they were talking about McKenna and it's not that you don't like me?" His eyes are hopeful.

I think about his response, about everything he's said or done. "You *have* been flirty with McKenna and some of the other girls. The counselors aren't wrong about that. And you've been hard to figure out. You don't talk to me for days, and suddenly today you're tickling me with a calligraphy brush." I take the plunge and add, "I don't know what's real. How you really feel."

He's silent for a long time, and I start to worry that I said too much or that he doesn't have feelings for me. But didn't he just say that he was upset because he thought I didn't like him back?

Finally, slowly, he says, "I can see why you thought I was flirting with the other girls. I was just trying to be friendly, but maybe I went too far." He pauses. "That's not completely honest. It made me feel good when McKenna flirted with me, so I flirted back to keep it going. Maybe that does make me a player, I don't know." He sighs. "Being the new guy has been harder than I expected. I'm not just new to camp, but I'm also new to this country. And the other guys treat me differently because I'm younger."

"I'm really sorry," I say. "I didn't realize that you were going through that." He's so cheerful and charming all the time. It's easy to forget that he's never been to Squee before, not to mention that he just moved here from another country. While I don't always like how she acts or what she says, I do admire McKenna for always making it clear when she's unhappy or disappointed. If you speak up, you can get support, like from Sūn Lǎoshī in crafts today. Does Harrison get any support? Maybe he feels like he has more in common with McKenna since she's new, too. I wonder if he likes it at Squee or if it's as hard for him as it is for McKenna.

He makes an apologetic face. "That doesn't excuse my behavior. I'm sorry I made you feel like you were, what did you say? Second place?"

I nod. "So what now? You can't keep avoiding all the girls in the group. And, um, I don't want you to ignore me."

Harrison's smile lights up his whole face. "Looks like I need to figure out where the line is. How to be friendly without being flirtatious." He leans forward. "And to convince you that you're not my backup plan. You're the only plan."

I feel well enough to rejoin Group 13 for lunch and afternoon classes. Lyr makes me swear never to scare her like that again. Ava pats my hand, Delaney smiles, and Piper wheedles an extra brownie from the cafeteria staff for me. McKenna nods, and Teagan jokes, "Do you see why I don't like crafts now?" which makes me laugh.

After dinner, I head toward my room to grab my sketchbook before joining the rest of Group 13 for a joint card game night in the living room. I thought it would be better to show everyone what kind of historical costumes I had in mind for our wǔshù performance in the Showcase and get their opinion before arranging it with the teachers.

Mom stands in the door of the nurse's office. She says good night to Dr. Ung and starts down the hall toward her room.

"Mom," I call out, and run to catch up with her. I promised Dad that I'd keep an eye on Mom, but I haven't talked to her in days.

Mom turns and gives me a hug. "Hi, Phoenny. I was just thanking Dr. Ung for taking care of you. Come on, let's talk in my room. I need to sit down." She looks exhausted.

She fills an electric kettle with water from the bathroom sink faucet and heats it. When it's ready, she makes a mug of green tea before sinking down on the edge of her bed. After a few sips, she seems to have a bit more energy. She looks at me over the rim of the mug. "A weasel hairbrush, huh? That's a new one."

I laugh. "Yeah, I'm going to be a lot more careful when choosing paintbrushes from now on. And maybe start carrying around antihistamine tablets and my inhaler, just so I'll be prepared if it happens again."

"That's a good idea," Mom agrees, "but it's probably best if Sarina or Winson carries them for you. You're technically not supposed to take medications unless you're supervised by a counselor or the nurse. Those are the rules . . ."

"I'm okay with that," I say.

There's a long pause while Mom sips her tea. There's something I want to talk to her about, but I'm not exactly sure how to start. "Um, Mom? How do you think camp is going this year?" I finally manage.

"What do *I* think about camp? Well, there have certainly been some new challenges to navigate, including safety concerns." She gives me a long, searching look. "What do *you* think about camp this year?"

"To be honest, I don't think it feels the same. There are good moments and bad moments, which feels really confusing because camp used to be mostly good moments. I think too much has changed."

Mom takes another sip. When she lowers her mug, she says, "Tell me, Phoenny. What has changed?"

"I don't understand why some of the new people came to Squee. We learn about Chinese culture here, and Teagan doesn't really want to know about it. McKenna doesn't want to learn Mandarin or wǔshù. Gemma says it's hard for some adoptees to be around cultural stuff, but like, we're surrounded by those things at camp. Harrison has a better attitude, but he says he doesn't know how to act around us. I think they feel like they don't belong here, and . . . and I kind of agree with that."

"Why don't you feel like they belong here, Phoenny? Aren't you always saying that Squee is your safe space, the place where you feel like you belong the most?" Mom presses.

"Well, yes, but . . . Maybe they're not Chinese enough for Squee. Except for Harrison—maybe he's too Chinese."

Mom cradles her mug between her hands and doesn't speak for a full minute. "Did you know that your nǎinai didn't want your dad to marry me?"

"Um, what?!" I'm completely taken aback. Năinai is seriously one of the nicest people I know. "Why not?"

"Because I wasn't Chinese enough. She said those exact words to my face and tried to convince your dad that I would never fit into their family." Mom stares down into her mug and then smiles to herself. "But you know what he said to her? He said, 'Culture isn't static—it evolves, just like people.' And then he told your năinai that she needed to expand her definition of being Chinese to include me."

"Wow," I say. "Go, Dad."

Mom grins at me. "That's when I knew he was the one for me." She puts down her mug and stands up. "I wish I'd known that the new girls in your group were adopted before camp started, so we could've been better prepared. They—and Harrison as a recent immigrant—are caught between cultures in a much different way than you or me. We're going to add some questions to next summer's registration form, so we'll be aware of different backgrounds and be more sensitive to everyone's needs. All campers deserve to feel like this environment can be a happy place."

I think about this. "Squee is evolving and expanding, too."

Mom gives me a hug. "That it is, sweetheart. And this is what makes me so furious about the online harassment we've received this summer. We can't just focus on how to make internal changes for the better. Now we have a whole new set of worries."

# CHAPTER TWENTY-TWO

When I reunite with Group 13, they're engrossed in multiple raucous games of Slap, smacking each other's hands and shouting in pain or glee. Smiling, I watch them for a few minutes. Mom's right about two things: There's room for all of us at Squee, and we can't let the trolls ruin this place for us. I wind my way through the crowd and stand at one end of the coffee table. I put my hands on my hips and address the whole group, loudly. "I have thoughts."

They fall silent, staring at me in confusion, annoyance, or amusement.

Sarina's mouth twitches. "What's up, Phee?"

Mentally, I channel Queena's and McKenna's big energy . . . "Online trolls suck. We need to cancel them."

Win tilts his head. "I agree with you. But how are you going to do that?"

With both hands, I point to Howie and Bran. "With them."

The two boys look at each other in confusion. "Us? What are we going to do?" Howie says, eyes wide.

"What you're best at." I grin. "Fighting." My mouth can hardly catch up to my brain. The ideas are flowing like a cascade of slippery satin. I tell the group we should have Howie and Bran spar onstage during our Showcase performance while the rest of us do some simpler choreography in the background. "We'll make a video and wear cool costumes. And then we're going to post the video on our social media accounts."

The counselors' eyes bug out. "What? We're not posting anything online." Sarina shakes her head.

"The trolls are *why* we're going to post the video online. Right, Ava?" I look at her and smile encouragingly.

Ava looks tentative at first, but then she nods vigorously. "I've been working with Cooper and his crew. They're still trying to figure out the identities of all the trolls, but they also want to see if there's a pattern. Like, if some of the trolls are using the same servers or finding us from the same sites. To do that, they'd like more data. Which means more comments. Posting a new video would generate more comments. Camp would be over by then, so it won't be dangerous for us and we can figure out how to prevent the trolls from posting again next year."

The counselors still look like they need convincing.

"We'll also ask community groups to post responses calling out the trolls. Maybe they can contact the local news stations for us, too. Instead of keeping quiet and hoping no one notices, we go big!" I raise a fist.

Maze raises her fist, too. "We will not be the quiet and submissive model minority they stereotype us as. Let's publicly shame the trolls for harassing innocent Chinese American kids."

"Exactly! And the video will also be proof that their comments don't work on us. Like Gemma said, we're going to show them our joy. The video is our act of resistance." I look around. "What do you all think? Haven't you experienced more microaggressions and anti-Asian hate the past few years?"

"I have," Lyr says quietly. "I take the T home from piano lessons, and someone kept trying to get me to talk to make sure I could speak English."

I hug her tightly while some of the others make sounds of support.

McKenna says, "I was walking home from school, and an older couple was sitting on their front porch. When I passed them, the woman shouted, 'Go back to China!' When people say stuff like that, it really messes with my mind. Like I said in crafts class—I don't really feel Chinese or a connection to China. So it's always kind of a shock that other people immediately treat me like I'm Chinese."

Piper puts her arm around McKenna. "It's a shock, and then there's no one to talk to about it that understands, because the people around us are all white," Piper adds.

Everyone has a story, including Harrison, whose soccer teammate accused his parents of stealing jobs from "hard-working Americans." By the time people are done sharing, they're all convinced that we should make the video, that it would be a good start in our fight to be who we are.

# CHAPTER TWENTY-THREE

The next morning in the cafeteria before the field trip, there's an ease in the air, like when the thread tension is released on my sewing machine and the stitches are loose, even a little loopy. McKenna and Teagan sit down at the table next to me, and McKenna catches my eye. She nods and smiles. Surprised, I smile back.

After breakfast, we climb onto the bus—all of us, including Group 12, so the whole Squad is together again. And even though Mom agreed that the trip was optional, all the Group 13 girls decided to come after all. On the bus ride, Win, Harrison, and the Group 12 counselors entertain us with a hilarious performance of "Little Apple" in Mandarin by Chopstick Brothers. Soon, Lyr, Fei Fei, Kir, and I, along with a few other campers from Group 12 are chiming in on the refrain, "Nǐ shì wǒ de xiǎo ya xiǎo píngguǒ er / zěnme ài nǐ dōu bù xián duō," and laughing.

Delaney turns around. "What does the song mean? What's so funny about it?"

"It's this bizarre love song about a little apple and her red face," Lyr says, giggling. "Here, I'll teach you the refrain."

Lyr patiently sings the lyrics several times until the girls get it. McKenna has a nice voice. So she's a dancer *and* a singer! The whole bus clamors for an encore, and we sing it for almost the whole way to the museum. Is it my imagination, or does Harrison look at me when he sings, "I've never disliked you / I like everything about you"? My face warms but I keep my eyes on his and sing back, "With you, every day is always fresh."

At the museum, we listen dutifully as one of the docents gives us a half-hour talk about the history of the collections. Then we separate into our camp groups and follow our counselors through the exhibits.

We wander through the Yin Yu Tāng, a super-old house from China that the museum shipped over here in pieces, then reassembled inside the museum. It's pretty cool, but when we hit the fashion and textiles collection, I'm transfixed. In addition to clothes, there are shoes and quilts and banners from all over the world. A lot of it is antique, but there are modern pieces, too. I study every detail of each item, taking multiple photos of everything.

"I would totally wear that," McKenna comments, startling me. I was so lost in the exhibit and all the ideas for clothing and art projects running through my head that I didn't even notice when she came to stand beside me. "I knew you liked art from crafts class, but I didn't realize until yesterday that you make clothes, too. What do you find so fascinating about them?" Her voice is sincerely curious.

I feel my face warm—it's always hard for me to talk about

my feelings when it comes to my art projects. "Everything, I guess," I say. "I know that sounds silly, but it's just amazing to me that people figured out how to spin yarn or thread out of animal hair or plant materials or"—I point to the ornate silk headdress in the display case—"the cocoon of a moth. And that those fibers can be dyed and woven or knitted into so many different things. Things that are plain and functional, or things that are both functional and decorative, that also express the maker's personality and emotion. Their inner selves," I finish slowly.

She studies the headdress. "I get that," she says. "I don't sew, but I like to express myself through my outfits."

"I really liked that corset-style top you wore," I tell her. "I was trying to figure out if it had actual plastic boning in it or if the seams were just sewn to look like it."

McKenna flashes a smile that looks almost shy. "It's just sewn that way. I love that top—it's actually really comfortable. Way better than the Victorian dress I had to wear for history class last year. That one had the boning you mentioned and laces to tighten the waist section. I could barely breathe."

A giggle pops out of my mouth before I can stop it. "I can't see you in a Victorian dress!"

"And you never will."

We move through the exhibit together, pointing out what we like and don't like about each piece. As I suspected, our styles are very different, but for once, our conversation doesn't go off the rails. We come to a Chinese wedding quilt cover printed with flowers. The pink roses remind me of the red rice dough rose McKenna received, and I decide to just say what's on my mind, to clear the air with McKenna the way I did with Harrison the other day.

"I was jealous about that rose you got," I say softly. "I thought Harrison gave it to you."

McKenna looks stunned. Then she admits, "Yeah, I know." She pauses. "I really wanted it to be from him. He told you it wasn't?"

I nod. "We talked about a bunch of stuff the other day, after he took me to the nurse."

"And?"

"What do you mean, 'and'?" I feel my cheeks get warm. "We just talked." I move on to the next display case quickly.

She looks at me closely and laughs. "*And* it looks like that went well." She hesitates and then adds, "I'm happy for you."

I can tell that she means it. "Well, you don't have to be *too* happy," I say lightly. "He's not allowed to date as a Squee CIT, so we have to wait until camp is over. Meanwhile, you have a date to the dance! I'm happy for you," I say, echoing her words. "Want to tell me who it is? Is it the same person who gave you the rose?"

"Nope, I'm not telling!" She grins. "You'll just have to find out at the dance."

I roll my eyes. "Rude."

McKenna chuckles. "Yeah, I know."

We reach the end of the fashion and textiles exhibit, but a new beginning to our friendship.

After the museum, the bus drops us off in Chinatown. First, the counselors lead us into a restaurant where we spread out over four large tables and order practically everything off the dim sum carts that roll by. We must be pretty noisy because I notice people from nearby tables glancing our way. But they just smile and keep eating. A couple of their kids run over and call us "jiějie" or "gēge" and ask us to play with them as if we really are their older sisters and brothers. Lina lets one little girl take photos with her phone camera, and Q finds some makeup in her purse and gives another child a mini makeover. More kids join us. Kir and Maze play "rock, paper, scissors" with them, except it's called s"cissors, rock, fabric" in Mandarin. McKenna and Delaney braid the hair of two other girls. I remember the stickers in my backpack left over from decorating our dorm door and pull them out. I hoist a small boy onto my lap, and he promptly plasters tigers and oxen all over my face.

I hear a familiar laugh and glance across the table. Harrison is smiling at me, starry-eyed, the way the Squad looks at Emerson. I blush, grateful for the stickers covering my cheeks.

"Do we have another field trip tomorrow?" Teagan asks. "I could go for more of these roast pork buns."

"No, there's no field trip," Win says. "But tomorrow is

going to be super fun anyway. We have lots of great activities to choose from on Sundays. And after dinner, it's Bingo Night! You're going to love it. Right, Sarina?"

"Right!" Sarina agrees. "Gemma and I and a few other counselors are doing spa treatments. We've got Korean face masks and all sorts of stuff for mani-pedis. You can relax and get pampered."

Teagan and McKenna glance at each other and raise their eyebrows. "That does sound pretty good," Teagan admits.

After stuffing ourselves, we have about an hour before the bus comes back to pick us up, so we do a little shopping. Win takes us to a grocery store, where we load up on Pocky and Calbee Shrimp Chips. We hit a few of the touristy gift shops, too, and McKenna, Teagan, Piper, Delaney, and Ava all buy bracelets made of pale jade-green beads with a gold charm of the character for good fortune dangling from it. Bran and Howie are super excited about something they bought, but they won't tell us what it is. Typical.

I doze on the bus, lulled by the food, the rocking motion, and the murmur of my friends' voices. I wish Squee could last forever.

After breakfast on Sunday, Win and Sarina gather the group to tell us about our choices of activities for the day. "Cooper and I are going to practice yo-yo tricks in the backyard in a half hour. So come out if you want to learn how to do some," Win says. "Harrison and Emerson are putting together a pickup game of soccer out on the field. Other choices include basketball, badminton, and Ping-Pong in the gyms. I think that's it for sports. You can also learn to make dim sum with Chen Lǎoshī in the cafeteria kitchen. And of course, as we mentioned yesterday, there will be a spa-stravaganza. Where's that happening, Sarina?"

"We've set up some lounge chairs on the patio behind the cafeteria," Sarina replies. "Everybody's welcome, not just girls. And if there's something else you'd rather do that we're not offering, let the front desk staff know where you'll be, even if it's just in your room. Don't forget that you need a buddy if you're going to be out of the dorm."

McKenna and Teagan follow Sarina, debating which face masks they want, while the rest of us slowly disperse. I thought Queena and Fei Fei would head to the spa station, too, but Kir persuades Q to play badminton with her, and Fei Fei wants to play video games with Ava again.

"Back to work on the camp memory book," Lina says. "I took a ton of pics this week and haven't had a chance to weed through them yet." She waves and heads up to her mom's room.

"That dim sum workshop sounds awesome," Maze says. "I'm going to go check that out. Want to come?"

Lyr and I shake our heads, but Delaney pipes up that she'll go with Maze.

"How's your contest piece coming along, Lyr? Are you going to work on that, or do you want to do something else?"

"I do want to work on my music," Lyr says slowly, "but I'd like to use one of the pianos in the Performing Arts Center. I need to hear what it sounds like on a real piano onstage instead of on a keyboard in our room." She frowns. "But I need a buddy. Could you bring your sewing stuff down there?"

"Did you say you're going down to the Performing Arts Center?" Piper asks Lyr. "Can I tag along? I was hoping to get to play the gǔzhēn a little more."

Lyr's face lights up. "Sure!" she chirps. "That would be fun. And then Phee doesn't have to drag all her stuff across campus. We could play another duet! Let's go ask my mom for the key to the instrument room. I'm sure she'll say yes." They wave bye to us, and Lyr practically skips away. Lyr and Piper spent time together at the museum yesterday. How much more do they need?

Maze waves her hand in front of my face. "Hey. Phee. Stop that."

"Stop what?"

"You're doom-thinking again. Don't worry, okay? Lyr is always going to be your BFF." She, Delaney, and I walk to the lobby together, and Maze pats my shoulder before they head to the cafeteria. "Go have fun doing your art, Phee," she says gently. "We'll come get you before dinner."

I nod and head for the stairs, but my feet feel impossibly heavy. There's no one in the first-floor hallway, so I take the elevator, feeling like a seam coming apart, stitch by stitch.

# CHAPTER TWENTY-FOUR

Back in my room, I take Maze's advice and lose myself in making her cupcake-themed appliqué T-shirt. I sketch a bunch of cupcakes in different sizes and colors, and with various decorations on top of the frosting. Then I cut out the different parts of each cupcake to use as pattern pieces. Once that's done, the real fun begins. I lay out all my fabric on the bed, deciding on one the color of bamboo leaves in the fall for yellow cake, and a deep loamy brown for the chocolate cupcakes. For the frosting, I have an ivory silk and a pale spring green from my cousin Dawn's prom dress.

With a chalk pencil, I trace around the stencils on the different fabrics and cut them out. Finally, I pin a yellow cupcake shape to the shirt and start sewing it on. The hum and whirr of the machine is comforting. I'm so focused on the work that I don't hear someone knocking on my door until they call my name.

"Phoenny? It's McKenna."

McKenna? What's she doing here? I lift my foot off the pedal, and the sewing machine falls silent. "Come in," I call.

She opens the door cautiously and doesn't step inside until I nod. "What's up?" I ask as casually as I can. What if I say something wrong and the friendship that we're building disintegrates like antique lace?

"Hi. I came back to get a bottle of nail polish and thought I'd lend you this, since Maze said you were working on a sewing project." She hands me a small bundle of white stretch jersey. I unfold it and discover it's actually her corset-style top. "You can figure out how to make your own, as long as you don't take mine apart," she says with a smile.

"Thanks, that's so nice of you. I actually think I brought some T-shirt fabric I could try this on." I get up and hang her top in my closet so I don't accidentally mix it into my stuff. I'm touched by her thoughtfulness. "Where did you get it? I don't think I've seen a top like that in the stores around here."

"Italy, actually. My mom still has a lot of family there, and I get a lot of my cousins' hand-me-downs. I'm hoping she comes back with a bunch of cool stuff." Her eyes roam around the room, taking in the piles of fabric, vintage clothes, and the makeshift ironing board I created out of a metal baking sheet I snuck out of the cafeteria, covered with an extra pillowcase.

"Your mom is there now? In Italy?"

McKenna nods morosely. "Both my mom and my dad are there. I wanted to go with them and visit my nonna, but the plane tickets are pretty expensive. Plus, my mom wanted me to try out Squee with my *cousins*." She gives me a dramatic wink when she says "cousins," and I laugh. That whole mess feels like a long time ago.

"I'm really close with my nǎinai and wàipó, too. I'd be super bummed if I couldn't visit them. They live close by, though." I clap my hand to my mouth. "I mean my grandmother on my dad's side and my grandmother on my mom's side. I'm so sorry—I didn't use the Mandarin to make you feel bad—it's just a habit."

She stares at me for a long moment, and then her jaw drops. "Oh my god, you heard me that first day! When I complained to Teagan about you mixing Mandarin words into your speech." I nod, afraid that this is the end of our almost friendship. "No wonder you didn't like me," McKenna says, laughing. "I'm sorry, too. I was taking out my frustrations on everyone." She holds up her right hand, pinkie extended. "Let's make a deal. You can use whatever Mandarin words you want in conversation, as long as you explain them to me. And I can use whatever Italian words I know when I'm talking, and I'll translate them for you. Even the swear words."

"Deal." We hook our pinkies together.

The cafeteria is buzzing when the Squad enters—sounds like everybody had fun with all their free time today.

"Win is waving you over," Q says disapprovingly. "Doesn't he know the Squad gets to eat dinner together?"

"Come eat with us anyway," Lyr urges. "Win and Sarina won't care."

Kir nudges Q. "Look over there—Cooper's arms are flailing. We're being summoned, too."

"I suppose I should go see what my steward wants," Q decides.

Maze snorts. "Your poor *steward* definitely doesn't get paid enough. See you later, Kir and *Your Majesty*."

When we finally sit down with our plates of chicken Parmesan and broccoli, the rest of Group 13 is already gathered at the table.

"We thought we should explain Bingo Night, since we have some fresh meat." Win pretends to cough. "I mean some new-timers."

"It's bingo," Teagan says. "Pretty sure we all know how to play. *Why* we're playing is still a question."

Sarina chuckles. "At Squee, we don't play regular bingo. Years ago, a bunch of counselors came up with the idea to merge truth or dare with bingo to make it more fun. It's hilarious." She explains how bingo winners have to do a dare in front of everyone to get their prize, which only confuses more of the new girls.

"But we already got bingo," Delaney says. "Why do we have to do something else if we've already won the game?"

Gemma giggles. "Remember the time I had to prove I knew the dance moves to 'Gangnam Style'?" Sarina and Win snort-laugh.

"Why do you have to prove anything?" Teagan's mouth twists. You said it's a mash-up of bingo and truth or dare. What's the truth part of it?"

Win waggles his eyebrows. "Instead of the letters in bingo just being letters, each one stands for a category. And in each of the squares, there's an activity or event instead of a number. If that square is called and you've done the activity listed in it before, then you get to mark it. You have to be honest about what you have and haven't done—you can't just answer yes to everything and get bingo right away. We all operate on the honor code, yeah?"

"Don't forget that you can get called out on it, too," Sarina adds. "If you claim to have bingo, sometimes the dare is to tell everyone the story behind one of the activities you marked off on your card."

Ava gasps. "That's diabolical!"

"You're telling me," Harrison says. "I read some of the cards and lists of dares yesterday, and some of them are totally chī sǐn."

Win flicks Harrison on the shoulder lightly. "Translate, bro."

"It means, like, bonkers," Harrison explains.

"I still don't get it," Delaney says. "What's fun about embarrassing yourself in front of everyone?"

"We're all in it together," Gemma reassures her. "We all genuinely want each other to win the prize, and we're all supportive of each other. It's like those game shows where people run obstacle courses. We laugh when you get knocked off into the water by a giant fist, but we know we're next."

"It's like that saying—'We're not laughing at you, we're

laughing *with* you,'" Win says with a grin. "It's a blast, okay?"

"You said that the letters each stand for a category," Teagan says. "What are the categories?"

Sarina pulls out a sheet of paper and draws a bingo card—five squares across and five down. "*B* stands for *Bodily Functions*, which sounds gross but is really about if you can wiggle your ears or roll your tongue into a cloverleaf shape or something. *I* stands for *Interesting Facts about Me*, which is a bunch of random things that you might have or like to do, like play *Minecraft* or something."

"*Fortnite* all the way, dude!" Howie high-fives Bran, drawing some eye rolls from Gemma and a grin from Win.

Sarina keeps going. "*N* stands for *Never Have I Ever*. You get to mark that square if you *have* done the thing listed. And *G* is for *Gosh, I'm a Bad Asian*, which is about the ways we feel like we don't measure up to the Asian standard. Lastly, *O* is for *OMG, I Can't Believe I . . .* That category has a bunch of things that we do at camp that you never thought you'd do."

"Half the fun is looking at your friends' cards and seeing what they did or didn't mark," Fei Fei says.

"Yeah," Maze adds. "Like if your friend marks 'Never Have I Ever Shoplifted.'" She stares at Fei Fei.

"Hey! Your dad said I could have whatever I wanted!" Fei Fei protests, laughing. "He didn't actually say I had to pay for it!"

Maze cackles. "The look on his face when you took an

entire crate of mangos and sauntered out the door!"

The faintest hint of a smile crosses McKenna's face. Suddenly, McKenna elbows Teagan and says, "Lip gloss," in a very unsubtle, smirking kind of way.

Teagan looks horrified. "Stop! We're not actually playing the game, McKenna!"

McKenna smiles wickedly. "This one time, Teagan 'accidentally' forgot to pay for some licorice-flavored lip gloss. She *says* she was nervous about going to the dance with her crush that night. So she puts on a ton of gloss and kisses him hello on the cheek. Then . . ." She takes a dramatic breath. "He. Literally. Threw. Up. Turns out that he got sick on black jelly beans one Easter and, ever since, the smell of licorice makes him barf." She laughs harder than I've ever seen, and it's impossible not to join in.

Teagan turns bright red, then sighs and chuckles. "I've never shoplifted again. Karma stinks."

The whole table is roaring. "God, I'm so glad you were just kissing him on the cheek!" Gemma wipes her eyes. "Can you imagine?" That sends everyone into hysterics again, with Howie pretending to smooch Bran, who then fake-vomits.

Sarina reaches over and pats Teagan on the shoulder. "Great way to kick us off, Teagan!"

Bingo Night is as rowdy and hysterical as ever. It's fun to learn weird new things about people, and there's not much I don't know about my friends after all our years together.

The tables in the Flex are decked out with colorful table-cloths and party streamers. A table and chairs are set up on the low stage in front of the movie screen. A large plastic bingo ball rests on the table and there are several microphones scattered around. I swallow hard, hoping that I won't be dared to sing again, like last year.

Lyr and I sit together at the Group 13 table, and my heart does a flippy thing when Harrison chooses the seat on my other side. I'm delighted, too, when Teagan and McKenna park themselves across from us.

I look around the table. Piper sits down on the other side of Lyr, and Lina and Ava sit across from them. Delaney, Win, Bran, Howie, Maze, Fei Fei, and Gemma round out the rest of the table to my right. Gemma gets up and passes out bingo dot markers, while Harrison tells everyone to grab a playing card from the stacks in the middle of the table. I feel the same sense of awe and satisfaction as when I've finished piecing together an intricate appliqué and then step back to see the whole picture.

Sarina and Cooper welcome everyone and explain the rules. They spin the bingo ball, and Sarina pulls out a slip of paper, handing it to Cooper. He reads it into the microphone. "Okay, campers! We've got a B for Bodily Functions, and 'attached earlobes' as the square. Everybody with attached earlobes gets to mark their card!" He reaches up to feel his own earlobe and laughs. "If you don't know what you have, ask your neighbor!"

Sarina leans over and peers at his ear. "Breaking news, everyone. Cooper does not have attached earlobes. No bingo for you!"

I stamp the square on my card and look over at Harrison's. He leaves his unmarked, and sure enough, his earlobes aren't attached. The one facing me is pierced, though. "No earring?" I ask.

Harrison makes a wry face. "Didn't know how conservative the Committee would be. My mum had a fit when I got it pierced."

"I don't think my mom would care unless it was, like, a bull ring through your nose."

"Good to know," he laughs. "No bull ring." He reaches out and gently cups my earring, his fingers brushing my earlobe.

Win clears his throat loudly, and Harrison quickly pulls his hand away and turns back to his bingo card. Lyr leans over a few times and points to squares that I should've marked off. I dot them dutifully, but I'm distracted.

Someone cries, "Bingo!" and I'm surprised to hear Matty's voice. He runs up to the stage with his card and shows it to Cooper.

"All right, Matty! You marked 'Never Have I Ever Moonwalked,' which means that you *can* do it. Or you think you can. Show us your best Michael Jackson moves to claim your prize!"

My little brother flawlessly moonwalks across the stage

and pumps his fist in triumph when Sarina hands him a gift card. I cheer and clap as loudly as I can, and Emerson's whistle splits the air. It reminds me how much Squee means not just to me and the Squad, but to all the campers. Matty gets picked on at school, but here he has friends and is supported and encouraged. He's a winner. He belongs. It's like what Mom said the other night. Năinai's definition of being Chinese enough had to expand to include her. How awful would it have been if my grandmother hadn't been able to change and accept that Mom belonged in their family? I see now how horrible it would have been if I continued to do that to our group's new campers.

We grab fresh cards, and this time, I focus on talking to everyone in the group, listening to their stories and laughing about the things they've done or giving sympathy about the mistakes they've made. Bingo Night isn't about the prizes or even the public embarrassment, I realize. It's about the bonding, the friendships, the discovery that, as Sarina put it, we're all in this together. Win catches my eye and gives me a thumbs-up, nodding like he knows what I'm thinking. And maybe he does.

Suddenly, Lyr looks over at my card and squeals, "Phee! You have bingo!"

At the exact same time, McKenna stands up and waves her card in the air. "Bingo!" she announces.

Oh, crap. It's a tie.

# CHAPTER TWENTY-FIVE

"No, I don't," I admonish Lyr, covering my card with my hand. "I don't have bingo. McKenna does. She gets the prize."

"Come on," she urges, ignoring my plea. "Look, you didn't dot the square about being able to do the Spock 'Live Long and Prosper' sign with your hand. I know for a fact that you can do that, since you taught me when we were seven."

Gemma cranes her head around Harrison and wags her finger at me. "Honor code, Phoenny Fang," she scolds me jokingly. "If you have bingo, fess up."

"No, I don't," I repeat, crumpling the card in my hand. "I missed one of the other squares."

"What's the big deal?" Harrison asks. "There are a ton of prizes—enough for both you and McKenna to each get one."

There's an invisible scarf wrapped around my neck, choking me. "That's not it. It's . . ."

Win snatches the crumpled card from my hand. He smooths it out and studies it while McKenna frowns down at him, and I stare morosely. Then he jumps up and throws his hands in the air. "We have a tie, ladies and gents! And you know what that means!" He points to Cooper on the stage.

"DANCE-OFF!" Cooper roars into the microphone, and the whole room erupts into cheers.

Nooooo, not a dance-off. I will go up there and sing again, but dance? No way. I glower at Lyr, and she has the good sense to look aghast. Lina's eyes are wide in sympathy. Behind me, I hear Fei Fei cheering me on. "You got this, Phee! You can do it!"

"Go on, Phee. It's all in good fun!" Harrison says.

"You know your way to the nurse's office now, right? Because I'm going to need medical attention of some sort very soon."

A look of alarm crosses his face before he realizes I'm joking and grins instead. "It can't be any worse than ribbon dancing."

So, so much worse.

He stands up and tugs me to my feet, gently pushing me toward the stage. McKenna flips her hair over her shoulder and strides up there ahead of me, as fluid as a lioness. I heave a deep breath and stumble after her.

There's no way I can dance as well as McKenna. She's had lessons. Since she was *three*. What would happen if I just refused to participate? I motion to Sarina that I want to talk to her off to the side of the stage. I mean just the two of us, but McKenna follows.

"Um, Sarina? Can I just hand over the prize to McKenna? She's going to win, anyway."

Sarina is surprised but sympathetic. "You sure? You know we're all friends here. No one is judging you."

"That's not true," McKenna says. "They're going to judge me if you quit, Phoenny. How do you think it'll look if you let me win? Everybody will think that I can't hack it, that you gave me the prize just to keep me happy." Her face is sincere.

I've entirely forgotten how to breathe. I was so focused on saving my own face that I never stopped to consider McKenna's. She just wants our approval. She wants to belong. Shame and guilt rush through me.

I struggle to take a breath. "I . . . You . . . You're right. I'll do the dance-off. I'm not trying to make camp hard for you. I wasn't thinking about you at all, just about making a fool of myself again. I'm sorry."

McKenna winks. "Trust me, you're going to be fine. You might even have fun."

"Okay," Sarina says. "I'm glad you both shared your feelings. We should probably talk more about this later, but for now, let's just get through the dance-off." She directs us to the front of the stage, a few feet apart.

Cooper cues up a video on the screen behind us. "Everybody ready?! Here's how we do the dance-off at Squee. I'm going to play a music video for us to watch first, and then Phoenny and McKenna will each have two minutes to show off their skills! They can do the dance from the video or just freestyle to the song. Then we'll ask you to cheer for the person you think had the best moves. The one with the loudest cheers wins this trophy and a fifty-dollar gift card!" Cooper holds up a large stuffed bear with a gold medal around its neck and a gift card taped to its paw.

The video starts, and the crowd of campers and counselors shriek. It's T-Swift's "Shake It Off." McKenna and I turn to watch the screen, and I see her smile grow wider and wider. There's a bunch of dance styles in the video—including ballet. I love this song, but right now it's making my stomach churn, and not with excitement.

At the end of the video, Sarina grabs the mike. "McKenna, you're up first! Show us how you shake it off!"

My jaw drops as McKenna transforms. Effortlessly, she switches from ballet poses to hip-hop steps to robot moves. She sways and pouts, and then, at the end of the chorus, she turns her back to the crowd and shimmies her rear end. When Cooper cuts the video, McKenna looks over her shoulder and winks. She's a pop star! There's complete silence when she finishes, but McKenna doesn't seem fazed at all. She turns around and blows a kiss to the audience, who all look a little stunned. Then the crowd cheers wildly.

Cooper recovers and says, "All right, McKenna! And now it's Phoenny's turn!"

The music starts again. Fei Fei gives me an enthusiastic double thumbs-up, and I know she's trying to make me feel better. It doesn't work. I sneak a peek at McKenna, and she's smiling confidently. I told her I'd do this, but I honestly don't have a dancing bone in my body. So I do the only thing I can think of—the Squee Dance.

The Squee Dance was made up by one of the counselors when Lyr and I were day campers. Dennis was an incredible dancer. He and his friends always wowed the crowd during the Variety Show. But he wanted everyone to feel comfortable dancing, knowing that a lot of us didn't. So he combined over a dozen different dance moves, and we all did them together at the end of each day, before we got picked up by our parents. Soon, campers started doing it whenever there was something to celebrate, or whenever we needed a pick-me-up, or just for fun. We taught the Squee Dance to new day campers for the next few years, but after Dennis graduated from college and couldn't be a counselor anymore, the dance kind of died out.

The opening moves come back to me. I forget some of them, but it doesn't matter. Isn't that the point of the song, anyway? My eyes find Matty—he's dancing, doing his own version of the moves, grinning like he's never had as much fun in his life. I keep my eyes on his as I flap my arms like a chicken, do high kicks, swing like Carlton from *The Fresh Prince of Bel-Air*, and a bunch of other wild moves before ending in an epic, cringey dab. I'm glad my face is hidden in my arm because I'm sure it's beet red. Like after McKenna's dance, the audience is dead silent, but I don't think it's because they're astonished. It's because they're embarrassed for me and don't know what to say.

But after a second, there's a collective holler from the campers. "Squee Dance!" shouts the Squad, and the crowd takes the cue, chanting "Squee Dance" over and over while laughing and clapping and whooping. I drop my arm and gape at the crowd—people I've known for years, who've always been friendly but have never given me this kind of approval. Even the ones I don't know are clapping, too. Teagan is laughing and shaking her head as though she can't believe I just completely humiliated myself that way. I can't quite believe it, either, but at least the dance-off is over.

But what about McKenna? I turn to her and am surprised again when she gives me a fist bump. "I told you you'd be fine!" she says.

Cooper comes forward and stands between us. "All right, everyone! This has been an exciting dance-off, and now it's time for you to make the final decision! If you think McKenna should win the dance-off, let's hear it for her now!" The audience screams and cheers and stomps their feet. "And if you think Phoenny should win, give her some love!" I'm so grateful when the Squad and a bunch of other campers and counselors clap and cheer, even if it's not as loud as for McKenna.

"We have a winner!" Sarina calls out. "McKenna Fitzgerald has some serious moves, am I right?" Everyone roars as

Sarina hands her the teddy-bear trophy and gift card. McKenna bows, her face radiant.

"And the runner-up prize goes to Phoenny Fang, for reminding us how awesome the Squee Dance is!" Cooper announces, handing me a gift card for ten dollars to Dunkin'. This time, I gladly accept the consolation prize.

The counselors decide that there's no point in going back to playing bingo after that performance, so Cooper turns on some music and we all hang out in the Flex. Some of the counselors teach the Squee Dance to the younger campers, and there's a lot of random spontaneous dancing all around the room. I sink down into my seat and let Lyr wrap her arm around me.

"You did great up there," she says.

"I'm just glad it's over," I reply.

McKenna leans across the table. "Why didn't you at least do the shake part?" She sounds genuinely curious.

I laugh. "Have you seen me in dance class? I can't shimmy like that. It's just . . . not me."

She nods thoughtfully. "You were brave to go so off-script like that. To refuse to do something you weren't comfortable with."

"And you were brave to dance in front of a room mostly full of people you don't know," I respond.

She turns pink and looks away, but when she turns back, there's a smile on her face.

"You were right about something else, too," I admit.

She raises her eyebrows. "Oh, really? Do tell," she says in pretend fascination, which makes me chuckle.

"I did have fun, even though I also did make a fool of myself."

I study the faces of the people around the table, people who are now my friends. That's the heart of Squee. Silly shared experiences like accidentally braining your counselor with a birdie, or falling over while doing wobbly wǔshù stances, or dancing completely out of rhythm to a song. It's about being together and figuring out who we are without our parents around to tell us what we're doing wrong or how we can be better. Squee is a chance to be ourselves for a brief, glorious, time.

I look into McKenna's shining eyes. "You know what? I've been trying so hard to force camp to stay the same so I can relive the same fantastic experience I had last year and all the years before that that I've been closing myself off to the truth. Which is that we are all evolving, so we can never have the same exact experience we had before. But I can choose to see this summer, this version of Squee, as something spectacular."

"Cheers to choosing to see the spectacular," McKenna says, pretending to raise a glass.

# CHAPTER TWENTY-SIX

We have hall meeting later that night. Without going into details, Sarina starts the meeting by giving both me and McKenna Snaps "for talking it out and putting yourself in someone else's shoes." McKenna rolls her eyes in a joking manner. I motion to her to take her turn next.

"Snaps to Sarina and Gemma for the awesome spa day," she says, snapping her fingers.

I notice that her nails are pale blue with blue-gray arcs on them. No. Not arcs. Sharks. "Your turn," she says, "since Sarina gave you Snaps, too."

"I have both a S'up and a Squawk." I turn to McKenna. "S'up with the shark nails?"

She tilts her head, amused. "I want to be an oceanographer. Okay with you?"

My eyes widen, but I nod quickly. "All right, my Squawk is that Squee is only two weeks long. It should at least be a month." I feel the same sharp longing ripple around me.

"What I think Phee is trying to say," Howie pipes up, "is that camp gives me the confidence to be me. Not just here, but at school."

"I like that I don't have to answer annoying questions

about being Chinese here," Bran adds, surprising me with his seriousness. "No one's asking me to do kung fu moves or help them with their science homework." He stares at us with a touch of defiance. "I don't even like science. I guess that makes me a Bad Asian."

"For adoptees, we still have to answer questions like that here at Squee, both from teachers and campers," Ava points out. "It never really ends for us. We always feel like 'Bad Asians' for one reason or another."

"And then you all are like, the opposite," McKenna says. "You're, like, Super Asian, because you know Mandarin and all about Chinese history and culture."

"#VeryAsian," I interject.

McKenna snickers. "You are *so* extra, Phee." It's the first time she's said my nickname. I don't mind.

"I'm not, though. I always feel like a Bad Asian because I don't like hot soup." When Delaney looks confused, I explain, "It's part of almost every Chinese dinner. There are even hot soups for *dessert*." I make a face.

"I'm a Bad Asian for refusing to take violin lessons," says Lina. "And piano lessons, and flute lessons, and cello lessons—basically any music lessons." She nudges Lyr. "Sorry. I like listening to music, not playing it."

Lyr squeezes Lina's arm and says, "I love you anyway," making the rest of us laugh. "I'm a Bad Asian for not being super competitive. It's nice to win contests, but I really just want to create music because it makes me happy."

Fei Fei takes a deep breath. "I'm a Bad Asian for being queer. How do my parents put it? Oh, right, they think I'm terrible because they won't get grandchildren. As if queer people don't have kids." Maze and Lyr put their arms around her, one on each side.

"You are not terrible, and we love you the way you are," Maze says gently. In a louder voice, she announces, "I'm a Bad Asian for being blunt and talking about things my dad thinks should be private, like my period."

Bran and Howie rear back into their seats and turn red. Harrison stares down at the floor. Looks like they're not used to hearing people talk about it, either. Only Win seems unfazed, and I remember that he has three older sisters.

"Yes! Let's all normalize talking about menstruation!" Sarina leans across the circle and high-fives Maze. "Everybody needs to be more open about it. Anyway, this is an awesome conversation, and I want to add that I've been feeling like a Bad Asian because I don't go to an Ivy League college. Or MIT or Stanford or one of the Seven Sisters. My mom never wants to tell her Chinese friends that I'm attending a community college, but the truth is, I'm getting just as good an education and we're saving so much money."

Win claps. "Let's hear it for going to the school that's the best fit for you, or no college at all! Speaking of best fits, I'm a Bad Asian because slippers are uncomfortable, and I won't take off my shoes in the house." He shrugs. "What can I say? I love my kicks."

Gemma looks around. "I guess I'll go. I'm a Bad Asian because I don't like going to dim sum." Fei Fei gasps melodramatically. "It's true," Gemma says. "I only made it through yesterday because I was with you all. It's too crowded, too noisy, and all the servers insist on speaking to me in Cantonese because I look like this." She points to her face with both hands. "And when white friends make me go, they keep asking me what everything's called, what it's made of, are they supposed to dip it in soy sauce, and on and on. It's exhausting. Once I lost my cool and shouted that I'm adopted and, even if I weren't, I'm not their personal tour guide." She laughs ruefully. "There may have been a few swear words in there, too. The good news is that they don't ask me to go anymore."

Teagan looks at McKenna and says quietly, "I'm a Bad Asian because I didn't find out about the Chinese Exclusion Act until this year. Some of my white friends had already learned about it somewhere and teased me for not knowing my own history. I feel like there's so much stuff I should just *know*, like by osmosis, but I don't even know where to begin."

"I wish more schools would teach Asian American history," Delaney agrees. "Unlike Teagan, I'm really bad at math and I don't like any of the STEM subjects. My teachers all seem to expect that I'll be good at all those subjects because

I'm Chinese American. And then when they realize I'm not, they're all disappointed in me. Like I'm making extra work for them, or not living up to the model minority stereotype or something. I guess that makes me a Bad Asian."

"So does it make me a Good Asian if I like all the shows and dim sum and actually want to go to Chinese School?" Ava asks, and we all laugh. "But I'm a Bad Asian, too," she continues. "I've watched a lot of C-dramas and realized that what I consider important is really different from what most Chinese women think is important. Like, they're looking for stable jobs and relationships that give them security, while I want to do my own thing and go after my dreams, even if it's risky. I like that in the US, girls are being brought up to believe they can do or be whatever and whoever they want."

Piper bites her lip. "I could list a bunch of ways, but for now I'm going to say that I feel like a Bad Asian because I'm not sure I want to go on a heritage tour or look for my birth parents. It's not that I don't want to go to China—I do, but not right away." She looks at Gemma, who smiles at her sympathetically.

"Wait. What's a heritage tour?" Howie asks. "Is that the same as a heritage camp?"

"No, it's a trip for adoptees to visit their birth country," Gemma answers. "In our case, the Chinese government has partnered with tour companies to take adoptees and their families around the country. You visit landmarks, participate in cultural activities, and can visit your finding location and orphanage if you want to. Some of my adoptee friends have reconnected with their foster parents in China."

"Oh," Bran says. "That sounds cool. I've been to Taiwan, and it was really fun."

"Visiting the motherland makes you a very Good Asian," Win teases. "Bonus points for moving there as an adult—you get an actual medal for that. Not like the rest of us who can barely call ourselves Asian because we've never been there."

"Sure, it sounds fun to you," McKenna says sharply, "but it sounds like an emotional nightmare to me. I don't want to go, either. I don't want to see the bridge where I was left. What if I look for my birth parents and never find them? Or worse, find them and have them say that they really didn't want to keep me? Like, maybe I cried too much or was too ugly, so they were glad to relinquish me." She crosses her arms. "I'm probably the baddest of the Bad Asians because sometimes I wish I wasn't Chinese at all. I wish I was white." She looks both angry and like she's about to burst into tears.

Gemma gets up and envelops McKenna in a bear hug, then sits beside her. "That's a totally valid way to feel," she tells the other girl. "I've felt like that myself. Like it's a constant struggle between being obviously Chinese because of my face and not feeling truly Chinese."

Again, I'm reminded of my conversation with Mom and

how Năinai made her feel like she wasn't Chinese enough. I feel bad because I did the same thing to these girls. But all the ways we express our identity is enough.

Harrison clears his throat, and I realize he's been quiet this whole time. "I don't know what it's like to be adopted, but I can relate to a lot of what you've been saying. Actually, to what everyone's been saying. It's different for me because I grew up being part of the dominant culture. And now I'm not anymore. Before I came to camp, people in my new town were already treating me differently. Even here at Squee, I'm discovering that I'm also different from you all, because I don't know American culture." His eyes flick toward me and slide away. "A lot of my friends in Hong Kong were jealous that I moved here. Honestly, though, all I want to do is move back. That's my Bad Asian story—I'm ungrateful for this opportunity to become an American."

"You didn't have a choice in coming here," Gemma says. "Just like I didn't. Why should we feel grateful about it? The way I see it, we *lost* things—my birth parents, your friends—we should be allowed to be resentful and grieve."

As her words sink in, the new campers give little signs of their agreement—nods, shared glances, small nudges. They seem lighter somehow, like they've shed cloaks of wariness they've been wearing on a long journey.

"Thanks, Gem. That helps." Harrison lets out a long breath and runs his hands down his thighs. "Is this what therapy is like?" There are chuckles and low laughs from the whole group.

Sarina smiles. "Thank you all for being honest and sharing your feelings—I know that's not easy. And big thanks to Gemma, McKenna, Teagan, Delaney, Ava, and Piper for your work helping us understand what it's like to be an adoptee. Not just now, but over the past week at camp. I'm sure it was tough to share some really personal stories in front of strangers, especially non-adopted strangers. I hope Squee continues these hall meetings in the future—I feel like we're diving into what it's like to be Chinese American and learning a lot from each other." She looks as if she's going to end the meeting, but Ava raises her hand.

"I'm already sad that the first week of camp is over and we only have six more days," Ava says.

Just like that, I feel the sting of tears. "It's always so hard to leave," I say.

"But that's why we should make this week as fun as possible," Lyr continues.

Maze's voice is gruff. "You don't have to say goodbye to us. Squee is special, but the people matter more than the place. We'll always be friends. We'll always be in touch."

"Maze is right." Sarina's voice is gentle. "It's okay to be sad and to miss Squee. But *we* are Squee. Our shared experiences here, both good and bad, are Squee. And we can continue to do things with each other once camp is over. It won't be exactly the same, but that doesn't mean it won't be joyful in a different way."

There's a long silence as everybody tries to process what Maze and Sarina said. Fei Fei sniffles, and Lyr holds her hand. Then Lyr clasps her other hand around mine. I reach my other hand for Sarina's, and the hand holding continues around the circle until we're all linked like a crocheted ring.

# CHAPTER TWENTY-SEVEN

Early the next morning, I approach Gāo Shīfu at his table in the cafeteria to discuss the Showcase and our plan to vanquish the trolls. I take Lyr with me for emotional support and Harrison in case my Mandarin isn't good enough. He says he speaks Mandarin with a Cantonese accent, but I ask him to come along anyway since having a counselor on our side will probably help, even if he's just a CIT.

Between the three of us, we manage to explain what we'd like to do. A simple fight scene starring Howie and Bran, with us in the background. Everyone in cool costumes. Record and upload our performance to our social media account.

It goes more smoothly than I could've imagined. Even though Gāo Shīfu wasn't aware that a Showcase performance could be more than a simple "have your students do a few basic moves" event, he immediately realizes how important it is to us. He agrees to do this favor for me since Mom is such an "old friend" of his. Win was right to focus on the teacher's friendship with Mom.

In class, Gāo Shīfu puts the counselors and CITs in charge of leading us through the basic routine of stances, punches, and kicks, while he takes Bran and Howie to a corner of the room to teach them the steps for the performance. He said it would look better if it wasn't a real fight, but one that was choreographed, like the fight scenes in movies.

Ten minutes later, it becomes clear to everyone that Gāo Shīfu is taking the Showcase performance seriously. Maybe a little too seriously. His voice keeps getting louder as he drills the boys over and over again. By the end of class, Bran's and Howie's faces are grim and exhausted.

"I'm sorry, guys," I tell them on the walk to the classroom building. "I didn't know Gāo Shīfu was a tiger parent in a wǔshù uniform."

Howie shrugs. "It's okay, Phee. My regular wǔshù teacher is pretty strict, too. I could do with less yelling, though."

"If we were in Westeros and I had a sword . . ." Bran mimes cutting off his tongue. He laughs when he sees my shock. "Don't worry, Phee. I'm just kidding. Gāo Shīfu isn't that bad. I know he wants us to look good during the Showcase." He turns to Howie. "Let's practice more after dinner. Then he won't have as much to yell about in class tomorrow." The two of them run along the path, fighting each other with imaginary weapons.

Sūn Lǎoshī meets us in the hallway outside the classroom. Her face is creased with worry. "I'm so sorry, Phoenny," she says. "I had no idea that people could have allergic reactions to the paintbrushes. This has never happened to me before."

"It's okay, Sūn Lǎoshī. It's never happened to me before, either, and I use paintbrushes all the time. It's not your fault."

"Well, for the next few days we are going to have two setups," the teacher announces. She points to the room next door. "I've cleaned and set up another classroom with entirely new materials. All the brushes are synthetic, and there are no animal products in any of the art supplies, just to be extra careful." She offers a half smile. "Phoenny, I hope you will be comfortable there." She gestures to our regular room. "In this room, we'll have our traditional brushes and supplies, for those of you who still want to experiment and learn with them. I'll be spending my time teaching with the traditional materials, in order not to cross-contaminate. But you'll have a very talented teacher in the new classroom, too." She smiles again. "Okay, please choose a room, and we'll begin."

Sarina, Gemma, McKenna, Teagan, Ava, Delaney, and Piper enter the regular classroom, and to my surprise, the boys follow them. Lyr shoots a glance at Piper's back disappearing through the doorway, and for a split second, I'm afraid that she's going to choose Piper over me. But she doesn't. She slips her arm through mine and pulls me into the new classroom. "You can't weasel your way out of class today," she teases, making me snort. Maze, Fei Fei, and Lina step in after us and we gather around the large table, wondering who our teacher is going to be. There isn't another adult in the room, unless Win counts, and I'm not sure he does.

Harrison comes in after Win and sets a pitcher of water on the table. He and Win pass out sheets of newsprint and tell us to cover the surface with them, to help absorb extra liquid. Then Win hands us each a sheet of rice paper and a brush with a bamboo handle, while Harrison sets an inkstone and black ink stick on the table in front of each piece of paper.

Lina looks at her watch. "Win, when is the teacher getting here?"

He smiles mysteriously. "He's already here."

"I thought you were studying engineering," Lina says. "I didn't know you knew how to do brush painting, too."

"I don't . . . but Harrison does. Right?" He breaks into a grin as all five of us gape at Harrison, who stands at one end of the rectangular table with a set of materials in front of him. He fidgets with one of the brushes.

"Well," he begins, "this was not what I expected to be doing this week, and I don't have any experience teaching, so I hope you all just bear with me."

"Way to inspire confidence, dude," Win says sarcastically. "Come on, you're awesome at painting! Tell them about the shirts, yeah?"

Harrison shifts his weight to his other leg. "Right. The shirts." He's kind of adorable when he's nervous. He looks over at me. I gesture to my own shirt with both hands and move them apart and down, in a *look at what I'm wearing* and *I'm taking a bow* kind of move. His eyes crinkle at the corners as he catches my drift and smiles. I'm wearing another one of my creations today, broad strips of cotton in different colors, cut and sewn on the bias so the stripes run from my left shoulder to my right hip, the frayed seams showing on the outside like fringe.

He clears his throat. "So," he says in a more confident voice. "I may have been the one who painted the rabbit on your camp shirts."

My mouth drops open again. "Wow," I say breathlessly. Harrison had painted the amazing design that was printed on every single camper's shirt, even the day campers. I had worn his creation that first day during the group photos. I love that I have another piece of his artwork, even though he didn't create the rabbit painting especially for me, like he did the ogre.

"Well, now I'm convinced that you're an expert," Maze says dryly. "I'm pretty sure we all are, so teach away!"

We nod in agreement, and he smiles back at us. Win gets a text and leaves the room, waving to Harrison to keep going.

"Okay, let's start by making some ink. They sell ink in bottles, of course, but I think the traditional method is more fun."

Some of us have done this before in our various Chinese school classes, but none of us stop him. Harrison pours a little bit of water from the pitcher into the inkstone, so it wets the raised flat part and runs down into the sunken part on the other side. Following his lead, we take our ink sticks and rub them through the droplets of water left on the flat part, moving it back and forth until enough ink has been dissolved into the water. Grinding the ink stick against the stone is calming, and it's neat to see how the water gets darker and thicker.

Harrison says that we're going to start by writing our Chinese names, and he shows us how to hold the brush to do calligraphy. The hand placement always feels so unnatural, so unlike holding a pencil. We dip our brushes into the ink we've made and get rid of the excess by running the brush against the lip of the inkstone.

I don't wipe off enough ink, apparently, since my first stroke is more of a blob than a dot. I make a face and try writing the next stroke. A horizontal line should be easy enough, but it's too fat at the starting end and too thin at the other. Sewing is so much easier than painting. I sigh and look over at Harrison's paper. His characters are fluid and beautiful, of course. "*Ko* is Cantonese for *Gāo*?" I ask. "The word for *tall*?"

"Yes. They sound pretty different, don't they? I only understand about seventy-five percent of what Huáng Lǎoshī says in Mandarin class."

I chuckle. "And I tune him out seventy-five percent of the time, so you're still understanding more than me." I watch as he writes the characters for his first name and am pleased when I can read them. "Hóngshān. Harrison. It's cool how they sound alike. Did your parents plan that?"

He looks pleased. "I'm not actually sure which came first, the Chinese name or the English one. Or which one is better."

I think about that for a moment. "Why does one have to be better? Most campers have names in both languages. Bran has as many Chinese names as he can come up with," I laugh. "Hey, we're like your design for the camp shirt—a blend of East and West." I put a hand on my hip in mock irritation. "Speaking of which, how come you've never said you could paint? "

He chuckles and stares down at his paper. "I don't talk about it a lot. I play football—I mean soccer—for school, so everyone thinks I'm just an athlete. Or they look at me and . . ." He stops and turns red.

For a moment, I don't understand why he's embarrassed. And then it hits me. "They look at you and see someone who looks like they could be in a C-pop boy band." I don't mention that I thought those exact same things when I first met him.

He nods, still blushing. "And then they treat me differently, and it messes with my head. It's flattering, but it's also empty. Sometimes I crave the attention, but then I wonder if they really like me for me. I usually keep my art to myself because it feels more real that way." He clears his throat and says, loudly, "Okay, everyone, let's move on to painting something pretty simple. How about pandas?"

I mull over what Harrison said while making more ink blobs. How people treat him differently because he's handsome. How that makes it hard for him to trust their motivations. I bet he was mad at Emerson and the other male CITs because they judged him by his looks and the attention he gets for it. Maybe he's not a player. Instead, he's a teenager dealing with other people's assumptions, just like McKenna and all the assumptions I made about her.

# CHAPTER TWENTY-EIGHT

This week in sports, we've moved on from the jiànzi and are playing Ping-Pong. Finally, a sport where I don't have to have a lot of foot coordination. We're playing doubles again, so I just have to stand behind my half of the table while Lyr keeps watch on hers.

After sports, we head to music class and find that Peng Lǎoshī has arranged all the chairs in a big circle and there is a black plastic case on each one. They look a little like violin cases. "This week we are learning the èrhú," the teacher says. "This is another classical Chinese instrument, like the gǔzhēn, but it uses a bow." He picks up his own instrument from the table in the back to show us. "Some people call it the Chinese violin or Chinese fiddle, but it is very different from the Western violin or fiddle. For one thing, the bow is attached and doesn't separate from the strings. There are only two strings—that is why it has 'èr,' the word for 'two,' in its name. And maybe most unusual, the sound is created by the vibration of the python skin across the front."

"Real python?" Howie says. "Awesome!"

"Poor snakes," Lyr murmurs.

I have to confess that I agree with Howie for once. The

python skin is kind of cool, and I love the pattern of the scales. I have about a yard of a snake-patterned fabric that I've been holding on to for a while because I'm not sure what to make with it yet. Maybe an èrhú appliqué shirt is in order.

We choose our chairs and start opening the instrument cases. Suddenly, Harrison, who has been hanging off to one side of the room with Sarina and Win, dashes over. "Stop!" he cries, and practically slaps the top of my èrhú case down. I yank my hand away before it gets crushed. He motions to the teacher. "The bow! What's it made of?"

Startled, Peng Lǎoshī stammers, "H-h-horsehair. Just like a violin bow."

Harrison turns back to me. "You're not allergic to horses, are you?" His eyes are wide, alarmed.

"What? No. No, I'm not allergic to horses. I used to ride ponies when I was little." I can't believe how worked up he is. I touch his arm lightly. "It's okay, I promise."

Harrison takes a deep breath and nods. He looks up and is clearly startled to find everyone's eyes on him. "Uh, sorry. I just didn't want a repeat of Friday," he says, turning pink.

"Phoenny is allergic to weasels and ferrets," Gemma informs the teacher. "She had a reaction to one of the calligraphy brushes last week, and I think we're all still a little nervous when she's around animal hair. We didn't realize how much of it we have at camp."

The normally reserved man puts a hand on his chest like

he just had a heart attack. "Of course, of course. I understand. Director Fāng informed us about your allergy, Phoenny, but I didn't think you might also be allergic to other animals. Thank you for stepping in so quickly," he says to Harrison. "I would be devastated if any of my students became ill because of my class."

"No problem. I'm sorry if I overreacted." He returns to the back of the room. Over his head, Win and Sarina share a long look, which makes me uneasy. Lyr catches my eye and gives me a *we're going to talk about this later* look and I make an *okay, fine* face back.

Peng Lǎoshī tries to teach us how to play the èrhú. Instead of making music, though, the screeching and squeaking that we produce sounds like wailing cats and frightened hamsters.

The teacher walks around us, trying to give encouragement and get us interested. "The èrhú is used in many different types of music," he says, sounding like an entry out of Wikipedia. "Of course, it is used for traditional Chinese music, including music for fan and ribbon dances. It is also used for contemporary music, including rock, pop, and jazz. Maybe you have heard of Nine Inch Nails?" He looks around, but only the counselors nod their heads. "Okay, how about *The Legend of Korra*?"

All our heads snap up. *The Legend of Korra* and the original series, *Avatar: The Last Airbender*, were my and Lyr's favorite

TV shows a couple of years ago. We'd binge-watch on weekends when she didn't have music events, and Emerson and Matty would join us, too.

"Ah, I have your attention now," Peng Lǎoshī gloats. "Yes, the èrhú was used in the music for the series finale. So, even though it is an ancient instrument, it is still relevant today. Modern musicians are rediscovering and reimagining what èrhú music is." He smiles at us. "It is old and new, East and West, at the same time."

Just like our names, and Harrison's shirt design, and maybe even some of the clothes I make. There are so many threads that connect us to our different cultures.

# CHAPTER TWENTY-NINE

The living room is empty when we file in for Counselor Time. Perfect for today's journaling activity. McKenna and Teagan help Maze and me drag several heavy wooden tables together in a spot underneath the leaded glass windows overlooking the front yard. The other girls gather various chairs until we've assembled ten seats around the tables so we can all sit together. Bran and Howie have decided to journal outside, which means they're really playing with their yo-yos instead. Sarina hands out unruled composition books as our journals, while Win, Gemma, and Harrison set out craft materials on a coffee table in the middle of the room.

The box of ribbons makes me think about all the fabric I brought to camp. It would be cool to incorporate some of that in my journal. I raise my hand and call Sarina over. "Can I run up to my room and get something? I'd like to glue some fabric scraps into my journal."

"All right, since we're in the dorm. But come right back down," she says.

"I will," I promise, then dash upstairs.

In my room, I grab the little plastic bag of scraps I've been collecting, left over from Lina's and Maze's T-shirts and other previous projects. Most are too small to make anything else with, but I like to use the scraps to stuff pillows or plushies.

Back in the living room, I pick up a bottle of glue, a pack of markers, and a ruler. Then I linger over the box of scissors, digging through them to find the ones with the wavy edges.

The girls of Group 13 work on our journals, chatting about the different activities we've done at camp so far. Even though I was sad when we split up to do different things, I have to admit that it's fun to hear about how they spent their free time. Maze brags about how the teacher said her soup dumplings looked and tasted the best in the dim sum workshop. Delaney says it's all true and that she ate fifteen of Maze's dumplings. Lyr and Piper play short recordings of their jam sessions together, and it's like listening to professional musicians. I die laughing when McKenna and Teagan tell us a horror story about using the Korean microneedling pen during their spa experience, complete with their reactions when they discovered how painful it was. Fei Fei has been playing *Rise of the Alien Wombats* with Ava so much that she dreams about being Captain Yeoh. And Lina tells us funny stories of what the other groups are doing, as seen in the photos for the memory book.

After we ask, Lina gets her laptop and shows us the photos she's taken of our group this week. It's interesting to see how we really kept to ourselves the first couple of days. Squad stuck with other Squad. Adoptees only hanging out with each other. But by Friday, we're mixing it up more. I point to a photo of me and McKenna standing side by side in the museum, staring at an exquisitely beaded black gown by Alexander McQueen. "I had no idea you were even there!"

Lina grins. "Stealth is my middle name. You want the photo? I'll text it to you." I nod.

"Send it to me, too!" McKenna calls out. I smile. She and I have come a long way since the first day.

In my journal, I sketch the dresses I designed for myself and Lyr for the big dance. But instead of coloring them in with pencil or marker, I dump out my little bag of fabric scraps and sort through them, picking out pieces of the two vintage blue qípáo in my dress as well as the cream satin and gold brocade for Lyr's. I snip them into the right shapes and glue them into place on my sketch.

"Has he asked you to the dance yet?" Fei Fei grins and pokes me in the arm.

"What? No. He's not allowed to. It's kind of a bummer since it's my last dance as a camper." That heavy wet sweater feeling is back.

McKenna still won't tell us who her date to the dance is, and none of the other girls have been asked, so we move on to other topics, like what we're going to do for the camper Variety Show tonight. Some kids take it really seriously and bring instruments and props and costumes, but there's no pressure to actually perform since parents and grown-ups don't come—just campers and counselors. The Squad has always treated it as a fun event where we can be silly, so we don't figure out what we want to do until right before the show. Last year, we did an impromptu skit where we wore all white and pretended to be old-timey milkmen who were lost in the desert and dying of thirst but couldn't drink any of the milk we were carrying because we were all lactose-intolerant.

"You should show off those muscles of yours, Maze." Lyr grins. "You could lift heavier and heavier things and end with lifting Win."

"I could maybe lift Lina over my head, but definitely not Win. His arms are way more ripped than mine."

I giggle. "Maze, you're fangirling over Win's arms!" She stands up and tries to swat me from across the table.

Fei Fei eyes me mischievously. "Let's do a Squad flash mob. Of the Squee Dance!"

I groan. "You had to bring up the Squee Dance again. Noooo, it's not going to happen."

They completely ignore me and discuss what song to use and who will take photos since Lina will be dancing with us. I put my head on the table and pray that they're just teasing me. Eventually, they give up, and we make plans for an epic, ten-girl musical number. What's better than a squad of eight? A band of ten.

# CHAPTER THIRTY

We're all getting ready for the Variety Show when Queena calls out, "Phee!" "Where's that blanket of yours—the one with all the patches? We need it tonight!"

I look around my room blankly until I remember that I lent the quilt to Matty on Movie Night. "I'll go grab it from Matty," I tell Q before heading down the emergency exit stairs, forcing myself to pass Harrison's floor and popping out on the first floor. All the room doors are open, and boys are rushing around, yelling at each other. Yep. Exactly like what's going on in my hallway.

I find Matty's room and knock on the open door, poking my head in. "Matty?" I spot my little brother and his roommate on their beds, throwing things at each other. "Please don't tell me you're wearing underwear on your heads?!"

Matty whips the black briefs off his head. "Hey! It's supposed to be a surprise! And they're ski masks."

"The door was open. I just came to get back my patchwork quilt. I won't tell anyone about your costumes." This, of course, is a lie. I'm going to tell all the girls the second I get back upstairs, because it is too priceless to keep to myself. I grab my blanket from the floor, hoping it doesn't smell too bad after spending a week with two ten-year-olds. They're adorable, but also slobs.

"They're robber masks, too," the roommate blurts.

Matty shushes him. "Stop talking about the raid!" He slaps his hand over his mouth. "Phee, please don't tell anyone. I swear I'll bring back Oreos for you. Or give you the rest of my candy." He holds up a pinkie.

I grin. "Pinkie promise. Oreos in return for my silence."

The Variety Show is hilarious. Emerson and Jackson are the emcees, and they have everybody cracking up between the performances. We cheer for all the gymnasts tumbling around the stage, the budding violinists who sound as bad as Group 13 on èrhú, and the legions of Rubik's Cube solvers. Win, Cooper, and a couple of other counselors team up and show off their amazing yo-yo tricks, tossing and catching in sync. The audience roars when Matty and his roommate go onstage with their undie masks and cardboard skis and act out wild and impossible jumps as a video of a ski run plays on the screen behind them. They end by pretending to crash into the base lodge, with legs and skis sticking up.

We'd signed up as one of the last performers, giving ourselves a stage name. When Emerson calls out "The Band of Ten!" we run out onto the stage.

There are excited whispers as we set up our equipment and get into position—Lyr behind her keyboard, Maze front and center, Piper beside her with a guitar slung across her chest, and Teagan behind a drum set that we borrowed from the Performing Arts Center. The rest of us are grouped around them. McKenna and I are toward the back, because she's tall and I'm not a good singer or dancer. We are all decked out in as much vintage and upcycled clothing as we could find—most of it from my wardrobe, but Lyr had some, too. Lina has her appliqué shirt on, Q has my patchwork quilt pinned to her shoulders as a cape, and Maze has gone full Goth in head-to-toe black. I'm wearing my ruffled baby-doll tunic, Fei Fei chose my poppy-flower shirt, and Kir picked one of Lyr's boho-style dresses. Lyr is wearing the other boho dress she brought, topped by a red beret she borrowed from a girl in Group 11. Gemma let me use the face paints, and I drew cats on everyone's eyelids.

"Hello, Squee!" Maze shouts into the mic. "We are the Band of Ten, and we're going to play 'Growing Up'by the fabulously talented band The Linda Lindas!" The younger campers squeal, and I grin.

Jackson hits "play" on his laptop, and the music video starts up behind us as we launch into the song and jump around on the stage. Lyr and Piper are playing their instruments for real, while Teagan just pretends to jam on the drums. The only time I don't really mind singing in public is when I'm with my friends. Even so, I keep my voice low. But when we get to the lyrics "We'll sing to people and show / What it means to be young and growing up," it feels like that moment when I try on a new piece of clothing I made. I look into the mirror and feel proud of who I am. Armed with that confidence, I let my voice free, belting out the words with all my closest friends.

Tears sting my eyes and my voice cracks when we reach the end of the song, crooning "We'll take the good with the bad / All of the times that we'll have / Make every moment last . . ." And just like in the video, we collapse together in a heap.

The crowd cheers and claps and whistles for us, and we stand up to take a bow. Looking out into the sea of faces, I know I'll remember this moment forever. Especially because, right in the front row, Harrison is grinning and holding up his cell phone flashlight, just like at a real concert.

# CHAPTER THIRTY-ONE

"I still can't believe you both fell off the stage," I greet Howie and Bran as they enter the cafeteria the next morning.

There'd been a huge ruckus last night inside the Flex, and then everyone had poured out of the building when the ambulance arrived. Counselors and staff had shooed us into Agnes and then basically put us in lockdown. We were allowed to sit in our rooms or the hallway and talk, but staff kept us from leaving our floors. None of the counselors or CITs were around, either. Word was that they all got called into a meeting with the Committee to find out what had happened and how.

"That was just me," Bran says. "Howie fell off the ginormous stack of chairs we were using for a prop." He sits down and leans his crutches against the table.

"So what's the damage?" Maze asks. "I mean, besides to your heads. We already knew you both were a little off even before you did your skit last night."

"Ha, ha," Howie says sarcastically. "Bran just has a badly sprained ankle. I fractured my fibula." He raises his right leg and shows off the big plastic boot strapped around his right shin and foot. "Cool, right?"

Lina frowns. "Not cool. Say goodbye to performing in the Showcase."

I hadn't even thought about that yet. My stomach starts to hurt. "Oh no. There goes the fight sequence. What were you guys thinking last night?"

"Swords," Howie says, as if that explains everything.

Bran nods. "Yeah. Swords. We got toy ones in Chinatown and acting out a scene from *Game of Thrones* was a no-brainer. I'm sorry we messed up the Showcase performance, though. I was actually looking forward to it."

"Maybe Gāo Shīfu will still let us do it," Howie says. "We can use our crutches like weapons, Jackie Chan—style."

I shake my head. "I bet Dr. Ung would have something to say about that."

"We should come up with a completely different performance," McKenna says. "It doesn't feel fair to leave Howie and Bran out of the Showcase, even if it was their own fault."

I nod. She's right. Either we're all in the show or none of us are. The problem is that, even with twelve brains working on it, we can't figure out what kind of performance to do.

The group splits up again for crafts class. Win pulls a chair up to the table and sits with us, but otherwise lets Harrison teach. He shows us examples of animals rendered in the Chinese brush painting style, then gets us started on mice, which are pretty easy. Then he moves us on to rabbits, which are also basically just blobs of fur with ears and a tail. He moves over to the other table, letting us chat and paint freely. He's a good camp teacher, going with the flow and not being all rigid about making us do better, like Gāo Shīfu.

The hardest part is controlling how dark my ink is and how much water to use to dilute it. I'm aiming for a soft gray bunny, but I seem to only make invisible bunnies of all water, or charcoal-black bunnies. I look over at Lyr's paper, where she's decided to give her bunny a long dragon tail.

She shrugs at me and giggles. "It's a xiǎolóng bun, get it? I know the characters for soup dumplings don't mean 'little dragon' in Mandarin, but it sounds the same. And everyone thinks a bāo is the same as a bun, which made me think of bunnies. And voilà! A little dragon-bunny dumpling is born." Everybody groans at her mixed Mandarin and English pun.

"That's so bad, I have to try." Maze adds thin lines of cross-hatching to her rabbit's body and pointy leaves to the top of its head, like a spiky crown. "Look, it's a bōlúo bun." I can't stop laughing at the poor, pineapple-bun-bunny mashup.

Fei Fei paints her bunny sitting peacefully in a giant lotus flower, holding a piece of lotus root with its distinctive holes showing. "Mine's a liánróng bun," she says. "His name is Zen."

"Mmm, that makes me hungry. I love lotus seed paste buns," I tell her.

Lina's bunny tops everyone else's. She paints a steamed bun, with the swirls of the dough and the little pucker at the top where the dough is pinched together. Then she gives it bunny ears, eyes, and whiskers. "It's a bāo bun, or a bun bun in all English. Her name is A Bun in Two Worlds." We compliment her on her brilliance.

"Very meta," Win comments, admiring our work. "These are great. I'm going to show them to Sūn Lǎoshī next door. Keep painting." He glances at Harrison, who is still busy doing his own thing at the other table, and nods at Gemma, who has been sitting quietly in the corner on her phone. My bunnies are punless disasters, but I give them to him anyway.

When I turn around, Harrison beckons me over to his table. I gasp when I see what he's been working on. "This is amazing," I tell him, staring down at the paper. A multicolored Chinese phoenix flies above a mountain range. A Chinese character is painted to look like a misty cloud. Like his rabbit design, this painting is both traditional and modern at the same time.

"What does this say?" I point to the Chinese character.

"Chōng," he says. "It's a rare literary word that means "to soar," used especially for birds. I looked it up last night, after your band sang onstage." He takes a breath. "I painted it for you."

My heart skips a beat. "I . . . I don't know what to say. It's beautiful, Harrison. Thank you."

"Say that you'll see me after camp ends," he says, dropping his voice so the others can't overhear.

Startled, I blurt, "Like a date?" I wonder if I'm allowed to date yet.

"Yes, exactly like a date. Since we can't hang out alone at camp."

I can feel the heat in my cheeks. "Um, on one condition. Bring me Swedish Fish after the raid tonight."

He coughs. "How do you know about the raid?" He makes a wry face. "I forgot. Nothing gets by the Squad. Speaking of which . . ." He points behind me with his chin.

I turn around to find the rest of the Squad openly eavesdropping on us. I roll my eyes at them, and they all start laughing. Gemma looks up and smiles. "Gemma knows about us?"

He nods. "We're good."

"Then I better get back before Win returns," I say. "And you should get back to teaching, Ko Lǎoshī. But to answer your question, yes, I'll see you again."

"Great," he breathes. "I'll give you the painting this afternoon when it's had a chance to dry more. I'm really glad you like it."

We walk back to the main table together. Side by side but not together together. Not yet. Not until camp is over.

# CHAPTER THIRTY-TWO

At lunch, I tap my spoon against my glass to get everyone's attention. "The online trolls are still out there. Do we still want to stick it to them and make a joyful video?" There's a chorus of yeses from the table. "Okay, great. I agree with McKenna that it's not fair to leave Bran and Howie out of the performance, so wǔshù isn't an option. Besides, I pretty much suck at it." The group cracks up. "I've been trying to think of something we could all do together but haven't come up with anything good. So I'm asking you all now to brainstorm with me. You're all smart and talented and creative. We got this!"

After a moment, Fei Fei starts clapping, and everyone else joins in. I smile gratefully at them. And then I roll my eyes dramatically and smirk. "Come on, stop that. We haven't figured anything out yet. Think, people!"

"What about repeating our cover of The Linda Lindas song from last night?" Delaney asks. "Everybody loved it, and we could easily add in Howie and Bran. Or the 'Little Apple' song? Win and Harrison can be lead singers like they were on the bus to the museum."

Fei Fei claps excitedly. "Squee boy band concert!"

I glance at Harrison, and he grimaces at me. I have to stop

myself from giggling because Sarina would totally notice. Win seems pumped by the idea, though, and suggests using the Squee Dance as choreography for one of the songs.

"This is a weird idea, but we could do a card game tournament," Ava suggests. "It was really fun to watch our Slap contest. Maybe the parents could even bet on which of us they think will win."

Sarina clears her throat. "Phee, thank you for starting this brainstorming session. I think creating our own performance is a great option. But let's not forget the purpose of the Showcase is to show the parents what you learned at camp, so they'll keep sending their kids back. And it's a heritage camp, so the performances all have to relate to Chinese culture in some way."

We slump in our chairs, deflated. I think about singing "Little Apple" on the bus and dressing up for the Variety Show and . . . something is unfurling in my brain like a bolt of cloth, an unbound sail, a pair of feathery wings. An idea, hidden in the folds, just beyond reach. I almost have it . . .

"Phee?" Lyr's voice slips between the threads. "Do you have an idea?"

I blink, the cafeteria coming into focus again. McKenna stares at me, and I stare back, wide-eyed, wondering.

"What?" she whispers.

In my head, I spread those wings and uncover the prize— an idea. "A fashion show," I murmur, and then I repeat myself so the whole group can hear. "A fashion show."

McKenna's eyebrows draw together, and she says "What?" again, but this time there's a hint of interest.

Win makes a sad face. "Phoenny, I love that idea, but the Showcase performances are supposed to highlight what you learned at camp, remember?"

"It will," I tell him, "And it'll be more than just one class." I look around the group. "Think about it—we could include something from each class we took. Lyr and Piper, you could play the music for the fashion show using the traditional instruments. We could brush paint Chinese characters on banners—that would use the skills we've learned in both crafts and Mandarin class. And so on. We could each pick what class or activity we liked best and figure out how to incorporate it into the show."

"Aren't you forgetting something? Like, the whole point of a fashion show is the *fashion*," Teagan points out. "Where are we going to get that?"

"Phee!" the Squad shouts in unison, and Lyr squeals.

I look across the table. "And McKenna," I say firmly. "I can't do it without you."

A range of emotions crosses her face. "Why me?" Win and Sarina are looking at me curiously, too. They've had a front-row seat to the drama between us.

"Because whether you meant to or not, you came to camp and challenged everything I thought I knew about Squee, about being Chinese American, and about being enough exactly as we are. That's part of our camp story this year. You helped write it." I smile. "Also, you have more fashion sense in your perfectly polished pinkie finger than the rest of us combined."

"You taught me a lot, too," McKenna says, her ears getting pink. "And why didn't you just say that in the first place?" Then she laughs and adds, "Let's do it. Let's have a Squeetacular Fashion Show!"

I hug her while everybody else gives us Snaps.

The rest of the day feels like how Kir describes a race—keeping herself restrained and at a steady pace but filled with tension and waiting for the right moment to unleash a burst of energy. I go through the motions in sports, music, and Mandarin classes, and when Counselor Time arrives, I let it all out. There's no time to waste—we have so much work to do.

For the first half hour, everyone comes up with ideas for incorporating their favorite camp activities into the show. Lyr and Piper have their heads together, discussing which C-pop songs they could accompany on gǔzhēn and èrhú. McKenna and I trade ideas for the overall theme.

"What do you think about a banner? In English and Chinese?" I ask her.

She presses her lips together. "I like that idea," she says slowly. "But are we going to have to involve Huáng Lǎoshī for the Chinese translation?"

"No, thank god. We have a native speaker right here." I tilt my head toward Harrison, who is talking to Win across the room.

"Perfect," she says, relieved.

"He is, rather, isn't he?" I joke, and she tosses a sofa pillow at me.

I catch it and lob it right back. "One sec. Gotta go arrange something." I walk across the room.

Harrison looks up at me and smiles. "What's up?"

"A banner, hopefully." I quirk an eyebrow at Harrison. "Here's what I was thinking . . ."

For the rest of the afternoon, we are a frenzy of activity. Harrison practices painting really large Chinese characters, while Delaney and Bran use stencils to trace the English word on fabric. Fei Fei and Ava walk around, asking each person what part of camp they want to represent in their outfits or incorporate into the show. Maze, Lyr, and Piper go upstairs and return, lugging my sewing machine, sewing equipment, boxes of fabric and vintage clothes, and Lyr's keyboard. Howie falls asleep, still on painkillers for his broken bone.

McKenna and I drape fabric and clothes over the sofas and chairs and study them. Because we don't have enough time to design and make twelve whole outfits from patterns and cloth, she and I decided to do what I do best—repurpose everyone's old clothes and add to them from my fabric stash to create something new. As soon as a camper has been interviewed by Ava and Fei Fei, they are sent over to us with an index card of notes that Ava took. They give us the clothes that they don't mind being cut up and repurposed, and McKenna and I suggest color combinations and styles based on their responses to the interview questions. Once everybody is happy, I sketch the final outfit in my notebook and McKenna bags the clothing, fabric, and index card together so they're all in one place. Lina does her thing and takes photos and videos of everybody. She's excited to create a "behind-the-scenes" documentary of the fashion show to play in the background while the actual fashion show is happening.

Just before we need to stop for dinner, Harrison, Gemma, Sarina, and Win approach me and McKenna. The four of them stand there with their arms crossed, looking irritated.

"Um, is there a problem?" I ask.

"The problem is that you haven't asked us what we want for our outfits," Win snaps. His biceps are pressed against his chest, making them look even bigger and more menacing.

"Uh, you all wanted to walk the runway, too?" I ask. Four more outfits to cram into the three and a half days we have left. Goodbye, sleep. But how can I refuse? I look around at the piles of fabric and bags of outfits to complete. "Okay, of course, sure," I babble. "What kind of outfits do you want?"

Sarina's bright laugh cuts through my stress. She steps forward to hug me. "Relax, Phoenny. We're just messing with you. We're not mad." The other three drop their arms and break out in wide smiles.

I sink onto the sofa, my knees still trembling. McKenna says, "That's not funny. You almost gave her a panic attack."

"Sorry," Gemma says, still grinning. "But we would actually love to have special outfits for the show, even if we're just introducing the group and holding the banner. Nothing fancy, though." She opens her backpack and pulls out four plain black T-shirts.

"Just an appliqué on each shirt," Harrison says, "of this." He slips a folder out of his pack and opens it to reveal a painting of a Chinese character, done in black ink on rice paper. It's the same character on the phoenix painting he gave me yesterday.

"What's it mean?" McKenna asks.

"It means 'to soar,' which I thought was perfect because of both your names."

Wait. *Both* our names?

Harrison continues. "*Phoenix*, because birds soar, and *McKenna*, because it means 'ascend,' which is a synonym for *soar*."

"Also, because both of you are leading this group to new heights." Win sweeps his arm to encompass all the campers.

My eyes follow his gesture, and I see heads bent together over various projects. Everybody mingles, laughing and working. I get a little choked up. "The Squad is dead," I murmur. "Long live the Group."

"Ugh," McKenna grumbles. "Can't you come up with something better than 'the Group?' It sounds too much like therapy."

I turn, ready to push back, only to find her grinning from one perfectly bejeweled ear to the other.

# CHAPTER THIRTY-THREE

"Phee, I can't wear that," McKenna says later that evening. She lifts the top half of a qípáo and holds it up against Teagan's body. "I'm sorry."

"Why not? It would be perfect since you're opening the show and I'm at the end. That's the top of the same qípáo I used in my outfit's skirt." I decided to wear my dance dress for the fashion show—one less outfit to make. I'm going to be too busy sewing to go to the dance anyway. "Look, it goes great with this skirt you said we could use."

Everyone in Group 13 is crammed into my and Lyr's room, even Bran and Howie. Kir and Queena came along, too. Fourteen people in one tiny dorm room staring at me makes me feel panicky and claustrophobic. Must keep it together.

But McKenna shakes her head. "I'm really not comfortable wearing this style of Chinese dress." She looks at the confusion on my face and sighs. "I wore one when I was little, and my mom said I looked like a 'little China doll.' It made me feel really icky."

I wrinkle my nose. "That's awful. I hate when people tell me I look like a China doll, too. It's so skeevy." I reach out and take back the qípáo half.

"Exactly!" McKenna says. "Like we're just here to smile and look pretty and be, like, I don't know . . ."

"Arm candy," Maze offers.

"The exotic flower," Piper mutters.

"The submissive Asian girlfriend," Fei Fei adds.

"Like we're objects and not actual people," Lina says. "I'd have been mad if my parents had said anything like that to me, too."

Howie and Bran are wisely silent, for once.

I bite my lip and ponder the problem. McKenna is the only one who still hasn't decided what she wants her outfit to look like, and it needs to be just right to set the tone for the rest of the show. "Okay, what other clothes did you bring that we can work on?"

She shrugs. "You can use anything I brought. Take a look through my closet and drawers."

All fourteen of us cross the hall and crowd into her and Teagan's room. Her closet is crammed with clothes. This all fit in her suitcase?

"We can use anything?" I ask, incredulous. "Some of this stuff is really nice. Are you sure you don't mind if I cut it up?"

She makes a face. "I'm not attached to any of this stuff, really. Just the corset-style top that I loaned you. A lot of it is hand-me-downs from my Italian cousins. There's some stuff my mom gave me that she didn't want anymore, either."

"That makes me feel better. My grandmothers give me

their castoffs, too, and I love making new things out of them and feeling that they're holding me close when I wear them."

McKenna smiles. "That's a great way to think about it. But I still don't know what to wear for the fashion show."

"Close your eyes," I tell McKenna. "Now, what would you wear if you could wear anything? What do you see yourself wearing when you're happy?"

After a minute, she starts talking. And then I know exactly what to suggest. As I hoped, she loves the idea.

Gemma's voice comes from the open doorway. "I'm all for teamwork, but right now it's time for bed, everyone."

Harrison appears behind her. He points to Bran and Howie. "Come on, guys. You get to go down the elevator."

Later, Lyr and I lie in the semi-dark yellow light coming through the open windows from the streetlamps on campus. "You and McKenna seem to be getting along really well," she says. There's a touch of jealousy in her voice that I recognize because it sounds like me.

"Maze gave me good advice when I was upset about you spending time with Piper. She told me to stop doom-thinking, and that you would always be my best friend. So I'm telling you now that I will always be your best friend, too." I hear her breathe a sigh of relief. "Okay, now that we got that out of the way, tell me how the music for the show is going."

"It's going great! Péng Lǎoshī was so excited about our idea and the theme of the show that he offered to help us. He's planning to accompany us on the pípá, and he's definitely going to help us record the music with the fancy equipment in the Performing Arts Center."

"That's awesome. I'm so glad you thought of making a recording so you can strut your stuff on the runway, too."

Lyr laughs. "And I can't wait to see all the outfits!" Her voice sobers. "It's a lot of sewing, Phee. Are you sure you can do it all before the Showcase? I don't want you to be completely overwhelmed."

"It *is* a lot, but I'm planning on asking you and the others to help as much as you can."

"Good," she says. "I'm up for anything, O Fearless Leader."

I laugh, my eyes going to Harrison's painting which I'd hung on the bulletin board above my desk. Win had called me and McKenna leaders, too.

By some stroke of luck, the light from the window falls across the painting, making the mountains glow. It isn't until just now that I realize by using red paint for the mountain range, Harrison had included himself in the painting. His name means "tall red mountain."

He'd painted me soaring above him.

# CHAPTER THIRTY-FOUR

Even though I should be sewing every minute that I'm awake, the Squad persuaded me that there was still time for one more prank. So, after an hour of gabbing with Lyr in the dark, we get out of bed and put on our shoes. I poke my head out the door, verify that it's all clear, and then we both slip into the hallway. Starting with Kir and Q's room, we tap on doors as we make our way back to the emergency exit. Soon, all ten of us are huddled on the landing of the stairwell.

I look at my phone. "Okay, he says that they made it to the snack closet. Victor is trying to pick the lock before the front desk staff come back from patrolling outside. We've got to move, now!"

We sneak downstairs to the first floor and quickly gather in front of my brother's door, which is just a few rooms away from the lobby. Ava stands guard, ready to give the signal if she spots anyone coming. Fei Fei and Piper pull stacks of large red plastic cups out of their backpacks. They hand them one by one to me and Lyr, and we create a row of cups across the width of the hallway, their rims just touching each other. As we start to set up a second row, Teagan, McKenna,

Delaney, and Q unscrew their water bottles and start filling the empty cups.

Q runs out of water and hands the empty bottle to Kir, who runs into the bathroom to fill it while Q pulls another bottle out of her pack. The same happens when another person runs out of water—they pass the bottle to Maze, Lina, or Kir to refill. It takes a lot of trips to fill up all the cups, but we are so organized that in six minutes, we have twenty rows of cups, brimming with water.

It takes us another eight minutes to create a second barrier of twenty rows right before the emergency exit door. By this time, Ava has gone up to the second floor, run down the hall, and joined the water bottle brigade. The second barrier takes longer because we have to use the kitchen on the second floor to fill the water bottles.

Lyr giggles quietly. "Thank god they have to stay in the snack closet until the next patrol!"

My phone buzzes just as Lina snaps a quick picture of our achievement. "They're on their way," I whisper, and we scurry back into the emergency exit stairwell. Cautiously, we open the door a crack and peer out.

Kir snickers. "They're never going to be able to hurdle that, not even if they're long jumpers."

Thirty seconds later, six CITs and a handful of campers run through the doorway from the lobby and turn the corner. Emerson comes to a screeching halt at the sight of the cups, windmilling his arms to keep from falling into them as he gets bumped into from behind. "Stop!" he whispers loud enough for us to hear him.

They study the barrier in confusion. Jackson looks up and spots the one farther down the hall, near our hiding place. He points to it, and there's more heated whispering. They've just figured out that they can't go up the main staircase, run across to the emergency exit, and go down that staircase to get to their rooms. They either have to risk jumping across the cups and probably knocking them down and getting water everywhere, or they'll get caught when the night monitors come by. Which is soon. There's no time for them to empty all the cups, although Andrew tries. He picks up a cup in each hand, but they're so full that the slightest pressure causes water to overflow and run down his arms and onto his legs as he walks to the water fountain and dumps them in. "Crap," he says, and we giggle.

Emerson's head snaps up, and he spots us peeking. The other boys see us, too. They shake their fists at us and mouth bad words while Lina snaps photos and Fei Fei takes video. In the back of the group, Harrison waves; then he and Victor lope up the stairs. They're the only two who have a room on the second floor. We hear grown-up voices speaking in Mandarin in the lobby. The night monitors are about to do their rounds! We stay just long enough to see a couple of boys panic and try to jump over the cups, creating a wave of water as they crash into them.

We laugh hysterically upstairs in my and Lyr's room as we look at the pics and watch the video.

"Your brother's even cuter when he's mad," Q observes, making us laugh even more.

My phone buzzes. The text from Harrison simply says *"Well done, you"* followed by rows of fire emojis. At the very end there is a heart-eyed emoji, which make my own heart flip again.

In the morning when I open our door, there is a paper bag hanging from the doorknob. Inside are five bags of Swedish Fish and a package of Oreos.

The days fly by in a flurry of classes, fabric, and fashion. The others help make a stencil of Harrison's calligraphy character, then trace it onto a length of patterned red silk and cut out four appliqués. Since the appliqués are each one single piece, it only takes me ten minutes to sew each one onto the front of a T-shirt. The counselors' outfits are done. Most of the campers' outfits are done, too, and parts of several others are ready to be put together. But there's still so much to do.

Before I know it, it's the night of the big camp dance, and the Showcase is the day after tomorrow.

"I'm not going," I insist to Lyr and the others. "I have to keep working. The fashion show was my idea—I can't let everyone down."

"It's the last Squee dance, Phee," Fei Fei wails.

"You'll let us down if you don't come," Maze growls. "Not to mention Harrison. He's been making eyes at you every chance he gets, but you're so busy sewing clothes that you don't even notice."

That makes me feel happy and sad at the same time. "What's the point? Harrison still isn't allowed to date me while we're at camp. Sarina and Win are probably going to watch us like hawks, so it's not like we can even sneak in a dance."

Lyr links her arm in mine, and Fei Fei takes the other arm. "The point is," Lyr sighs, "it won't be the same without you. We always go together, the whole Squad. And now that we're the Squad Plus, you absolutely cannot sit this one out." She pouts at me comically, and I have to laugh. Since when are we calling it the Squad Plus? It sounds like cold medicine.

McKenna adds, "Don't you even want to see who my date is? After asking about him all the time?"

"But I don't have a dress to wear," I tell them. "I'm wearing the dress I originally planned to wear to the dance to the fashion show instead. If I wear it tonight, it won't be a surprise at the Showcase."

McKenna starts riffling through my dresser and closet. "Wait. What's this?" She pulls out a little wad of silk from my fabric stash and shakes it out. There's a collective "Ohhhh" from the Squad Plus.

"No, I can't wear that," I protest. "It's . . . it's . . ."

"It's perfect, Phee. You're wearing it, and that's final."

"You sound just like me," Q says to McKenna. "I approve." They grin at each other. "Makeover for Phee?" Q asks.

"Absolutely," McKenna says. "Grab your kit and meet back here in five." They disappear into the hallway.

Maze groans in mock dismay. "Oh no, not two of them. How ever will we survive?"

Lyr takes the dress from McKenna. "I'll iron it for you right now," Lyr says. "No more excuses."

"Okay," I say, resting my head on her shoulder. "Twist my arm."

The Flex is already dark and crowded by the time we arrive. The glaring fluorescent overhead lights are off, and the counselors have strung multicolored twinkle lights along the walls and between the pillars. Win, Bora, and another counselor are DJ'ing up on the stage where I'd made a fool of myself doing the Squee Dance. There's no designated dance floor because the whole room is tiled, so campers are dancing in small groups all around the room. Others are milling around or standing along the walls or trying to chat with each other over the music.

We walk to the center of the room, all twelve of us, the girls of Group 13 plus Q and Kir. The Squad Plus. People stop and stare, moving aside to let us through. Months ago, the Squad had decided over group text that we were going to wear colors to the dance. No more little black dresses, no more hiding in the shadows—we were going to show ourselves off. The new girls got on board—borrowing from each other if they didn't happen to bring a lot of color. Some have raided my fabric stash. Ava is wearing a length of orange chiffon like a scarf, and Piper has looped a couple of yards of fuchsia satin over her shoulder and pinned it to her waist on the opposite side, like a beauty pageant contestant's sash.

And then there's McKenna. She took my pinking shears to her floral sundress and cut a wide strip from the bottom hem. Tonight, she's put her hair up in a high ponytail, wrapped the fabric around her head, and tied it in a big bow toward the front. The headscarf accentuates the high planes of her cheekbones and her delicate features. A boy breaks away from where he and his friends are standing by the side and strides toward McKenna. He's wearing a black shirt with a silver tie and dark jeans. His hair is slicked back. I literally don't recognize William until McKenna says his name. He says something I can't hear, and she follows him to another part of the dance floor.

Lyr and I look at each other and burst into giggles. William is McKenna's secret admirer and now her date. That was unexpected.

I scan the back of the room and spot a group of turquoise T-shirts in the back right corner. They're setting up the "bar"—really, just a drink station of giant coolers full of water, lemonade, and fruit punch. On another table, there are bottles of ginger ale and soda water to make your drink fizzy if you want to. Harrison looks up from where he's mixing lemonade powder into a cooler full of water and spots me. His smile flashes in the dark, lit blue and green by the twinkle lights. He turns and says something to another CIT near him, who comes and takes over stirring the lemonade for him. He makes his way toward us, not sparing a glance at anyone else.

"Phee," he breathes, and the way he says my name unravels the knots in my stomach. "You look beautiful. Your dress is amazing. When did you find time to make that?"

"I whipped it up before breakfast this morning," I tease. When his jaw drops, I laugh and shake my head. "I'm kidding. I'm not a morning person at all. I actually made this back in the spring, from a vintage Japanese kimono I found in a thrift store."

It had taken me a week to carefully pick apart the stitches holding the lavender silk outer fabric and its cream-colored silk lining together, and then separate each panel of the outer fabric. It was a surprise to find that kimonos are essentially constructed of long panels of fabric about ten inches wide. I took the lavender panels and sewed them back together on the long edges, then rotated the large piece forty-five degrees and marked my pattern on it like a regular piece of cloth. Two more weeks later, I had a slip dress with diagonal panels and an asymmetrical hem. The lines of it skim my body before gently flaring at the waist, which is why I'd been hesitant to wear it until now. The look on Harrison's face makes me glad I waited.

"Want to dance?"

I swallow nervously. "Won't you get in trouble?"

His expression turns mischievous. "They told me I couldn't ask you *to* the dance as my date. They didn't say I couldn't actually dance with you once you were here. Anyway, camp will be over in a matter of days. What are they going to do to me?"

I look around before answering. Lyr shakes her head, but the rest of Squad Plus are making encouraging faces. Behind Maze, I spot Sarina, who isn't looking especially pleased by the sight of me and Harrison standing so close together. Before I can warn him, she strides over and puts her arms around my and Lyr's shoulders. "My pandas!" she exclaims. "We need a Group 13 dance!" She sees Q and Kir and adds, "Plus friends!"

It's obvious to everyone what she's doing, but we don't complain because she's Sarina and we love her. Also, I don't want to put her in the awful position of having to tell my mom. So we form up into a large circle; Harrison stays on my right and Lyr is to my left. Gemma appears out of nowhere dragging Emerson by the wrist, who gives me a *don't you dare say anything* look. I bite back a laugh. Fei Fei looks dismayed, though, so I go over and whisper in her ear, "You never know until you ask, right?" I squeeze her shoulder, and she nods, looking determined.

We jump and sway and fling our arms around, grinning. I'm acutely aware of Harrison and sneak glances over at him. Our hands accidentally smack into each other's, which sends a ripple of electrified silk up my arm.

It's exhilarating and nerve-racking, and half an hour later, I'm exhausted. I turn to Lyr. "I need a drink. Want to come?" She nods, and we head toward the drink station.

Harrison joins us. "Let's go see if there's any lemonade left."

The moment we near the makeshift bar, one of the other CITs grabs him. "Thank god you showed up. We ran out of ice and water and the campers are about to pass out, or lose their minds, or both." She shoves a large orange water cooler jug into his chest, and Harrison has no choice but to hang on to it. He just stares at her for a moment, until she barks, "Water and ice, Harrison!"

I touch his shoulder. "Come on, I'll show you where to get it. We have to go to the cafeteria kitchen."

"But it's locked," Lyr says. "What are you going to do, break down the door?"

"I've got a way," I tell her. I turn to Harrison. "This way."

Lyr watches us go. "I'll go distract Sarina," she says. She really is the best friend ever.

# CHAPTER THIRTY-FIVE

I lead Harrison through the back doors and up the rear stair-case. Was it just ten days ago that I led the Squad up here to steal eggs? It feels like a lifetime. I try the handle experimentally. It's locked, like Lyr knew it would be.

"What now?" Harrison asks, setting the cooler jug on the floor. There's a series of marks on his camp shirt where the wet side of the cooler had been pressed up against him. His hair is messy, and he's sweaty from dancing. Suddenly, he doesn't seem so out of reach anymore.

I smile. "Watch this." I turn to the wall, where there's an emergency fire hose stored in a recessed metal cabinet. The glass door of the cabinet is unlocked, and I swing it open. Then I reach up, above where the hose is coiled, and feel around the sides of the cabinet. "Got it!" I pull my hand out of the cabinet and show Harrison the magnetic key box. "We run out of water and ice at the dance every single year. One of the counselors got their hands on the key to the kitchen a few years ago and made a copy without the director finding out. They keep it hidden in here and only tell other counsel-ors about it."

"That's brilliant," Harrison says as I unlock the gray door

and hold it open for him. "But you're not a counselor or CIT, so how did you find out about it?"

I shoot him a look. "Who do you think filched the key from his mom, the director?"

Harrison laughs and picks up the empty cooler. "Your brother's not so bad. I wish he thought the same about me."

"It's not that he doesn't like you . . ." I start. "He just—"

"Still doesn't trust me," Harrison finishes.

"So prove him wrong," I say, and his eyes glitter in the dark. I usher him through the doorway and let it close gently behind me. Harrison follows me through the darkened food service kitchen, lit only by the dim yellow light coming through the windows in the cafeteria beyond. Without streetlights, the place would be pitch black. The giant ice machine is around the corner, and he sets down the cooler while I open the bin.

We both grab the plastic scoops from their holders on the side of the ice machine and start filling the jug. The chilled air rising out of the machine feels good against my face. "Okay, let's stop," I tell Harrison when the cooler is half full. "We can fill the rest with water. There's a faucet thingy over there, by the stove." He heaves the container up and walks in the direction where I pointed, while I close the bin.

"This thing?" He points to what looks like a garden faucet, except it's on a pipe that rises three feet above the floor. A flexible metal hose with a nozzle is attached to the mouth of the faucet. "Why's it so far off the ground?"

"My mom says it's called a pot filler—it makes it easier to fill up big pots when they're on the stove. I guess you boil a lot of food when you're cooking for a whole college."

Harrison turns on the faucet and grabs the hose, directing the flow of water into the cooler. "Perfect for filling water jugs, too."

After a few minutes, it's full, and I shut off the faucet while he screws the lid on the jug. He tries to pick it up and manages to get it a few inches off the ground before letting it slide back to the floor with a thunk. "Oof, that's heavy," he says.

I mentally smack my own head. "I forgot that the staff uses a cart to move the filled jugs around. It's in the main lobby. I can run and get it." I take a couple of steps toward the exit, but Harrison stops me.

"Wait. Let's try this first," he says. "You grab one handle, and I'll grab the other. We can probably carry it between us. But not down the stairs. To the elevator."

"Oh, good idea." We take the handles and lift. But since Harrison is taller, he lifts his side higher and the jug tilts toward me. Some of the water that was around the rim drips onto my dress.

"Oh, crap. Sorry." Harrison lowers his side so it is level, and we shuffle out of the kitchen.

We stop and set the cooler down in front of the elevator, and I go back to lock the kitchen door and hide the key.

When I return, I pick up the handle on my side again, but Harrison just stands there, his head cocked to one side. "Do you hear that?" he asks.

I listen, but I don't hear anything unusual. To be honest, I'm feeling a little cranky. I'm thirsty, and now my dress is wet and the pressure to finish the outfits is weighing me down again. I'm starting to regret coming to the dance. I'm surprised when Harrison gently pulls my hand away from the jug and leads me past the elevator, down the hall toward the front of the building. He stops when we reach the open area in front of the cafeteria doors.

"Listen. You can hear it better from here."

All I hear is the muffled sound of the dance coming up from downstairs, the occasional bark of laughter, the sound of people chatting. I raise my eyebrows at Harrison.

"They're playing a slow song." He raises his hand, still holding mine, and places my hand on his shoulder. He smiles. "May I have this dance?"

My heart races and my mouth is suddenly drier than it was before. I nod, and he rests one hand on my shoulder while the other curves around my waist. I reach out and put my left hand just above his hip, and then we're swaying to the beat of the music, although it might be my heartbeat, too.

I take it back. There's nowhere I'd rather be than here.

We step out of the elevator just as Lyr bursts through the doors to the dance hall, Sarina on her heels. "There you are!"

Lyr says breathlessly. "I was just telling Sarina that you probably had trouble getting into the kitchen." Her eyes are wide, begging me to play along.

"Yeah, whoever used the key last stuck it behind the hose, so it was really hard to reach," I say, sounding equally out of breath, but for different reasons. "And we didn't have a cart, so we had to lug the cooler between us." To make my point, I drop my side of the cooler, and Harrison, caught off guard, drops his side with a grunt. Sarina looks from me to Harrison, then back to me. She eyes the water jug and the drips on my dress. I hope my excuse explains why my face is so red. She must decide to believe me, or at least to let it go, because she moves over to grab the handle I just let go of.

"C'mon, let's get this thing inside. Campers are freaking out that they're going to pass out from dehydration." Sarina rolls her eyes and motions for Harrison to pick up the other handle. Together, they easily lift the jug and carry it into the Flex.

Lyr studies my face. "Something happened!"

I place the back of my hand to my forehead and pretend to faint. "We slow-danced! It was . . . it was . . ." I don't have the words.

"Magical," Lyr says.

I nod. "Magical. It really was. We danced for two songs and then I got nervous that Sarina or Win was going to catch us, so we came back."

"Good call. I had a really hard time keeping Sarina from running after you. McKenna noticed and distracted Sarina for a bit by claiming Howie stole her headscarf. William helped, too, by asking her to help look for McKenna's earring." Lyr looks at me a little shyly. "Did he kiss you?"

"No," I tell her, "but it seemed like he wanted to. I'm glad he didn't, though."

"Really? Why? Didn't you want to?"

I feel my cheeks get even warmer, if that was possible. "I did, but not like that, where it could get us into trouble. I mean, in a few days he won't be my CIT anymore. And then we won't have that problem of him being staff and my being a camper. We can just be friends. No more rules."

Lyr links my arm with hers and tugs me toward the dance hall. "I think you mean *more than just friends*," she teases.

I groan. "I don't know. It all just feels overwhelming sometimes, you know? I'm not sure that I'm ready to have a boyfriend. I didn't come to camp expecting someone to like me, much less a CIT. We haven't known each other that long, either."

"Time is different at camp," Lyr says. "You've spent more than twelve hours a day with him for the past umpteen days. That's longer than most middle school relationships even last. I think you're stressing about the fashion show and camp ending and finding reasons to blame that stress on Harrison."

"You're right. My emotions are all over the place. I need

a moment. Would you be mad if I sat here for a little bit? I'll come back in and find you when my head is clearer." I flop down on one of the sofas in the space.

"Are you sure?" Lyr looks longingly at the doors to the Flex.

I push her gently. "Yes, I'm sure. Go have fun. I swear I'll be there in ten minutes." She gives me a smile and slips back into the dance.

*Camp ending*, Lyr had said. The pressure inside my head and chest builds. Only two days left of the magic. And despite the mixed messages from Harrison, the roller-coaster friendship with McKenna, and the online trolls, it's been amazing. Things with Harrison turned out better than I ever expected. Same with McKenna, whom I can see becoming almost as good a friend as Lyr. As much as I want the fashion show and our video to be a success, I don't want camp to end. But it will. We'll all leave Squee, and it'll be like it never existed.

My chest feels even tighter, and it's hard to breathe.

A hand touches my shoulder, and I jump. "It's just me," McKenna says. "Are you okay? Lyr told me you were out here, and I came to check on you." I blink up at her. She squats down in front of me and stares into my face. "Phee. Take a deep breath for me, okay? Like this—in—two—three, out—two—three. Good. Do that again."

She coaches me for another minute until the knot in my chest loosens, and I'm breathing normally. Was that a panic attack? I've never had one of those before.

McKenna sits down on the sofa next to me. She doesn't say anything, just waits me out.

"I'm really stressed out from everything," I finally say. "I don't want camp to end. Maybe if I sit here and *not* finish the outfits, then we won't have the fashion show and Squee won't be over."

"I don't want camp to end, either." She shakes her head. "Isn't that weird? When I got here, I wanted it to be over as fast as possible. And the first few days felt like an eternity. But then I started to have a little bit of fun, and then a little more, and now I don't want to leave. It would be great if sitting here meant Squee wouldn't end, but it doesn't work that way. This is not a magical time-stopping sofa. Even if you don't make the rest of the outfits and the fashion show doesn't happen, Squee will still be over." She pats my leg. "So come on. Let's make the most of it while it's still going on. Didn't you say you were going to be present at camp? Well, you can't be present at the dance if you're out here on a non-magical sofa."

She stands and starts to pull me to my feet, when we hear people coming through the doors to the Flex behind us. "What was it you wanted to talk to me about, Fei Fei?" Gemma's voice carries across the room.

Quickly, I pull McKenna back to the sofa, and we curl up so our heads aren't visible above the back of it. I hold a finger to my lips so she knows to stay quiet.

"I . . ." Fei Fei says, and then falls silent. Then she blurts, "Do you like Emerson?"

Gemma clears her throat. "I don't know. We're just getting to know each other a little better," she says carefully. "Fei Fei, do *you* like him?"

"What? No." Fei Fei laughs and sounds more like herself. "I mean, he's handsome, but no. I don't like *Emerson*."

"Oh?" Gemma says. There's a pause, and then she says "Oh," again, more softly. "I'm really flattered, Fei Fei. I think you're fun and hilarious and sweet, and it's been great to hang out with you at Squee. But—"

"But you don't like me that way," Fei Fei interrupts, her voice full of angst.

"But I don't like *girls* that way," Gemma says gently. "I'm pretty sure I'm straight."

"So it's not personal?" Fei Fei says brightly. "Like, if you *weren't* straight, you might consider dating me?"

Gemma laughs. "If I weren't straight and you were three or four years older. For the next two days, how about you keep being a camper and I'll keep being your CIT?"

"And what about after camp? What will we be then?"

"How about FWT. Friends who text. You want updates on my pet iguana, right?"

I peek over the back of the sofa in time to see Fei Fei and Gemma pinkie-swear before returning to the dance. I'm so proud of Fei Fei for sharing what's in her heart because I know that isn't easy. I hope she won't mind that we heard her private conversation.

"We should get back, too, McKenna. I told Lyr I'd only be out here for ten minutes."

"Are you okay now?" McKenna asks.

I nod. "Fei Fei and Gemma reminded me that there is life after camp. With friends who text."

"Don't forget the iguana."

# CHAPTER THIRTY-SIX

The rest of the dance is wonderful, and I manage, with the help of Squad Plus, to stay present and positive. It also helps that Harrison's work shift ends soon after I return to the Flex, and he doesn't leave my side until the dance is officially over.

Back in Agnes, we stay up most of the night working on the outfits. Squad Plus helps pin, cut, and even do some hand sewing. Queena irons seams and hems. For someone who claims she never does chores, Q is surprisingly good with an iron. She shrugs when I mention it and says that she helps a friend from school straighten her hair with a flat iron, so this is kind of the same.

Sarina stops by to tell us it's time for lights-out, but when she sees what we're doing, she gets Gemma and they come back to help. They ooh and aah over their appliqué T-shirts and promptly try them on. As each girl's outfit is finished, she models it for us. Some girls go off to their rooms to catch a few hours of sleep, while others return after brushing their teeth and curl up on our beds. It's like a combined sleepover and arts-and-crafts party, and even though I'm still stressed about finishing on time and carrying off a successful fashion show, I'm also happy. I've always done my art and sewing alone or with

Lyr keeping me company while composing her own music, so to have everyone helping fills me with a warm, fuzzy feeling.

We try to stay quiet, even though there doesn't seem to be much point since most of the girls from our end of the hall are all in my room. But I guess we're not doing a very good job, because my phone buzzes around two in the morning.

"Oh no," Lyr says. "Tell me that's not your mom."

I look at the screen. "It's not." I scan the message: **Everything all right, Phee?** I stare at the three blinking dots. **Heard a loud thump. Sounded like a body. Or maybe an ogre.** I chuckle.

Teagan brushes herself off after trying to do a pirouette for Lina and landing in a heap on the floor. "What?" she mutters in response to my laugh. "I get uncoordinated when I'm exhausted." I make what I hope is a sympathetic face and turn back to my phone, typing with both thumbs.

**Everything's fine. What're u still doing up?**

**Bunch of us just finished creating, printing, and folding all the programs for the Showcase. My hands are full of paper cuts. U sure you're all right?**

Weird.

**Yeah, I'm fine. Why?**

281

Someone said they saw you alone in the room
outside the Flex and you looked upset. 'Wanted
to apologize if I did something wrong.

Was stressed about costumes but all the
girls helped and they're nearly all done now.

Cool. Can't wait to see. Goodnight.

Night.

I look up to find everyone's eyes on me. "What?" I say, trying to sound innocent.

Fei Fei laughs. "There's only one person that makes you all swoony smiley like you are right now."

I feel my face warm, but I can't deny it. It was sweet of Harrison to check on me.

Sarina studies me for a long moment. "You really like him, don't you? It's not just because he's older and looks like—"

"Wang Yibo!" my friends squeal, giggling hysterically. I really hope Harrison didn't hear that from downstairs.

I bite my lip and manage a squeaky "Yes? And he's not that much older than me. A little over a year."

"Well," Gemma pipes up, "I can tell you that he really likes you, too. Goes on and on about how talented you are, and how helpful you are, and how funny you are. Won't shut up about you." She makes a retching sound that sends the rest of the girls into another fit of giggles. My cheeks burn.

"I'm glad to hear it," Sarina says. "Just keep it quiet for a couple more days, okay? I like your mom, but she laid down the law about relationships with campers during counselor orientation. And if you guys get together after camp is over, then I'm going to pretend that nothing happened here."

"So you don't actually think there's anything wrong with me and Harrison going out?" I'm stunned.

Sarina's eyes narrow. "Does he ever make you do anything you don't want to do?"

"No!" I say emphatically. "Nothing like that. He's actually been really sweet and thoughtful. It's just . . ."

"Sparks," Fei Fei supplies. "Lots of sparkly sparks."

I want to sink into the floor and disappear. But Sarina grins and relaxes. "Okay, good. Keep it that way until after camp!"

"I promise." Two more days, I tell myself.

I feel like a pair of distressed jeans the next morning—the kind that's been put through a washing machine full of rocks until they're limp and frayed. Sarina kicked everyone out of the room around three a.m. so Lyr and I could get a few hours of sleep. But even though the costumes were all done, a new set of worries kept me awake. What if Mom and Chŭ Auntie find out about the fashion show and prohibit us from doing it? What if the tech fails? What if I trip walking down the runway? It would be the worst, most UN-spectacular way to end camp.

We shuffle our way to breakfast, and I pause for a moment in the upstairs lobby, remembering the dances Harrison and I shared here. Was that only just last night? It feels like ages ago. The memory of his hands holding me and my head resting on his shoulder sends little fizzy bursts like sequins through me. Even if everything else goes wrong, at least I'll have that perfect moment from camp.

"How are you two so full of energy?" I glower at Fei Fei and Queena. "You're like . . . the . . . you know . . ." My exhausted brain cells can't come up with any examples. I sigh.

"Like the frog from that old puppet show who does this," Kir says, and flails her arms around her head, making us all laugh.

Fei Fei leans in and fake-whispers conspiratorially, "We took a cue from our wise elders and hit up the coffee machine."

"Eww, that stuff is gross," Piper complains as she sets her tray down next to Lyr. So far, it's just the ten of us. None of the counselors or CITs have shown up yet, and I bet Bran and Howie are still asleep.

"It's not that bad if you add this." Queena holds up a packet of Swiss Miss cocoa mix and shakes it in front of my face. "I mean, it's not Dunk's iced latte with mocha swirl, but . . ."

A slender arm shoots past my head and grabs the packet. "I could kill for a Mocha Frappuccino, but I guess this'll have to do," McKenna says.

Maze laughs at my dismayed face. "I got you covered,

Phee." She pulls out another box of cocoa packets from her backpack and hands it to me. "Courtesy of the Ma Family Market."

Soon we're all lining up at the coffee station with tall glasses filled with ice and cocoa mix. I'm stirring my drink when I hear a voice over my shoulder. "Is that for me?"

I turn and hand my glass to Harrison. "You can have a teeny-tiny taste." I allow. "But I seriously need to caffeinate myself today or I'll really be an ogre. So if you like it, go make your own. Maze has more cocoa stashed in her pack."

Harrison pretends like he's going to guzzle my mocha but takes a small sip instead. A dreamy look slides over his face. "Wah—"

"Hóu jeng," we all chime in Cantonese, laughing as he turns pink.

Despite our iced mochas, morning classes are brutal.

In crafts class, Sūn Lǎoshī has set out silky red cords and bowls with jade-colored beads and gold ingots made of plastic. In front of each chair is a small corkboard with several sewing pins stuck in it. We all sink down gratefully into the chairs. "For our last class, I thought I'd teach you to make good-luck charms," the teacher says. "The art of Chinese knotting is called Zhōngguó jié and there are special meanings for certain knots. The first one we're learning today is the simple lucky knot. Every Chinese knot is made from only one length of thread, to symbolize a long life without any setbacks."

I lean over and murmur to Lyr, "I'd settle for not tripping during tomorrow's performance." She nods in sympathy and squeezes my arm.

We follow Sūn Lǎoshī's instructions, using the pins to anchor the loops of the slippery cord in place. My knot is a little lopsided, but I think it still looks pretty good. Teagan mutters under her breath the whole time, while we all struggle to tighten the knot before it springs apart in our fingers. Sūn Lǎoshī has us string two beads onto each of the free ends of the cord and tie small knots to hold the beads in place. Finally, we brandish our completed charms for her inspection.

"Excellent!" Sūn Lǎoshī says. "I think you are ready to try the two by four bāo treasure knot. It's a little trickier, but just remember to be patient and tighten slowly. Watch me carefully." Her nimble fingers weave the knot on her corkboard and then pull the loops taut, leaving a complicated-looking ball-like knot with the two cord ends hanging down. She then pushes the dangling ends through the hole in an ingot bead and makes a knot below it. "There! Ready to try?"

Half an hour and a few tears later, we dangle our treasure knot charms from our fingers. Most of them, mine included, are messy balls with loops sticking out where they're not supposed to be. Only Win's knot is perfect, with three small, equally sized loops like the petals of a flower. I look over at Harrison, who is frowning at his creation. He catches my eye. "I think I'll stick to brush painting," he says.

"Hopefully they'll bring us good luck anyway." I sigh and attach the charms to the key ring hanging from my backpack. Lyr does the same, while McKenna tucks the knot through her ponytail holder. The red and gold pop against her dark hair, and I feel a twinge of the old jealousy. "You're so chic, McKenna."

"It's annoying, amirite?" Teagan adds, putting an arm around her friend to take away the sting. "But I love you anyway."

McKenna makes a face at Teagan, then looks at me with an expression that mirrors my own envious one. "You're kidding. Your belt is way cooler than this cheap charm."

"Really?" I look down at the tie-dye headscarf that I'd braided with purple and pink leather straps I took off old purses. "Thanks. I guess it's good that you and I came up with the designs for the fashion show. We are, like, style mavens."

Everybody laughs, and I smile across the table at McKenna. She twirls her ponytail and smiles back. Maybe we got off on the wrong foot, but we're standing together now.

# CHAPTER THIRTY-SEVEN

The last night of Squee for the oldest campers is a lock-in party, where we stay up all night locked in a large room next to the cafeteria. I've heard of lock-in parties in high schools after graduation, which sounds fun—everybody is celebrating the next step in their lives. But graduating from Squee is the last thing I want. It feels like growing out of a favorite, super-comfortable T-shirt.

The counselors for both Groups 12 and 13 bring in games, arts-and-crafts supplies, and lots and lots of munchies. We drink sweet chrysanthemum tea in cans, make s'mores in the microwave, and later, when we get midnight hunger pangs, there are Cup Noodles to revive us. After so little sleep for the past several days, I'm ready to crash after finishing my ramen. I only eat the noodles, of course, because soup is ick. But no one will let me sleep. Finally, I tell them that I'm getting more chips, but instead I lie down in the corner behind the s'mores station, hoping the tablecloth hangs down enough to hide me from view. Maybe I can catch a quick catnap before anyone notices I'm missing. I close my eyes and put my arm across them to block out more light.

Two minutes later, I hear footsteps approach, and someone

lies down next to me. "Lyr, let me sleep," I groan. "I'm going to be a wreck during the Showcase otherwise."

"I'm not Lyr," a voice says, and I fling my arm off my face and open my eyes to see McKenna staring at me.

"Oh. Hey." I turn and prop myself up on an elbow, so we are face-to-face.

"So you're exhausted?" she asks. "Me too, and I'm not even the one who did all that sewing last night. I can't believe the outfits are done."

"I know, right? But it wasn't just me. Everyone helped. You were there until the bitter end, too."

McKenna makes an *oh, please* sound of dismissal. "I pinned things together. You did most of the heavy work."

"And you did most of the styling and design. You have a great eye."

Her cheeks turn pink. "Thanks for saying that, and for asking me to do the fashion show with you. I have to admit that I've had a good time this past week. I'm really going to miss Squee."

"You mean you're going to miss William," I tease.

Her blush deepens, and she makes a little scrunched-up face. "Fine, him too. I wish we could've gotten to know each other more before camp ended."

"For what it's worth, I'm sorry we got off on the wrong foot. We would've had more time to get to know each other better if I hadn't been so judgmental."

She looks away and then back at me. "I'm sorry I kept jumping to conclusions about you."

I pick at a loose thread in the carpet. "If you couldn't tell already, I don't like change. I like traditions and rituals. I like understanding where all the pattern pieces go and having all the seams line up." I pause for a moment, thinking. "You and I, we're like pieces cut from the same cloth. We are both Chinese American, and to the rest of the world, that makes us the same," I say slowly. "They look at us and believe that we both must think and act the same. I sigh and roll onto my back, staring at the ceiling. "But we're not a monolith. We're all individuals, with our own unique histories and experiences, likes and dislikes. We're not interchangeable just because we share an ethnicity."

McKenna nods. "We're all trying to figure out what it means to be Chinese American, or Asian American. Sometimes we'll have things in common, like our love of fashion. And sometimes we'll be far apart, like you hate soup and I drink gallons of hot and sour soup every winter." She elbows me jokingly.

I make a face. "You like hot and sour soup? I'm seriously reconsidering our friendship right now."

McKenna laughs. "You don't know what you're missing."

"Listening to everybody talk about what made them a 'Bad Asian' made me realize that there are so many different ways to be Asian. There's no one 'right' way. All of us are 'Asian enough' the way we are."

McKenna smiles and says softly, "Asian enough. I like the sound of that." She sits up and smacks me on the shoulder. "Now get up and come back to the group. We need to choose a new name. This Squad Plus thing is worse than the coffee in the cafeteria."

"Right?!"

Bleary-eyed, we hit Maze up for more hot cocoa packets and start the next morning with iced mochas again. I look at the wobbling scoop of scrambled eggs on my plate and push it away.

"Okay, folks, I'm super sad to say it, but it's the last day of camp," Sarina says, "and I just want to say on behalf of me, Win, Gemma, and Harrison that it's been a great experience. We had a few hiccups, but we worked them out through honest communication, and I think we've all learned a lot and grown together. Thanks for being such awesome people—I'm really glad that you all were in my group." She holds up her mug. "Cheers to Group 13!"

We toast each other with our drinks. When Harrison clinks his Hydro Flask to my glass, my mocha tastes more bitter than sweet.

Maze looks around the table. "We decided that the Squad is no more and calling ourselves the Group or Squad Plus is too dorky, right?" We nod our heads. "So what *did* we agree to call ourselves from now on?"

Teagan groans. "Everybody voted for something different.

Bran wanted 'Legion,' but people thought it was too military-like. Howie wanted 'Herd' but—"

"But I said that made us sound like cows," Fei Fei says. "I suggested 'Pod,' but Lina said that we're not orcas or iguanas, then Lyr suggested we call ourselves whatever the collective name for pandas is, since that's our group mascot."

"I googled it, and it turns out that a group of pandas can be called either a *bamboo* or an *embarrassment*," Ava says, rolling her eyes. "At that point we were all too embarrassed to keep going, so we stopped without making a decision."

"Maybe we don't need to call our group anything at all," Piper says. "Instead, we could just assign an emoji panda to be the symbol of the text thread." We all think that sounds like a great idea.

Three hours later, we're back in the cafeteria for our last meal together as campers and counselors. We're hot and sweaty from the dress rehearsal, since we're the last group to perform. We kicked everybody out of the auditorium in the Performing Arts Center, locking the doors so no one else could come in. We all want the fashion show to be a surprise—even the brochures just say, "Group 13—Finale." Now we're as ready as we're going to be. The outfits survived the experience and are tucked away backstage, ready for us to put them on again. It was a big reveal for Harrison, and the look on his face was priceless. His grin was so wide when I gave him his own SOAR shirt that it looked positively painful.

"Everyone at camp already has a T-shirt with your artwork on it," I'd said to him. "We're all wearing them today. Why's this shirt different?"

He shook his head slowly, considering his words. "I'm happy that my design got chosen for the camp shirt, of course, but these shirts just feel . . . more special, somehow." He looked at me with an admiration that made me squirm. "The fabric you picked out for the appliqués is amazing. It's not just a solid red—it has all these different shades of red that add another dimension to the design. And I'm just, you know, really happy that we could work together on something and have it turn out so great." His cheeks had turned a little pinker by the time he'd finished talking, and I'm sure mine had, too.

"So you'll wear the shirt after camp?" I teased.

"I might never take it off," he said solemnly, and we both laughed, remembering that day.

# CHAPTER THIRTY-EIGHT

Lunch passes by in a haze, and before long, I look up and we're sitting in a packed auditorium and the Showcase has begun. The other groups' performances feel like they each last a zillion years. I fidget through them, rubbing the hem of my shirt, unable to concentrate.

Lyr's concern is etched on her face. "Whatever happens, we'll be okay."

I lean my head on her shoulder. "I know. I'm just being silly and feeling sad even before camp ends."

"It's not silly," Maze says. "It's just early PCS."

"PCS?" I ask.

"Post-camp syndrome," she says. "It's a real condition. But treatable."

"Oh, yeah? What's the treatment, Dr. Maze?" I feel a tiny smile form.

"To have a group get-together as soon as possible."

Queena turns around in her seat. "I decree that this get-together shall take place next weekend."

Finally, Group 10 finishes their painful èrhú rendition of a traditional song, and Group 11 takes their places on the stage. As the campers in Group 10 return to their seats, we stand and follow Group 12 down the aisle and through the side door that leads backstage. Numbly, I follow Kir, who is in front of me.

"Not that way!" Lyr whispers from behind me. She grabs me by the shoulders and steers me toward the girls' dressing room.

Inside, I take a deep breath. Gotta get with the program. Lyr hands me my blue dress, and I slip into it. The moment she zips up the back, I feel calmer, clearer. This dress, this show, these people—they're who I am and how I want to spend the last day of Squee. I turn around and hug Lyr tightly. She squeaks in surprise.

"You've got this," she reassures me.

"*We've* got this," I reply. "We're going to give everyone a show they won't forget and show those trolls they can't keep us down."

We're all ready and in position just as the music for Group 12's ribbon dance comes to an end. They did a great job, judging by the applause from the audience. I peek out through the curtain in time to see Kir and Q turn around and give me heart signs.

As soon as the stage is clear, I signal to Win and Sarina.

"Here we go," Sarina says to all of us.

"Break a leg, yeah?" Win grins.

Howie raises his crutch. "Way ahead of you!"

The counselors pick up a large roll of cloth and walk

through the part in the middle of the back curtains and toward the front of the stage, unrolling the cloth as they go. The spattered painters' drop cloth we found in a storage closet was cut and stitched together to make our own "red carpet," with the help of several cans of ruby-red spray paint. When the carpet is in place, they go and stand behind the podium at the side of the stage.

Sarina leans toward the microphone. "Welcome, parents, friends, and sponsors, to the first ever SCCWEE fashion show!" Win repeats her words in Mandarin.

From my hiding spot in the wings, I can see Mom's and Chǔ Auntie's surprised expressions. They look a little nervous, too, but it's too late for them to stop us now.

Out on stage, Win signals to the people in the control booth. The house lights dim, and a spotlight appears on the back curtains, centered over the red carpet. The music starts, and people lean back in their seats as the soothing sounds of the èrhú sweep over them. I signal to Harrison and Gemma, who step through the curtains together, each carrying a tall pole attached to the ends of the banner. They stride confidently down the runway, their red-and-black SOAR shirts on full display. At the edge of the stage, they move apart, unfurling the banner between them.

Appliquéd on top of my quilt are the Chinese characters for the idiom hǎi kuò tiān kōng, which Harrison suggested after listening to my intentions. Literally, it means, "the sea and sky are vast and unconstrained." Underneath the characters, we put the English translation: boundless. Like my grandmother expanding her point of view to accept Mom into the family, we have removed our boundaries to make room for all of us at Squee. Like my quilt, which is made from bits of Chinese and American fabrics, we have revealed how we are all patterns, all textures, all at once.

Harrison and Gemma let the audience admire the banner for another minute before moving to the side and clearing the runway.

It's showtime.

Several things happen at once: the music changes, a screen lowers at the back of the stage, and McKenna makes her entrance. She's wearing a simple black jumpsuit that makes her look even taller and more elegant. From stage right, she struts to the center of the stage and makes a sharp left turn onto the red carpet, accompanied by an upbeat Mando-pop song. At the end of the runway, she takes her hands out of her pockets and does a perfect pirouette. A short black silk cape billows out behind her, drawing a gasp from the audience. Embroidered red-and-gold koi fish swim in graceful arcs across the cape. It was the closest thing I had to shark-patterned fabric, I'd told McKenna, and she'd laughed.

McKenna strikes a few more ballet poses while Lina's documentary plays on the screen behind her. When the photos from crafts class appear, McKenna turns her back to the audience again and points at her head. Holding her updo in place is a large hair comb, embellished with pink roses. They're the rice dough roses she and her friends made the first day. We'd hot-glued them to the comb. Yesterday, William had given her a tiny rice dough shark, which she'd added to the center.

The parents and younger campers cheer when they see the connection between the photos of crafts class and McKenna's hair comb. With a last look over her shoulder, McKenna sashays down the runway and exits left, as Lyr enters stage right. She's wearing her long black concert skirt, paired with a halter top made from the same gold brocade as her dance dress. The qípáo-style mandarin collar lengthens her neck. Lyr carries an èrhú in her arms, and when she reaches the end of the runway, Win runs over with a chair. She sits down and plays the same tune as the runway music while scenes from music class scroll across the screen. The audience cheers when the video shows Peng Lǎoshī on pípá and Piper on gǔzhēn, completing a trio with Lyr. In the front row, Lyr's parents are trying to clap and wipe their eyes at the same time. I feel a little teary, too, watching my best friend perform.

One by one, each of the members of Group 13 walk the runway and show off their outfits and their talents, accompanied by a blend of Chinese and American music and photos and video clips of our time at Squee. Each of their upcycled ensembles contains a swatch of Chinese fabric—the pocket square in Fei Fei's suit, the sleeves of Bran's shirt. Howie wears his black martial arts uniform, now trimmed with emerald-green silk, and he's tied a matching sash around his forehead. He does a few tricks while on crutches, wowing the younger campers.

Delaney flutters across stage holding Chinese fans and wearing a flowy chiffon dress decorated with silk cherry blossoms. Maze carries a tray of egg custard tarts, her white chef's jacket embellished with black Chinese knot fasteners instead of plastic buttons. She hands the tray to Sarina, who gets off the stage and serves the dàntà to the sponsors, drawing jealous groans from the younger campers.

Piper, Lina, Ava, and Teagan all take to the runway, adding their own flair and choreography. Piper's guitar is strung across her body, and she leaps into the air, kicks her legs out, and lands, playing a loud chord. Lina pretends to snap photos all the way to the edge of the stage, where she strikes a bunch of hilarious social-media-worthy poses. Not to be outdone, Ava pretends to be in gamer mode, fending off alien wombats with Howie's toy sword. I'm shocked when Teagan does a series of perfect cartwheels all the way down the runway and then back handsprings on her return. She never once mentioned being a gymnast and didn't do it in rehearsal.

Finally, it's my turn. Before I step out of the wings, I glance across the stage and catch Harrison's eye. He smiles encouragingly. I take a deep breath—everything has gone fine with the fashion show, and I just have to trust that things will work out the way they're supposed to between us.

I don't strut, or sashay, or even stride on the runway. I focus on walking without stumbling and I make it to the front of the stage. Mom and Dad are sitting in the front row, beaming. And just behind them are Năinai and Wàipó—I had no idea they were coming to the Showcase. I do a couple of twirls and poses, enough to make sure that my grandmothers see both their qípáo refashioned into my dress. I hold up my prop—another of Harrison's "Soar" character appliqués—and pretend to snip it out. Behind me, photos of the past week appear, all of us hard at work on the fashion show. The final photo is of me at my sewing machine, lost in the magic of creativity. I hadn't wanted Lina to end the documentary with me—it was a group effort, I'd argued, so the last photo should be of the whole group. I got outvoted.

I turn around and beckon my friends back to the stage, where we all take a bow. The cheers are deafening. We get a standing ovation. My grandmothers are crying, Mom and Chŭ Auntie are crying, we're all crying.

Sarina and Win dry their eyes and start the credit roll, calling us each by name and having us step forward while they tell the audience what our roles in the fashion show were. The counselors make it clear that each person in Group 13 had a part in making the fashion show a success, and then they thank everyone for coming and invite them to head into the atrium for refreshments. The aisles clog as the younger campers try to be the first to get cake.

"Emergency exit!" Harrison announces, and all sixteen of us rush backstage and through the fire door, ending up in the loading dock area. From there, we head around the side of the building and enter the atrium through the front doors.

Wearing our fashion show outfits, we are instantly recognized and swarmed by parents and campers alike. They pepper us with questions about everything, from how I learned to sew to why our theme was "Expansion." Most of all, they want to know if SCCWEE will have a fashion show every year and if their camper can be in the "fashion show class." We tell them to email the directors and request that camp offer the "class" again next year, with the same instructors. Maybe McKenna and I will be back at Squee next year after all.

# CHAPTER THIRTY-NINE

"Phoenny? McKenna?" Win strides down the aisle of the empty auditorium and finds the rest of Group 13 sitting on the edge of the stage, chatting and eating cake.

"What's up?" I ask.

"Coop says the video of the fashion show is great, but it needs a better intro. Something to hook the viewers. I thought the two of you should do it," he says.

McKenna shrugs. "Okay, but what do we say?"

"How about explaining the show's theme," Sarina suggests, "like you just did to all the parents who came up to you."

Two minutes later, McKenna and I are sitting on stools on the stage, with Fei Fei literally powdering our faces.

"Ready?" Win asks from the front of the stage, where he has his phone camera trained on us. "Three—two—one, and action!"

"Hi. I'm Phoenny."

"And I'm McKenna."

"We are campers at Summertime Chinese Culture, Wellness, and Enrichment Experience," I say.

"Squee for short," McKenna adds.

"And our camp demonstrates and celebrates all the beautiful ways there are to be us. American Born Chinese," I say.

"Transracial Chinese Adoptees," says McKenna.

"Immigrants, Mixed Race, Mono or Multilingual, queer and questioning, and so much more," I look at McKenna.

"All at once and intersecting," she says.

"That's what we're trying to do with this show," I say.

In unison, we announce, "Welcome to *Expansion*, the first ever fashion show by the Summertime Chinese Culture, Wellness, and Enrichment Experience! We hope you enjoy it!"

"Cut!" Win says. "That's a wrap! You two were brilliant, as usual." He sends the video to Cooper, who immediately adds it to the video of the fashion show and then uploads the whole thing to Squee's social media.

Once the video is up, Win announces the number of total views it's gotten every few minutes. It's a lot. Former counselors and campers liked and shared the video, and it seems like it might go viral. Cooper and his crew are keeping track of the comments and looking for patterns. So far, there haven't been too many trolls leaving nasty messages. A few tried and got ridiculed by former campers, so they stopped commenting. Maybe they'll get canceled that way, without Cooper's team needing to track them down. We know this probably isn't the end of online trolls at Squee, but it does feel satisfying to watch our community rally around us.

Mom and Chŭ Auntie had asked us to stay instead of going back to our rooms to pack up but didn't tell us why. Now they reappear, leading a group of adults. I recognize a bunch of them. It's the Committee, who help keep Squee running smoothly. Mom tells us to form a receiving line, so we stand in a row with our backs to the stage.

The Committee members go down the line and shake our hands. They tell us how much they loved the fashion show, make us promise to come back as CITs and counselors, and thank us for making the video as one way to address the online troll problem. A couple of them approach Gemma and the adoptees and ask for their help forming an advisory group so Squee is better prepared to support adoptee campers next year. Gemma tells her that the advisory group should have both youth, young adult, and adult Chinese adoptees, and the Committee members wholeheartedly agree.

Tears prick at my eyes as I feel both Lyr and McKenna slide their arms around my waist, one on each side. Camp has turned out to be pretty spectacular after all.

# CHAPTER FORTY

"Okay, Group 13!" Sarina announces. "Let's head back to Agnes and grab your stuff! Don't forget to stop in the lobby and check out with me and Win, or else you won't get your memory book!"

Back at the dorm, we throw things into duffel bags and suitcases. We start a huge group text thread with all the campers from Groups 12 and 13 in it. Then the counselors and CITs whine until we add them to the group. A dragon emoji for Group 12 and a panda emoji for Group 13 are the only labels the group text thread gets.

We wait until everyone is done packing to bring our stuff down to the lobby. Win and Sarina are already there, a crate of memory books at their feet. The lobby is packed with campers from all the overnight groups, their luggage, and their parents. None of it deters Fei Fei.

"SQUEE DANCE!" she hollers, and every camper drops what they're doing and moves to the middle, gently pushing parents to the edges of the room. Without any advance planning, everybody understands we're part of a flash mob.

Kir sets her portable speaker on the front desk and taps a

key. "Ready, set, go!" she yells as the notes of "Little Apple" blare into the air.

We flap and kick and jut out our chins, laughing wildly. We are not in sync as we floss and Swagg Bounce and attempt the Woah, but somehow most of us manage to do the dab at the same time at the end. It is messy and noisy and utterly spectacular.

We say goodbye to Sarina and Win, who are in charge of supervising other counselors to put away all the craft, game, and classroom materials. Too quickly, friends start to leave, with promises to keep in touch. Some, like Lina, we'll see as soon as Chinese school starts again. Others who live farther away, like Piper, will take more of an effort to visit, but I think Lyr will make it happen. Lyr nudges me, and we watch Parker help carry Kir's bags to her family's car. He stops to talk to her for a minute afterward, and to our surprise, they shake hands. Even he can mature, I guess. When he returns to the lobby, Howie and Bran razz him, but he just ducks his head and shoves his hands in his pockets.

Finally, all our friends have left, except for William, McKenna, and Teagan. McKenna goes over to sit with William, and we try not to eavesdrop. When Harrison appears, having finished his CIT duties, I pull him completely out of the living room and into the snack closet.

He looks around, amused. "That reminds me. Look what

I found in my room." He waves a little bag of Swedish Fish in my face. I snatch it from him and he laughs. "There's my little ogre." He studies me. "So camp is over."

A wave of sadness crashes through me. "I know. I'm devastated."

"I'm not," he says. "I'm also not your CIT anymore."

My mouth forms a little "O" but no sound comes out. My heart races as he looks into my eyes.

"Can I see you tomorrow?"

I manage to whisper, "Yes."

"Hóu jeng," he says, and pulls me close.

Harrison and William are gone, leaving me and Lyr with McKenna and Teagan. We sit on the navy velveteen sofa under the watchful eye of Sister Martha Finchley, chatting about nothing and everything.

"You both don't actually live that far from me and Lyr," I say, studying the map on my phone. "There might even be a couple of bus lines that we can take to meet up at a coffee shop or something. Or I could ask Emerson to drive me to one of your houses."

"I would definitely choose Emerson over a bus," Teagan says.

I sigh. "Not you, too. Anyway, he likes Gemma."

She laces her fingers together and narrows her eyes. "May the best girl win."

We burst out laughing. "You're hilarious," I tell Teagan.

She grins. "You didn't think so two weeks ago, when I first arrived."

"And look at us now! We've come a long way."

McKenna smirks. "You mean *you've* come a long way, learning not to assume the worst about people."

"So what now?" Lyr asks.

"We keep evolving," I say. "The four of us are going to take on the world!"

"Let's tackle eighth grade first," McKenna says.

# AUTHOR'S NOTE

As a second-generation Chinese American who spent most of my childhood in rural Ohio without many others who shared my identity, I wanted my children to be exposed to their cultural heritage from an early age. I especially hoped they could find a group of other Chinese American kids and experience a sense of belonging that I didn't have when I was young. When I found out about the New England Chinese Youth Summer Camp (NECYSC, necysc.org), a Chinese culture camp located near my home, I was thrilled. My children became day campers as soon as they were old enough. I became a parent volunteer and then a member of the organizing committee. There was so much joy at NECYSC, from campers, counselors, and committee members alike, that I knew I had to write about the experience of being part of such a special community. Squee's basic structure and many of its activities are based on NECYSC and my memories of it, along with memories shared by former campers, counselors, and committee members.

NECYSC was founded in 1986 by Chinese American immigrants and attended by their American-born children. Over time, I watched as camp expanded to include a diverse mix of Chinese immigrants (from both China and Taiwan), American Born Chinese people (ABCs), multiracial people, transracial

Chinese adoptees, white parents of adoptees, and even several white children with an interest in Chinese culture. These varied and intersecting identities fascinated me. With few exceptions, everyone got along, thanks to communication that resulted in compromises and changes. There were difficult adjustments, but the reward was seeing how campers grew to love camp and often returned year after year. Like Phee and her friends, my children and I found camp to be a safe space where we didn't have to explain ourselves or prove anything. Then, as writers often do, I wondered, "What if? What if some campers suddenly *did* have to explain themselves and their culture? What if this environment ultimately made some campers feel like they weren't Chinese enough?" And, as the Covid-19 pandemic wore on and anti-Asian violence spiked, I wondered, "What if camp was no longer a safe space?" All of these questions inspired and influenced *Summer at Squee*.

There are many Chinese heritage camps across the United States, including both day and overnight camps, and even camps for families! Being of Chinese descent is generally not required. Here are a few to research further:

- Chinese Family Camp: ourcfc.org
- Heritage Camps for Adoptive Families: heritagecamps. org/chinese-heritage-camp/
- Midwest Chinese Family Camp: chinesefamilycamp.org
- Hip Wah Summer Program: hipwahsummerprogram.org

I have endeavored to capture a wide range of Chinese

American experiences in this book, including those of transracial adoptees. There are too few children's books written by adoptees about their experience, and I call on the children's literature industry to seek and publish them. As a non-adoptee, I'm not looking to replace or talk over the voices of adoptees. Instead, I sought to listen to members of the transracial adoptee community and reflect what I learned from them. My research included interviewing former NECYSC campers and counselors, reading memoirs, essays, and academic literature, watching documentaries, and consulting adoptees and experts in transracial adoption.

Here are a few resources for more information about both ABC and transracial adoptee experiences (for young adult and adult readers):

• Red Thread Broken blog: redthreadbroken.wordpress.com

• *Research on Diversity in Youth Literature*, sophia.stkate.edu/rdyl/ (Volumes 1–4) and iopn.library.illinois.edu/journals/rdyl/index (Volume 5)

• "Somewhere Between" documentary: somewherebetweenmovie.com

• Therapy Redeemed: therapyredeemed.wordpress.com

It is my fervent wish that all children will find a book that reflects their identity, written by someone who shares their lived experience. Every child should have the opportunity to feel that they belong and that they are enough, because they are.

# ACKNOWLEDGMENTS

I'm indebted to the wisdom of Dr. Sarah Park Dahlen, Meredith Seung Mee Buse, and others, whose labor, pedagogy, and/or critical feedback helped me learn more about the perspective of Asian American transracial adoptees in the US and the challenges they face, though please note that any errors are my own.

Thank you to my brilliant editor, Joanna Cárdenas, who believed that I could weave a whole story from a two-sentence snippet of a plot, and worked tirelessly to make sure the resulting fabric was strong. Erin Murphy, you are not only my shield but my bridge. Thank you—without you, my stories and I would still be marooned on the Isle of Shyness and Self-Doubt.

Boundless gratitude to Team Kokila for their editorial insights: Namrata Tripathi, Zareen Jaffery, Sydnee Monday, and Eunice Tan. Tabitha Dulla, Nicole Kiser, Ariela Rudy Zaltzman, and Jacqueline Hornberger did a stellar job clipping loose threads and patching holes (i.e., all the things amazing managing editors, production editors, and copy editors do). Many thanks to Zhui Ning Chang and Alina Chau for their Mandarin and Cantonese expertise and advice. I've been squee-ing over the page designs by Asiya Ahmed, and Karyn Lee—I'm honored that your gorgeous art graces the cover of this book. You've conveyed all the fun, excitement, and insecurities of summer camp while also showing how Chinese Americans are not a monolith!

The contributions of New England Chinese Youth Summer Camp (NECYC) former campers and counselors Jeffrey Chan, YiYi Chen, Wesley Chiu, Matt Cho, Kara Chuang, April Chung, Andrew Fei, Caroline Lucy, Bennett Wang, Evan Wang, Jesse Wang, Bryan Xian, and Anthony Xue were invaluable. Thank you for sharing your memories and experiences. And to all the NECYSC Committee members that I had the honor of serving with, especially Christopher Chiu, Dr. Lisa Gallagher, and Simone Lee, you have made my life richer with your friendship and inspired me to write this book. I'll never forget the good times (and stress!) we had at camp.

Beloved friends and writing partners Sarah Park Dahlen (yes, you're named twice because you deserve it), Dawn Dentzer, Sheri Dillard, Debbi Michiko Florence, Maria Gianferrari, Joanna Ho, Betina Hsieh, Mike Jung, Jung Kim, Lisa Robinson, Lois Sepahban, and Paula Yoo kept me from falling apart at the seams on more than one occasion. A magical weekend at the Highlights Foundation's Asian and Asian American Voices retreat gave me the courage to press on with this book—thank you for being in community with me.

For Wàipó, who taught me to sew—I love you and miss you. Anita, Ezra, and Feo—let's wear our sunglasses at night and stay forever young sharing memories of CFC. Tim, Evan, and Bennett—you are the warp to my weft. I am only whole cloth with you.